I0709551

Also By Jass Richards

This Will Not Look Good on My Resume

The Road Trip Dialogues

The Blasphemy Tour

The Blasphemy Tour

Jass Richards

Magenta

The Blasphemy Tour
© 2012 Jass Richards

ISBN 978-1-926891-45-3

Published by Magenta

Magenta

www.jassrichards.com

Cover design by Stephen James Price based on a concept by Jass Richards

Formatting and layout design by Book Looks Design

The letter to Dr. Laura is out and about on the internet, uncredited. The "Worship me...," "Fine, I evolved...," and "There's a reason..." bumper stickers are also out there, uncredited. The rest of the billboards, mugs, and so on are mine.

Thanks to Ellie Burmeister, who provided comments about the penultimate draft.

Thanks to the Ontario Arts Council for their support.

Library and Archives Canada Cataloguing in Publication

Richards, Jass
    The blasphemy tour / Jass Richards.

ISBN 978-1-926891-45-3

    I. Title.

PS8635.I268B63 2012   C813'.6   C2011-905662-3

Thanks again to Bill — for his younger self.

ev slowed as they approached the border at Fort Erie and chose a car lane that had virtually no line-up. Carefully manoeuvring into the narrow lane, which was marked by concrete dividers on either side and a huge concrete pillar on the driver's side—whose function intrigued, and absolutely eluded, her—she pulled up snug behind the car in front of her.

Almost instantly a voice boomed out over the speaker. "BACK UP YOUR VEHICLE!!" Simultaneously, a border guard appeared out of nowhere and walked briskly toward their car, making forceful 'back up' signs with his hands.

"BACK UP YOUR VEHICLE NOW!!" The voice commanded.

"All right, all right," she grumbled, puzzled by their urgency, and put the car into reverse. She grabbed onto the back of Dylan's seat for leverage, turned to look behind, and started to back up.

"Rev!" Dylan said almost immediately. But too late.

She heard the clunk. Then the clatter. And when she turned to face the front again, she saw that the rear view mirror on her door was gone, clipped by the concrete pillar. So that's what it was for.

She mumbled something as she opened her door to retrieve it.

"REMAIN IN YOUR CAR!!"

"Oh, for Pete's sake," she ignored the command. It was just a rear view mirror and it was sitting right there.

"DO NOT EXIT YOUR VEHICLE!!"

She exited the vehicle. More or less.

"Shit," she muttered.

Dylan didn't dare glance over—he was staring straight ahead in disbelief, exclaiming with full Irish, "Bloody hell—" Besides, he knew what had happened. "Please tell me you fell out, you're on the ground, and you're going to stay there," he managed to say.

"Yes, yes, and—" she tried to stretch her legs, but apparently her knees were doing their very best imitation of concrete— "don't have any choice. I hate this growing old—" she growled.

"Yes, well, we can commiserate about the tragedy of being over forty later. Perhaps when we turn sixty. Because at the moment we're surrounded by half a dozen border guards. All of whom are seriously armed."

"What?" she popped her head up.

"Men with guns!" Dylan shouted.

"Oh." She ducked back down.

"PUT YOUR HANDS WHERE WE CAN SEE THEM!!"

Dylan raised his hands.

Rev also raised her hands. Her head hit the pavement. "Shit!"

Dylan winced. "Are you—still conscious?"

"Yes. Unfortunately. I really—"

"—used to have abs. I know."

"STEP OUT AND AWAY FROM THE VEHICLE."

Dylan did as he was told.

"STEP AWAY FROM THE VEHICLE!" The voice repeated.

"Just give her—" he looked over at her— "an hour."

"Oh shut up."

Two of the three guards who had been aiming at Dylan swivelled to Rev.

"She was talking to me," Dylan said quickly. "Rev?" He was afraid to look directly at her in case that looked like they were colluding to—do something.

"M'AM, KEEP YOUR HANDS RAISED, STAND UP, AND STEP AWAY FROM THE VEHICLE!!"

She grunted. And cursed again.

"He called you 'm'am'," Dylan said out of the side of his mouth. "That should give you—motivation."

Although the Chief Officer had, spread out in front of him, their passports, birth certificates, drivers' licenses, and DBR cards (Dylan's homemade DO BLOODY RESUSCITATE!! cards), he still asked.

"Names?" His pen was poised over the lengthy, and sadly empty, form in front of him.

"Chris Reveille."

"Dylan O'Toole."

"Address?"

Rev told him.

"And where is that exactly?"

"A bit northwest of Sudbury. Near the border between Ontario and—Montreal," she said with a straight face.

Dylan quickly looked away to hide the grin.

"And Penticton?" The officer looked at Dylan.

It was too easy. "Same general area," he replied, pursing his lips.

In the year since Rev and Dylan had quite by chance reconnected, some twenty years after they'd gone through teacher's college together, he had introduced her to life as a housesitter. As a result, they divided their time between her cabin on a lake in a forest (a bit northwest of Sudbury) (near Montreal) and Paris, Portland, Peru, or wherever else he could get a housesit. (Penticton was simply where most of his stuff happened to be in storage; long ago when he had applied for a driver's license, having a fixed address seemed like a good idea, and nobody, apparently, had checked to determine whether the address he'd given was actually residential, so using it a few years later when he applied for a passport seemed—wise.) In fact, the speaking tour they were at that moment starting so eventfully followed a mishmash route determined by the engagements arranged by Phil, their contact at the Consortium, and Dylan's housesitting arrangements.

"Phone number?" The officer continued.

"Oh, I don't have a phone."

He looked up at her.

"No one north of Toronto has phones yet."

Dylan snickered and quickly looked away again.

"So how can we reach you?"

"Well the mail comes through. Once the lake thaws. In August."

Dylan was shaking ever so slightly.

"'Course, the dogsleds run all year. Though the polar bears killed half of 'em last year. One even came right into my igloo."

A guffaw turned into a cough.

"I see. And what is the purpose of your travel to the U.S.?"

"Um, we're on a speaking tour," Dylan thought he'd better take over.

"This speaking tour. Is it a paid tour?"

"Yes."

"That is how you're going to be supporting yourself while here?"

"Yes."

"And so you have work visas?"

"Oh. Um—we're being paid an honorarium that is, I believe, exempt from—"

"Who's sponsoring this speaking tour?"

"The American Atheist Consortium."

The Chief Officer looked up from the lengthy form then. And one of the other border guards, having heard that part, walked over.

"Hey, I remember you two," he said. "You were charged with, what was it? Blasphemy! For what you wrote on that Right-to-Life billboard."

"Yeah, but we weren't convicted," Rev spoke up.

"Yes, we were," Dylan said, turning to her. How could she have forgotten? Of the two of them, she was the more worried about it. Being, of the two of them, the more formally employed. He just then noticed her glare.

"Oh yeah," Rev remembered, turning back to the Chief. "But we got a suspended sentence. The conviction was just—"

Dylan stepped in again. After all, he was the one who'd just royally blown it by announcing they'd been convicted. Though of course it was easy enough to check. As it no doubt would be. Now. He turned to the Chief, "The conviction provided a platform for the judge to make headlines, and history, by showing that *The Bible* is itself blasphemous, since what we had written on the anti-abortion billboard was *from The Bible*."

"'Blessed are they that bash their babies brains out'," the officer volunteered. "Or something like that," he added, when his superior gave him a scathing look.

"This speaking tour," the Chief Officer continued the interview. "What exactly are you going to be speaking about?"

"Well, I'm not sure it's any of your business," Rev chafed. "What?" she said to Dylan when he poked her. "He can't detain us just because we intend make good use of the freedom of speech while we're here. In your fine country," she added belatedly, turning back to the Chief. But then couldn't help further adding, "The one that gives such warm, fuzzy welcomes."

The officer put down his pen. And struggled for control. "You have to understand that post 9/11, we're just a bit more concerned about who gets into our country."

"I understand that. What I don't understand is how exiting one's car increases the threat level."

"Well as long as you're inside your vehicle, you're contained," he explained. "Obviously you're less able to put our lives in danger."

"That would be true if I'd planned to come at you with a knife. Or a piano wire."

The officer, and Dylan, looked at her curiously.

"But if I'd put a bomb in the car—"

Dylan noticeably slumped in his chair. The officer picked up the phone.

"—and was willing to give my life to Allah to get at the 72,000 virgins...what?"

So as they sat in the designated quasi-secure area, watching a team of Michelin men carefully unpack their car and set each item some distance away, in another designated quasi-secure area, Dylan idly commented, "It's 72 virgins, not 72,000."

"Someone's been doing research for our book," Rev looked over at him, smiling happily.

As soon as the trial was over, they'd been approached not only by the representative of the American Atheist Consortium suggesting a speaking tour, but also by a representative of a major publishing company offering a book contract. Which both delighted and annoyed Rev. Delighted, because she'd spent the last twenty years writing, and despite thousands of queries to agents and publishers, had not been able to get a single book published. And annoyed, because she'd spent the last twenty years writing, and despite thousands of queries to agents and publishers, had not been able to get a single book published.

"Well, the hadiths say 72," he qualified. "The Qur'an itself doesn't actually mention a number."

"What are the hadiths? The Biblical form of the hads?"

"No," he grinned, "they're sort of like addendums to the Qur'an."

"Hm. I've never understood the appeal of virgins anyway. I mean, wouldn't you want a woman with experience, someone who knows—"

"A woman who knows?" Dylan shuddered theatrically.

An hour later, they sat looking out at all of their belongings sitting on the pavement. Red tape, ironically enough, was being strung around the area in which said belongings sat.

"We could call Dim," Dylan suggested. Dmitri had been their lawyer for the blasphemy trial. He was also one of Rev's former students.

"Or we could call someone who actually knows law. Dim doesn't know dick."

"Actually—"

"Right, okay, he does know dick. Still, we need someone—"

"Who knows *American* law."

"Alan Shore! We could call Alan Shore!"

"Do you have his number?"

"No."

"Then we can't call Alan Shore. Even if he *were* real."

"Spoilsport."

"How about your buddies at LSAT? You're still writing questions for them? I mean, while we're doing this tour thing?" Freelance test development was Rev's employment. She wrote critical reasoning questions for the LSAT. Questions like 'If X, Y, and Z are true, which of the following is also true?' And 'Which of the following would most undermine the argument made in the passage above?' It's the kind of job someone with a degree in philosophy did. When they weren't driving a cab. Dylan, on the other hand, wrote travel articles. Which fit perfectly with his housesitting lifestyle. And his almost history degree.

"Yeah. Which is why we're not calling them."

"Oh. Right."

"Let's just call Phil. Surely the Consortium must have legal counsel on call."

"And you know," she said a while later, as they continued to stare out the window, since it was the only show in town, "even if there *is* a potential bomb in the car, that wouldn't necessarily be a threat. It's *looking* at it that could turn it into a real bomb. And even then, there's only a fifty-fifty chance of that happening."

"Hm."

"So maybe we should tell them to stop looking."

"I don't think the Chief would appreciate the finer points of quantum indeterminacy."

"Still. He should have said that there's potentially a bomb in our car. Not that there's a potential bomb in our car."

"You could tell him *that.*"

A while later still, Dylan said, rather listlessly, as he handed Rev a Pepsi he'd gotten from the vending machine in the room, "So I guess there's no point in asking whether we could fix the car while we wait."

"You could do that?"

"Well, no." He took a long drink from his own Pepsi, then stretched out in his chair again. "I thought we could find a phone booth, I could go inside, and come out MacGyver."

"You mean Superman."

"I was being patriotic. Being at the border does that to me.

Another half hour and I'll break out in the national anthem."

"No you won't," she scoffed.

"I might. If I knew the words."

She laughed. "We are *so* Canadian."

"Anyway," she said, "there aren't any phone booths anymore. Remember? They took them all away when cell phones were invented. By Satan."

"There's still phone booths," Dylan said. "There's just not any phones in them anymore."

"At least no working phones," she amended.

"And the ones that have working phones don't have phone books."

"Or you could come out as Benton Fraser," she said after a moment.

"I like how MacGyver dresses better."

She laughed. "And yet, don't you remember your first practice teaching assignment? You went all young Republican on me. Gone was the rat's tail, and the earring, and the lime green t-shirt," she poked at the lime green t-shirt he was currently wearing. "You were such a—disappointment."

"Yeah, well. Look how that turned out."

She smiled. He'd ended up quitting his first teaching job, which had been up on some reserve, after just three days. To join a band called *A Bunch of Drunken Indians*. He played tambourine.

"At least I didn't get fired," he said. "Countless times."

"I could count them," she said cheerfully. "If I had four hands."

"Speaking of which, maybe Dad'll come, and rescue us both. You'd fit right in on the mothership."

"Hm." She seemed lost in thought.

"What were we talking about?" she finally said. "What was your point—with the phone booth?"

He thought for a moment. "Can't remember."

"Geez," she said, "it's like we're still—shit!"

She sat up straight and looked out anxiously at all of their stuff. Sitting nicely exposed on the pavement.

He had suddenly had the same thought. "No, didn't we use it all before—"

"Yeah, in a Betty Crocker kind of way."

"Oh. And where exactly are your—" he hazarded a guess "—brownies?"

"Well, more like 'pudding in the middle'—brownies. They're in with the sandwiches," she answered his question.

"Okay," he said, thinking quickly, and standing up to do so. "In an hour or so, if we're still here, we'll just casually say we're hungry, we've got food in the car, could we please just—"

"Right. First giggle and they'll know."

He giggled. "You're right," he sat down. "We'd never pull it off."

"Well, let's not worry. Unless they bring in a—uh-oh."

A grey SUV had pulled into the lot, and clean-cut young man in a uniform got out. He opened the back passenger door and a dog got out. A huge floppy dog. A very eager and excited, huge floppy dog.

"Wow. What is that?" Rev wondered aloud. "Looks like a cross between a Great Dane and a—"

"Bear." Dylan looked at the dog with interest.

"Yeah. I thought police dogs were, well, police dogs."

"There is no such breed. They're all German Shepherds."

"And that's a bit stereotyped, don't you think?" she asked.

"What, you think they should hire French poodles instead?" he giggled.

"Well, actually, the French—"

"Or Siberian Huskies!" he blurted out, gleefully.

"Why don't we have a dog?" she wondered aloud a short while

later, as the Chief Officer presumably explained to the K-9 unit, of two, whatever needed explaining. "Why isn't there a Canadian something? Regardless," she got back on track, "that's gotta be an explosives-sniffing dog, right? So we're okay."

"You mean they specialize? To that extent?"

She shrugged. "Ask an Epistemology prof something about Metaphysics and he'll refuse to answer on the grounds that it's not his field."

"Really? That's a bit—something."

"'Articulate' is not the word you're looking for," she grinned.

"It's not, no," he grinned back.

"What kind of sandwiches?" Dylan asked another short while later, when the dog had apparently eliminated their two suitcases, his laptop, and their box of books and cds. Several miscellaneous bags remained.

"Tuna."

"Oh, good, yeah for sure we're okay. The dog'll *never* find tuna."

"Could work in our favour. The tuna might mask the—uh-oh."

The dog had found the lunch bag. And pretty much swallowed it whole.

Dylan pondered the situation. "What happens when—"

The dog had resumed checking out the remaining bags, then suddenly seemed to forget what it was doing. It sat down. And wagged its tail. Dylan grinned.

The officers conferred and then the Chief and the K-9 unit came into the building through the waiting room. Suddenly the room was far too small. Since the dog took up a full quarter of it.

"I'm sorry, sir," the dog's partner was saying to the Chief. "We just came from a scene, sir, and Peanut—"

Rev let out a small snort. The young man glared at her.

"—ate the evidence. That's why he—he's got the— He's hungry," the young man finished.

"And you didn't think to take him off duty?" the Chief glared at him. The young man, not—Peanut. It's hard to glare at a giggling dog.

"No, sir. It was a very small amount and given Peanut's size, I thought it would have no effect."

In the moment of silence that ensued, they all followed the Chief's gaze. Which was fixed on Peanut. Who was stepping once to the right, then once to the left—lifting his front paws absurdly high, like a Lipizzaner stallion—then cross stepping three times to the right, into the wall; he then repeated the pattern in reverse, left, right, cross step to the left. Into the wall.

"What the hell is he doing?"

"'Thriller'. Sir."

Dylan burst out in a delighted giggle.

"Me and the guys at the unit—after class— The K-9s are very smart, sir."

As the Chief started to leave the room, Peanut jumped and turned half way around, wiggled his bottom half, then jumped and turned again to face them. And wiggled again.

"That's not in 'Thriller'," the Chief said, stopping at the door.

"No," the young man agreed. And looked at Peanut curiously.

"Um, what kind of dog is that?" Dylan asked the young man, as the three—four—of them waited in the waiting room for various decisions to be made.

"It's a Newfie. A Newfoundland dog."

"We *do* have our own dog!" Rev said. The young man looked at her. "We're from Canada."

"Oh."

"And you really call them Newfies?" Dylan asked.

"Yes, why?"

"Oh, not important," Dylan smiled as he and Rev exchanged a look.

"Their thick coat and webbed feet make them perfect for swimming in the cold ocean water," the young man said, "such as is off the coast of Newfoundland. So I hear," he added.

"Never been?" Rev asked.

"No. Never been much out of here," he confessed.

"And that would explain it," Rev said sotto voce to Dylan.

"He's got webbed feet?" Dylan was staring at Peanut's paws, intrigued. "Can we see?"

"Sure. Peanut, come 'ere." Peanut got up from the quadrant he'd claimed and lumbered over. "I'm Jon Tucker, by the way," the young man said, reaching out his hand to Dylan. "But everybody calls me Tuck."

"Dylan," Dylan replied, shaking his hand.

"Rev." She joined in.

As did Peanut, who offered his paw.

"I miss Bob," Dylan said, smiling broadly as he shook Peanut's paw.

"He used to have a dog," Rev explained as she too shook Peanut's massive paw. "Bob. But Bob left him. For Fifi. Who lived on a farm. With lots of kids."

Tuck nodded with understanding. As did Peanut.

"You wouldn't leave me, would you Pea?" He ruffled Peanut's loose and very full coat. "You're my little Sweet Pea," he said in a gushy voice, and Peanut planted a big sloppy one on Tuck's face.

As the Chief walked in. And stared.

Tuck jumped out of his chair and stood. "Sir." He straightened.

Peanut, perhaps feeling the need to stretch a bit, sauntered past him through the open door into the larger office.

Dylan and Rev also got up.

"All right, here's the situation. I've made several phone calls," he sighed, "and this is what's happening. You," he pointed at the young man. "You're aware that eating the evidence is cause for dismissal."

Tuck looked devastated.

"Not you, the dog."

"Oh. Right. But—"

"We'll find you a transfer." He sighed again. Clearly this was becoming a long day.

"And as for you two," he directed his attention to Rev and Dylan, "we've got a meet set up for tomorrow morning. Our legal counsel will be here, as well as your Mr. Brightson and, presumably, legal counsel for the Atheist Consortium."

"But—" Rev objected.

"As for tonight—"

"We're not free to go?" Dylan asked.

"You're not cleared for entry yet, no. So I'm keeping your passports. And your driver's licenses. Your car hasn't been cleared yet in any case. We can't get another K-9 unit here until tomorrow." Tuck shrank the tiniest amount.

"You can have these back," the Chief handed over their birth certificates and DBR cards.

"As for tonight—" he ran his hand through his hair. "We've got a holding cell, but that's not really appropriate. Tucker, make a reservation at the nearest hotel. And provide transport."

"Yes, sir."

"And show them which bags they can take with them."

"Yes, sir."

"But we're not under arrest or anything," Rev clarified.

"No. Just—please don't go anywhere. I believe you'd agree it's in your best interests to be here for the meeting tomorrow."

Dylan nodded. Rev conceded a nod a moment later.

"Oh—" the Chief stopped on his way out. "I've had pizza brought in, you're welcome to—" he stopped in the doorway. The five large pizzas that had been perched on the corner of his desk were now five empty boxes on the floor. Peanut was asleep in the corner, grinning, and wagging his tail. The Chief ran his hand through his hair.

"So," Tuck said to Rev and Dylan, when they were all in his SUV and on their way out of the border station parking lot, Rev in the front, Dylan in the back with Peanut—his head, like Peanut's, sticking out the sun roof.

"Phtt, phtt, ummmrrpht, ummrrpht—"

"What the hell are you doing?" Rev turned to ask Dylan.

"Trying to get that jowls flapping in the wind thing going. Like Peanut."

"It's not working," she pointed out the obvious.

"No. It's not," Dylan agreed cheerfully.

"So," Tuck tried again, "Do you have any preference as to where we go for dinner? Chief said I can claim it as expenses."

"Pizza's good," Dylan said.

"So very good," added Rev.

"Okay, pizza it is. I know a great place close by."

"Phtt, phtt, ummrrpht, ummrrpht—"

He took them to Bette's Bar, a comfy basement bar furnished with old upholstered furniture and a couple of chrome and formica dining room tables. Peanut had obviously been there before and knew he was welcome. He made a beeline for the kitchen.

"It's got karaoke!" Rev shouted as they walked past the bar, with its few occupants, toward the small stage. She actually broke out into a trot.

"What's she going to sing?" Tuck asked.

"God only knows," Dylan muttered, remembering the last time she sang, which was in the car on the way, too much of the way, to Montreal. She was enthusiastically tone-deaf.

"Oh I love that song!" Tuck followed Rev onto the stage.

"No, I—"

Rev quickly made a selection, then stepped away from the machine, mic in hand, ready to sing. Tuck took the other mic and once the song started—she'd chosen The Beatles' "Ob-la-di Ob-la-da"—he sang along, adding harmony. Or trying to, given Rev's tenuous grasp of pitch.

Part way through the song, Bette and the entire kitchen staff came out to watch the horror that was Rev singing. Or to thank her for not choosing "Hey Jude". At some point Rev realized, somewhat impossibly, that Tuck had a really great voice, so she switched from vocals to air drums. The kitchen staff cheered. And went back to the kitchen. At about that point, Dylan decided to join them on stage. He played air tambourine. Tuck really did have a beautiful voice. He had amazing control not only of pitch, but of volume and timbre as well.

"Oh wow, this is just like old times," Dylan said when the song had finished. "Let's do another one," he said.

Bette had reappeared and caught Tuck's eye with her query.

"A couple large," Tuck called out. "No, make that three," he said. "I forgot about you two," he turned to Dylan and Rev. "So should that be four?"

"No, we can split a large," Dylan said.

"Make ours vegetarian?" Rev asked.

"One vegetarian," Tuck called out.

Bette nodded and returned to the kitchen.

"What was the Drunken Indians' favourite song?" Rev asked, turning back to the karaoke machine.

"'One little, two little, three little Indians'."

"You're kidding."

"Well, they'd changed the words."

"To what?"

"Kill Whitey."

Peanut strode out of the kitchen at that point, a grin on his face and tail wagging.

"Hey, you guys want a show?" Tuck asked.

"Sure, what did you have in mind?"

"Peanut, come 'ere!"

Peanut bounded up to the stage.

"Have a seat," Tuck gestured grandly. Rev and Dylan claimed a table and sat to watch. Tuck made a selection at the karaoke machine, then turned to Peanut.

"'Do ya wanna get rocked?'" he asked him in his best Def Leppard voice.

Peanut shimmied in excitement.

Tuck started singing as an old Tommy Roe song began to play. "'I went to a dance just the other night,'" he made a slow circle in the air with his right hand, and Peanut did a slow circle to the right.

"'I saw a girl there, she was out of sight,'" Tuck made a circle with his left hand, and Peanut did a slow circle to the left.

"'I asked a friend of mine who she could be,'" he continued. Peanut was totally focused on Tuck, trembling with excitement, waiting for—

"'He said that her friends just call her Sweet Pea.'" When he heard Tuck say his name, Peanut let loose for a moment with a full-body wiggle, then immediately concentrated again.

He stepped toward Tuck as Tuck stepped backward, completely in time to the music —"'Oh Sweet Pea, come on and dance with me'"— right, hold, left, hold, right, hold, left, hold. Then he broke out into a freeform prance and shimmy on "'Come on, come on, come on and dance with me!'" Dylan was wild with delight, hooting and applauding.

Then Peanut stepped backward, as Tuck stepped toward him, "'Oh Sweet Pea, won't you be my girl?'" Then broke out again in a silly freeform that was full of nothing but energy and bliss. "'Won't you, won't you, won't you be my girl?'"

Dylan almost had a stroke when he saw what Peanut did with the brief percussion solo that followed: a complicated eight-beat sequence of up, down, right, left, rollllll, up, hold.

The song changed key for the second verse, but the choreography remained the same. Slow circle to the right, then to the left, then, to Dylan's great delight, the forward and backward walk followed by the Peanut's over-the-top freeform for the chorus.

"That was fantastic!" Dylan bubbled as Tuck and Peanut finished the song and sat down at their table. Peanut didn't need a chair; he just sat at their table, and his head easily cleared the top.

"Thanks!" Tuck beamed with pleasure at Dylan's appreciation.

"How long did it take to teach him that?" Rev asked, equally impressed.

"Well, a while," Tuck confessed. "But—"

"But I'll bet he didn't mind."

"No, I don't think he did," Tuck ruffled Peanut's coat.

Bette brought out a pitcher of beer and three glasses. Peanut didn't drink beer, of course, but he apparently had his own water dish. At least, it had his name written on it.

"To Peanut and Tuck!" Rev raised her glass in a toast.

"Yeah!" Dylan clanked his glass to Tuck's then to Peanut's dish.

Peanut grinned and thumped his tail.

Bette returned with their pizzas, one vegetarian for Dylan and Rev, one pepperoni and mushroom for Tuck, and a double meat-lovers for Peanut. Rev and Dylan grinned when they noticed, as Bette set Peanut's pizza in front of him, that it was already cut into bite-sized pieces. Peanut stared at it, intently, then looked at Tuck, just as intently. Tuck made a show of blowing on the pizza. Peanut stared at it again, intently, then looked at Tuck again. Tuck blew on it again. Satisfied, Peanut dug in.

"He burned the roof of his mouth on the cheese once," Tuck explained. "Ever since, Bette doesn't bring his out until it's definitely cool enough for him to eat, but he insists just the same that I blow on it to make sure."

"Well of course," Dylan said.

"So," Rev asked, after they'd had a few bites, which was about the time it took for Peanut to totally finish his, and he had left the table, "how is it you two came to be in the K-9 unit?"

"Well, I majored in music."

"Ah," Dylan said, and Rev laughed.

"But I wasn't any good."

"You sounded pretty good up there," Dylan said. "You've got a beautiful voice."

"I—thank you. But it's not up to performance standard. Classical performance standard," he amended.

"You could sing non-classical," Rev said.

"Yeah. That's what I thought too. And I tried a couple times to get a band together, but, in the meantime, I switched my major to business."

"Well," Rev said, "they're so closely related—"

Tuck grinned. "You know how they say you should think about what you really love to do, what you would do even if no one paid you, and that's what you should do?"

"Yeah, whose bright idea of career counselling was that?" she muttered.

"Well, I realized I love to hang out in bars—"

"And you found someone to pay you to do that?" Dylan asked, wonderfully interested.

"No," Tuck laughed. "I figured I'd become an agent, a scout. I'd discover new bands and make them rich and famous. And myself in the process."

"Ah, so *that's* how you became a—" Rev feigned understanding.

"No, that was Dad," Tuck sighed. "He paid for my university. And when music didn't work out, and I switched to business, he said I had two years after I graduated, and if that didn't work out either, I had to join the academy."

"He was a cop," Dylan said.

"He was a cop," Tuck agreed. And sighed again.

"And it didn't work out," Rev stated the obvious. She was good at that.

"No. It seems they've got to be famous *before* you sign them. And if they're famous, they're already signed. Plus, I realized I'm not that good with the high end of things. I can prepare a killer business plan, and I schmooze well enough with the guys in the bands, but I don't do meets with the banks very well."

"So why the K-9 unit?" she asked.

"Oh, well," he said oddly, "I don't like guns."

"You mean they wouldn't let you have one," she took a guess.

"That too," he confessed sheepishly. "In the K-9 unit, the dog is the gun. Peanut's trained to defend and attack."

Rev and Dylan looked over at him. Doubtfully. Since he was lying belly up on the couch—the whole couch—paws hanging limply in the air. His eyelids were fluttering, and his tail was wagging.

Tuck reached for the pitcher. "A refill?" he asked.

"You're in charge of transport?" Dylan asked.

"I am," he said and turned his glass over.

"Then, yes, another round indeed!" Dylan held his empty glass under the pitcher's spout, Rev followed suit, and they each took another slice of pizza.

A little later, after Rev and Dylan had filled Tuck in on how they came to be where they were, Tuck asked, "So what's your speech about?"

"What speech?" Rev asked.

"Well, it's a speaking tour—so I assumed—"

"Ah. Right. Well Phil said—Phil's our contact at the American Atheist Consortium—he said we'd never get past the first sentence."

"Apparently we're speaking at a lot of Bible colleges," Dylan explained. "He's billed us as Bible Enlightenment."

"Which is not untrue," Rev interjected.

"No," Dylan agreed.

"So I have the first sentence written," she announced happily to Tucker.

"You do?" Dylan looked at her inquiringly.

"'Hello.'" She said.

"A little formal, don't you think?" he said. After a moment.

"What, you'd go with 'Hi'?"

"Yeah."

"People would never hear 'Hi.' We need at least two syllables."

"Okay, how about 'Good Morning.' Three syllables," he said proudly.

Rev considered that. Carefully. "What if it's afternoon?"

"Okay, 'Good Morning slash Good Afternoon.'"

"That's stupid. 'Slash'."

"Well we wouldn't actually *say* 'slash'," he groaned.

"So," Tuck just had to interrupt, "Do you two always have this much—"

"Fun?" Rev supplied the word.

"We do, yes," Dylan supplied the answer.

And they grinned at each other.

Once they were in their hotel room—motel room, actually—Rev walked restlessly around the beigeness, stared out the window at the highway, then sat on the edge of the bed.

"What?" Dylan asked.

"I want to be home," she said simply. "I want to look out and see the sun sparkling on the water."

"Okay, but…."

"I can't believe I agreed to—this. Eight months of one-night stands in cheesy motels." She flopped back onto the bed.

"Because it's not eight months of one-night stands in cheesy motels. It's an all-expenses-paid trip around the country." He sat beside her.

"Oh yeah. I keep forgetting we're getting paid," she sat up. And became distracted by that line of thought. "I remember when I first found out that some professors get paid to present a paper. I was floored. I'd always assumed you *didn't* get paid. I certainly never did. It *cost* me to present a paper. The gas to get there, the hotel to stay overnight…. And for what? An extra line on my cv that apparently had no value whatsoever because I wasn't tenure track. Sessionals can present a hundred papers and publish a hundred books and serve on a hundred committees and it doesn't count shit.

"Same with being a board member," she continued as he went into the bathroom to brush his teeth. "I'd always wondered, how can all these men with such high-powered, demanding jobs have the time, let alone the altruism, to serve on, like, ten different boards?

Then I found out they get *paid* to do so! And they go to all those board meetings while they're on the payroll of those other jobs! When I was served on the ethics committee of the local hospital—"

Dylan popped his head out. "You were on the *ethics* committee? Of a *hospital?*"

"Yeah."

"What happened?"

"What do you mean, what happened?"

"Well, I imagine—"

"What, that'd I recommend a policy of euthanasia for anyone who wanted it?"

"Well—yes."

"I did. Abortion too."

"But abortion's already legal."

"'Legal' doesn't mean 'available'. This was a hospital created by a merger between Civic Memorial and St. Virgin Mary Martha Margaret."

"It wasn't really called that, was it?"

"May as well have been."

"Ah. I take it they didn't go for abortion on demand."

"Don't think so. My recommendation wasn't ever really addressed. Wasn't taken seriously. As wasn't I." She pondered the grammar of that sentence for a moment before continuing. "So I quit. Wasn't getting paid anyway, remember?"

He flopped onto the bed. "Did you *ask* to be paid?"

"Well, no, if they don't offer, you don't—I should've *asked? That's* how it's done?" She turned to look at him.

"I don't know. Maybe."

"Well, when we got hired to teach, we didn't have to *ask* to be paid. It was a paying job, they told us how much, we accepted or not, end of story."

"You didn't negotiate?"

"Negotiate what?"

"Your salary."

Rev was stunned.

"How is it," she finally managed to speak, "that you know these things and I don't?"

"I don't know. Whenever one of my magazines offers an assignment, we dicker about the pay a bit...I thought it was standard operating procedure." He sat up. "Apparently it's not," he said in the awful silence.

"Maybe it is," Rev said. "For men."

Dylan considered that. "And maybe—I wonder—if they *had* been paying you, that hospital, I wonder whether you would've been taken more seriously."

Rev was silent.

"Wow," she eventually said. "So all my life, as I've been doing stuff for free, or for minimal payment, trying to be affordable, knowing, from my own experience, what it's like not to be able to afford shit, all my life I've been cutting my own legs out from under me? *That's* why I haven't been taken seriously? All my life?"

"It's a thought. People value something more when they have to pay for it."

She was silent. "Well that's stupid," she finally said.

"Doesn't make it not true."

"It's an interesting trilogy, isn't it," she said after a moment. "Not being taken seriously because you're female, and not being taken seriously because you're not paid, and women don't get paid. Or don't get paid as much. Begs the question which comes first, doesn't it."

"It does." Dylan returned then to the main thread with enthusiasm, "But not only are we getting paid, we're getting paid *well*. Our gas, our hotel—which will probably be more like the swimming-pool-included kind—and a per diem. Not to mention the fee itself," he added. "Didn't you figure we were getting paid almost as much for one speech as you used to get for a whole term's course?"

"Yeah. Which doesn't seem right. Maybe—"

"No, no, and again, no. The Consortium isn't as rich as the Vatican or any one of a number of televangelists, but they are supported by a good number of well-off individuals, I imagine. And, well, they're a consortium. They probably just asked each of their member organizations to cough up $10,000 and that was that."

"Yeah but—"

"And," Dylan wasn't finished, "Don't forget we're getting paid for more than just the speeches. Phil's setting up radio talk shows and newspaper interviews and so on and so forth. We're advancing the cause, remember? I dare say American atheists have been waiting for something just like this. Remember that bus campaign in the UK? The British atheists wanted to put signs on the buses to counteract the 'Non-believers are gonna burn in hell' signs. They figured if they could raise 5,000 pounds—"

"Yeah, and within days they had 100,000 pounds."

"Exactly. See? The American atheists know they need to do something too, something with big promotional value, and, like the British, they're willing to pay for it. Well, we're it. Dim and the judge did us a favour. Here we are, on this tour, on an all-expenses-paid trip across the country, with a book contract, no less. We're finally the right people in the right place at the right time."

"Yeah. You're right." She got up to do her teeth.

"I wonder why the States didn't just do the bus thing instead," she called out to him.

"Because they don't have buses. They don't believe in public transportation, remember? Doesn't use enough oil."

"Oh yeah."

"And," Dylan still wasn't finished with the main thread, "it's never more than a three-day drive from one gig to the next, so we'll be able to stay in one place for three or four days if we like. And don't forget the week's housesit in Myrtle Beach. We've also got a week in California. It'll be fun. We'll get to see and do new stuff. We already saw Peanut dance. That was cool, wasn't it?"

"Very cool," she had to agree, coming out of the bathroom.

"And you'd never've seen that if you were still in your cabin. Watching the sun sparkle on the water."

"Yeah."

"And let me remind you," he said, being so not a winter person, "that in a couple months, the sun *won't* be sparkling on the water. It'll be a barren white wasteland, with polar bears roaming into your igloo—"

"It is good timing," she had to admit, flopping back onto the bed.

After a moment, she said, "You know what we need?"

"Yeah, but Peanut ate them all."

"So maybe we should prepare a speech," Rev said, once they'd settled in for the night. "Just in case."

"Good idea," Dylan agreed, grabbing his laptop. "We could open with the billboard and court thing, segue from there to other contradictions in *The Bible*, which leads us to the matter of historical accuracy, which leads us to the matter of interpretation, both of which land us feet first in the matter of the authority of *The Bible*."

Rev carefully considered his suggestion. "Or we could tell knock-knock jokes."

Dylan compared the two in his mind. "My plan's more appropriate," he concluded.

"Which is just a little bit disturbing," Rev said, remembering the road trip that landed them on the tour.

"It is, isn't it," he agreed. Then wondered for a moment whether he was finally growing up. Then dismissed the possibility.

She rustled in her bag for her writing clipboard folder thing, and they concentrated, Rev settling into the chair with her feet up on the night table, Dylan stretched out on the bed with his laptop.

Five minutes later, Rev said, "What have you got?"

Dylan cleared his throat. "Good evening, boys and girls.'

"But—you taught high school."

"Yes, I did," he agreed. "And I'm wondering now, just when did I start thinking of high school students as boys and girls?"

"Yeah," Rev said, sadly. "They used to be peers," she thought back to her own teaching career. "A group in which you were clearly the oldest and in charge, but still."

"What have you got?" Dylan swept the rumination away.

Rev dramatically held her clipboard in front of her. "Good afternoon, boys and girls."

"You taught university!" he exclaimed.

"Your point?" she asked. "Whenever I challenged them, whenever I pushed them for reasons to support their claims, they ran to the Dean, whining, 'Professor Reveille doesn't respect our opinions, we're offended, she's not allowed....'"

"And if they'd come to you instead, and said 'Prof Reveille, we don't think you respect our opinions'—what would you have said?"

"'Yeah, well, your mother wears army boots!'"

Dylan smiled.

"By the way," Rev said, "I've never understood why that's considered an insult."

"And yet, we probably shouldn't say it. In our speech."

"Why not?"

"Because this is a country at war."

"Room Service!" someone called out just then, knocking on their door.

The next knock on their door was Tuck, coming to fetch them in the morning. He and Peanut were obviously morning people. Rev and Dylan were obviously not. As they got their act together, Tuck and Peanut went outside to play with Peanut's Frisbee.

Once they pulled into the border station parking lot, they got out and headed toward the building. Just as Tuck offered to go in search of coffee, since they had managed to pass not one coffee shop on their way, a K-9 unit pulled into the lot. They all stopped to watch as it parked close to the taped area in which the remaining contents of their car sat. A no-nonsense German Shepherd exited the vehicle and proceeded immediately to examine the remaining items, clearing one by one with impressive efficiency. Peanut let out a half-groan half-whine as he slumped to ground in a dejected heap, his head on his paws.

"I take it this isn't the first time he's had to endure this kind of— humiliation," Dylan said.

Tuck shook his head and squatted down to scratch Peanut's ears. "You'll get it next time," he said encouragingly.

"I thought he was fired," Rev said.

"Shh!" Dylan said, glaring at her, and quickly covering Peanut's ears.

"Hey, he's gotta deal with it sooner or later."

"You're so cruel."

"Yeah, well."

They entered the building then and sat again in the outer waiting room while Tuck went in search of the much needed coffee.

Shortly after, they saw Phil appear from behind some parked

vehicles, with a man they assumed was the Consortium's lawyer, so they went out to meet him. A BuffaloTV van also pulled into the lot, and its occupants, reporter and camera, scurried to get set up.

"Hey, Dylan—" Phil seemed to stare at Dylan's t-shirt for a blank moment, then continued, "And Rev, good to see you!" He was a youngish, relatively nondescript, bespectacled man. "How was your trip to this point?"

"Good, thanks," Dylan said.

"This is our lawyer, Sam Lyon. Sam, Dylan O'Toole and Chris Reveille."

"Pleased to meet you," he said, not at all pleased to meet them. "When we're inside, you two will let us do the talking."

"Sure, no problem," Dylan said, a little defensively. "What's with the tv crew?" he asked Phil.

"Well, since you couldn't just slip in under the radar," he smiled wryly, "we figured we'd make the best of it."

"So sue me for opening my car door!" Rev said, because Sam Lyon wasn't smiling, wryly or otherwise.

"No! There will be no suing!" Lyon said to her sternly. "We are settling this out of court, here and now!"

"Settling what, exactly?" she asked.

"Well, that's what we're here to find out."

By this time, the Chief had seen their arrival, and Tuck had been sent out to meet and greet.

"Hello, Mr. Brightson?"

"Yes."

"I'm Officer Tucker, if you and—?"

"Sam Lyon," he reached forward to shake Tuck's hand.

"If you and Mr. Lyon, and Mr. O'Toole and Ms. Reveille, would come this way, please. There's coffee and muffins inside," he said quietly to Rev, as he led them into the station's meeting room. Peanut followed, partly because he wasn't told not to, and partly because, well, there were muffins inside.

Once they had all been seated at the table—or on the floor, as was the case for Peanut—the Chief introduced the Border Patrol's legal advisor, a Mr. Grim.

"All right, we're here—" the Chief began.

"Has either one of my clients committed a crime?" Mr. Lyon jumped right in. "Have they been charged with anything?"

"No, but—"

"Then I demand—"

"—it is our duty to protect our people, and that means not allowing anyone we think might commit a crime to enter our country. We have discretion," he looked at Mr. Lyon. "You know that."

Peanut also looked at Mr. Lyon. In fact, he looked at each person as they spoke. He was paying attention, he was.

"You also know," Mr. Grim spoke up, directing his comments to Mr. Lyon, "that some states still have blasphemy laws on the books. Do you promise not to blaspheme in those states?" he turned to Dylan and Rev. "What's your speech about?"

Dylan sat forward in his seat. "Well," he cleared his throat, "we thought," he looked to Rev for confirmation, "we thought we'd open with 'Good Afternoon.'"

"Or 'Good Morning,'" Rev added.

"But we wouldn't say 'or'."

"No. We wouldn't say 'or'. We'd just say 'Good Afternoon.' Or we'd say 'Good Morning.'"

"And then?"

"Well, that's as far as we got. Phil said—"

"Someone in our office will provide assistance," Phil said quickly, only momentarily confused by whether to be horrified or amused.

"And the content of the speech will not be blasphemous, no."

"I propose that we allow Mr. O'Toole and Ms. Reveille to proceed, to engage in this speaking tour," the Chief announced. "on the condition of escort."

"Escort? On what grounds?" Mr. Lyon objected. "For what purpose?"

"To ensure that no crime is committed by or against Ms. Reveille or Mr. O'Toole."

Everyone heard the 'or against'.

"Are you speaking in Kansas?" the Chief continued smoothly.

Phil consulted their itinerary. "Yes."

"Then it's a win-win situation. You'll need protection. I need assurance. Are we agreed?"

Phil had to admit Kansas was of some concern, now that he thought about it. He nodded to Mr. Lyon.

"Agreed." Was that sadness in his voice?

"Tucker!"

"Yes sir?" He bolted upright in his chair.

"You're reassigned."

"Excuse me sir?"

"You're to escort Chris Reveille and Dylan O'Toole on their speaking tour—" he looked at Rev, no it wasn't quite a glare "— through our fine country."

"Yes sir!"

"Tucker is to receive a copy of their itinerary," the Chief said to Phil.

"Certainly," Phil handed him a copy right there and there.

"And," the Chief looked at Tuck, "you'll be briefed by Legal—*our* Legal," he looked pointedly at Mr. Lyon, "as to what can and cannot be done. Or said."

"Yes sir."

Mr. Lyon looked ready to object, but Phil put a restraining hand on his arm.

Once the meeting had adjourned, Tuck rushed into the hallway after the Chief.

"And Peanut, sir?" He and Peanut looked at the Chief expectantly.

The Chief thought for a moment. "He passed Attack and Defense?"

"Yes sir. Mostly sir."

"Fine, the dog is reassigned too."

"Ah—Chief?"

The Chief looked at a waiting Peanut.

"Peanut, I hereby—" Peanut's ass flopped to the ground in response to the official tone— "reinstate—" Peanut's tongue peeked out— "What the hell am I—" the Chief turned to leave, but Peanut started to look so crushed— "You are hereby returned to active duty," he finished.

Peanut would've saluted if he'd known how. Instead he jumped up, turned half way around, and wiggled his bottom half.

As soon as they exited the building, the team from BuffaloTV rushed up.

"A word please?" the reporter said breathlessly to Dylan and pointed her mic at him.

"Perspicuity," he replied, and giggled.

"You are Dylan O'Toole and Chris Reveille? Arrested for blasphemy in Canada? For putting graffiti—"

"It wasn't exactly graffiti," Rev interrupted. "We added a quotation from *The Bible* to a billboard."

"And what quotation was that?"

"'Blessed are they that taketh and dasheth thy little ones against the stone.' Psalms 137:9."

"Isn't that a little inflammatory?"

"It was—appropriate," Rev said ambiguously.

"It was a Right-to-Life billboard," Dylan explained. "If it had been one of those sexual assault billboards, we would've added the bit from Deuteronomy: 'As for the women...ye may take them as plunder for yourselves.' It's my favourite."

"You're in favour of rape?"

Phil took a step forward.

"What? No, of course not!" Dylan said. "It's my favourite for showing that there's a lot more in *The Bible* than people think there is. Because they haven't actually read it."

Phil took a step backward.

"So you're saying most people are wrong? About what's in *The Bible*?"

"Yeah," Rev interjected. "I'd say most people are wrong. That's actually my whole philosophy of life right there in a nutshell." Dylan poked her.

"What we're saying is you can't just pick and choose."

"You don't think people should choose what to believe?'

"No! Yes! People should most definitely choose what to believe. I'm saying you can't just choose the bits from *The Bible* you agree with and ignore the rest. Well, you can, I suppose, but then any argument that begins with '*The Bible* says' or maybe even 'God says' will be useless. I mean, *you* could say '*The Bible* says don't kill' but then *I* could say '*The Bible* says *do* kill.' Which it does. In Joshua, for example. See? It's a stalemate. Better we should just figure out whether it's okay to kill, yeah? '*The Bible* says' part is irrelevant. Completely unnecessary."

At this point, the Chief Officer happened to step outside to see

Mr. Grim to his car. The reporter rushed from Rev and Dylan to him.

"Chief, how will you explain to your children tonight that you're letting a couple convicted criminals into our country to roam the streets at night?"

The Chief rolled his eyes and turned to go back inside without a comment, but at a nudge from Mr. Grim, changed his mind.

"My children are in their thirties," he said, "so they don't need me to explain anything to them, let alone the fact that we have freedom of speech here, as well as freedom of religion, freedom of association, and freedom of movement. Ms. Reveille and Mr. O'Toole will, however, be escorted as they engage in their speaking tour."

"And why is that?"

"Because some states have blasphemy laws—"

"Wouldn't that contradict freedom of speech?"

"Yes, it would," Mr. Lyon stepped in eagerly. "We maintain that those states with blasphemy laws are in direct violation of the Constitution of the United States of America—"

"Now wait just a minute," Mr. Grim stepped in as well, "you know very well that those freedoms are not absolute. We have what we call 'fighting words'," he explained to the reporter. "Speech intended to incite others is illegal. And it may very well be that blasphemous statements fall into that category."

"Oh please," Mr. Lyon scoffed, "you're glossing over what, exactly, fighting words are presumed to incite: hatred and violence. If so-called blasphemy is intended to incite, say, the pursuit of truth, the examination of one's faith—"

"No that's not quite right, I'm afraid," Mr. Grim scolded. "Fighting words are defined as those which 'by their very utterance inflict injury or tend to incite an immediate breach of the peace'. Blasphemous statements are very likely to incite an immediate breach of the peace."

"So might the claim that Santa Claus doesn't exist, if uttered at a mall in December in the presence of crowds of children waiting to see said Santa Claus. I find it interesting," Mr. Lyon continued, turning back to the reporter, "that the very first case of fighting words, Chaplinsky vs. the State of New Hampshire, 1941, was against a person of religion. Walter Chaplinsky was a Jehovah's Witness."

And it was only with the greatest of efforts that Mr. Grim refrained from saying 'Yeah, well, your mother wears army boots!'

"So," Rev said to Phil once the media, and Mr. Lyon, had gone, "we meet you in Fort Wayne in a few days? That's our first gig, right?"

"Actually," Phil said, looking vaguely out to the parking lot, "there's been a few changes in our plans. Why don't we go somewhere for lunch and I can fill you in?"

"Sounds like a plan. Got somewhere in mind?" Dylan asked, as he led the way to their car. "We'll drive," he added.

"I passed an Asian buffet place on the way," Phil said.

"Fine with me," Dylan said, looking at Rev.

"And me."

"Okay—no wait," he stopped at their car. "We need to get the mirror fixed."

"That's right, we do," Rev said. Not in the least bit sheepishly.

Dylan looked at his watch. "It'd be convenient if we found a garage or something on the way. We could leave our car, ride the rest of the way with you, and if it's ready after lunch—"

"That won't be necessary," Phil said then.

"But—"

"I mean, yes, necessary to get the mirror fixed, but not necessary that the car be ready—that's one of the changes. We've decided to provide a vehicle."

Dylan and Rev expressed some surprise. Their car was perfectly up to the task. Mirror deficiency notwithstanding.

"Partly," Phil started to lead them toward a white rental truck, "because you'll need a bit more room, since I'm not going to be going along—that's another change in the plan. So there's stuff you need to take. And partly—" the white truck happened to pull away at that moment, exposing a bright, a very bright, lime green mini-van.

Dylan's face lit up at the color.

'American Atheist Consortium' was written in large letters on the side facing them. Rev walked around the van to see what was written on the other side. She half expected to see something like 'There are no gods. Deal with it.' Which was exactly what she saw. She let out a delighted snort.

"It's one of those hybrids," Phil said, their glee not quite registering, "so it's not the fuel-guzzling environmental disaster you might think. Though of course we're paying for the gas in any event," he trailed off.

"I was going to ask you, by the way," Rev said in a carefully casual voice, "—we'd like more money. Our per diem—"

"How much more did you have in mind?"

"An extra thousand would be nice."

Dylan poked her. She poked him back.

"I've been authorized to offer an extra two hundred. Seeing as we're asking you to be—"

"A moving target," she finished.

"I was going to say a mobile billboard."

"Is it bullet-proof?" she asked.

"Well, it's lime green."

"And a lovely color indeed," Dylan said, walking around it.

"We wanted black. With somewhat more discreet lettering, but Marketing told us—well, apparently there's actually been a study done, and black cars are—most apt to be shot at."

"Five hundred," Dylan suggested.

"Two fifty," Phil said.

"Okay," they said together.

"Though you know," Rev said, "that doesn't necessarily mean that colors have some non-gunshot-inducing effect. It could just mean that no self-respecting drug lord or gun runner would ever drive a—not-black vehicle."

"Either way," Dylan pointed out.

"Yeah," she agreed. "So why lime green?" she asked Phil then.

"Marketing said it would stand out," he offered. Lamely. "Which is—"

"That it will," Dylan said.

"So we may as well transfer all of your stuff now?" Phil asked.

"Sure."

Dylan and Rev walked back to their car and Phil got in the van to drive it two rows over.

When he got out and opened the back doors, Dylan saw several boxes piled inside.

"We can talk about those at lunch," Phil said, going to their car for a load.

"Mystery boxes," Dylan said, as he put their bags inside. "I like it."

They left their car at a dealers'—the mirror would be replaced, the guy assured them, with suspicious vehemence, by the time they returned to pick it up. In eight months.

"We'll pay the storage fee, of course," Phil had said, taking out a credit card.

A short while later they pulled into the parking lot of the Asian buffet restaurant.

"Good afternoon, you'll be having our lunch buffet?" The host greeted them, led them to a table, then invited them to partake in both the hot and cold buffets.

Phil waited until they'd all gotten a plate of food before beginning. This took some time as Dylan had to get a bit of everything and Rev had to give serious consideration to everything. Phil just got his favourites.

"What's that?" Rev pointed to something on Dylan's plate when they'd gotten settled at their table.

"Noodles with yellow and green bits. What'd you think it was?" He grinned.

"Funny guy." She reached out with her fork and tasted some.

"Well?"

"Noodles with yellow and green bits," she announced.

"Okay," Phil said, once that was established, "so first change, the vehicle. You know about that now. Basically we figured, since you're driving clear across the country, on our dime, we may as well really capitalize on it. You remember that bus campaign in Britain? Well, what we're trying to do with the van is something like that."

"Good idea. Really. Apart from the moving target part of it," Rev said, "I'm going to like riding in a vehicle that says 'There are no gods. Deal with it.'"

"Okay, that's good. We weren't sure. We thought, given the billboard event that started this whole thing, we thought this *would* be something you guys would like—"

"You thought right," Dylan assured him. "Apart from the moving target part. But you're willing to pay extra for the risk we're taking on, so we're good with it."

"Okay, good." Phil took a forkful of his chow mein, then continued. "Second change, as I said before, is that I'm not coming with you. I was going to be your AAC liaison, the one who—well, we'll get into what I was going to do, because you two are going to be doing it now—I've made out a list for you. We're looking for a replacement, but it may be a couple months."

"May we ask why you changed your mind?"

"Oh, sure, it's not really that I changed my mind. I'm actually a bit disappointed not to be coming along, now," he added ambiguously. "But my school—at first I had this semester off, but there's been a change in schedule, and the course I was going to take in January is starting now, in September. And this is the last time it's being offered. The professor is retiring."

"We didn't know you were in school," Dylan said.

"Yes, I'm getting a Th.D."

"A Ph.D.? In what?"

"No, a *Th*.D. Doctor of Theology. I'm a student at Yale's Divinity School."

"But you're—"

"—single-handedly responsible for diverting ten generations of ministers and priests," he grinned a little self-consciously. "I take just one course at a time. That enables me not only to keep my job with the AAC, but also," he paused, considering, "to be very vocal in class discussions."

"What a brilliant idea!" Dylan said. "What a brilliant life! You're like that woman in *Sweet November*!"

"What's it like?" Rev was intrigued. "Divinity School."

"Oh. Well, let me see. You have your true believers. They want to change the world, make the world a better place. By the time they lose their religion, so to speak—and most of them do—as I'm sure you know, studying religion is the best way to become an atheist."

They nodded their agreement.

"By the time they realize they've been duped, they figure they've invested too much to drop out and start all over again. And, too, by that time, many have a wife and kids to support. Same old same old."

"A sad, sad story," Dylan concurred.

"And the ones who *aren't* true believers?" Rev asked. "Why would they even enrol in a seminary?"

"Well, it's not so much that they aren't true believers, it's more that they're just comfortable in the church. Always have been and can't imagine another career. They did well in school, they're conservative, someone somewhere along the line said they'd make a good minister or whatever, and they just sort of went along."

"Sad, sad story," Dylan said.

"And then there are your go-getters," Phil continued. "They're the worst. They're there for the job. The money, the power."

"Sad, sad—"

"It's a tax-free income. Housing's provided. The hours are phenomenal—a few hours a day, and not even every day. Sermons are provided."

"Sermons are provided?" Rev was surprised. "Priests don't write their own sermons?"

Phil shook his head. "They're like news anchors. Someone else hands them the script. They just—present it. In fact, most seminaries have extra classes in that."

"In what," Rev snorted, "acting?"

"Yes," Phil was serious. "But generally speaking," he continued, "seminaries, divinity schools, they're boys' clubs. Most of the students are men. So it can be very competitive."

"But what do they compete for?" Rev asked, when she had recovered.

"Jobs mostly. There are good assignments and bad assignments. And there's a ladder of advancement. When two or men gather together, they're going to fight for power. It's no different in a divinity school."

"Wow," Rev said. "I'd never really thought about—any of that."

"It explains—well, I'm sure it explains a lot of stuff we don't even see," Dylan commented.

"Anyone going up for seconds?" Phil asked, standing. Dylan and Rev grabbed their empty plates.

"These places never have good desserts," Rev commented as she put a bit of this and a bit of that onto her plate.

"I'm sure Buffalo has a cheesecake place," Dylan said. "We'll find it."

"Okay, so," Phil changed the topic when they had returned to their table, "you're going to be managing the tour yourselves." He opened the file he had brought in with him. "Here's a credit card. You use it for gas, vehicle repairs, accommodations.

"Here's a cheque," Phil thought for a moment, then wrote out a cheque. "For your first month's per diem. You'll get one of these on the first of each month. Or thereabouts."

"How?" Rev asked.

"We'll send it to where you're staying. Here's your updated accommodations list. Hotel reservations—the ones in bold are the ones at which you can expect a per diem cheque to be waiting for you, ask at the main desk when you check in—it'll be FedEx—plus the names, addresses, and phone numbers of people who have offered their guest room or what have you. Some are Consortium members, and some are college-affiliates."

"Okay, if we're not exactly presenting the kind of enlightenment the Bible colleges expect, why would college-affiliates offer to put us up?" Rev asked.

"Well, either they don't know you're not presenting what they expect, or they do, and they're hoping to convert you."

"Hm."

"You'll also see a lot of empty dates. We've just made reservations for the night before and the night of. It's up to you if you want to arrive earlier or stay longer. You may not want to take the shortest route from point A to point B. And that's okay. You're not under any obligation to us beyond showing up for the engagements we make. Actually, now that you're our bus, so to speak, the more miles you cover, the better. Just be sure you're where you need to be for the speeches and whatever else Dorothy sets up.

"Speaking of which, here's the most current update of your engagements," he presented another sheet from the file.

Dylan and Rev scanned the list of colleges, radio stations, and newspapers. They had received a list before their departure, of course, but this list was significantly longer.

"Head office will be sending press releases in advance to each one—here's a copy of what we're sending, just so you know what they're starting with." He handed them the next item in the file. "Check in with Dorothy every day to get additions and cancellations. You've got her phone number and email?"

"We do," Dylan confirmed.

"As for those engagements, here's a preparation checklist." He presented yet another sheet. "This is what I was going to be doing." They scanned it as he continued. "You call the College contact the day before to confirm the engagement and to confirm that a table and two chairs will be provided outside the auditorium. Names and phone numbers are there. You show up an hour before you're scheduled to speak. Directions and maps are included. You set up the AAC table. That's what's in the mystery boxes. A cloth for the table, with our logo on it, and another one to hang from the podium. And material to put on the table: books, pamphlets, catalogues, CDs, member organization literature, etc. Some items are free, some have price tags. There's a price list inside the box. There's also a cashbox. There are also membership forms, though I doubt you'll be needing many of them. Email Dorothy when you need any item restocked. You'll get a sense of how many of what to keep on hand. She'll have stuff sent to you, again via FedEx, again to your hotel.

"And here," he presented the next sheet of paper, "are suggestions for your talks, speaking notes for the interviews. You're free to say what you like, of course, but please remember that to some extent you're representing not just the consortium, but atheists in general. We want publicity. Not alienation." He looked pointedly at Rev. Who opened her mouth, then closed it.

"You did a good job with that reporter this morning," he said to Dylan. Who resisted the impulse to stick out his tongue at Rev.

"Any questions? It's a lot to take in, I know. Sorry to spring this on you."

"No, we're good, I think," Dylan said. "It's very organized."

"And very clear," Rev added. Ambiguously.

"And you've got my number and email. Contact me, or Dorothy, any time with any questions, any problems at all. We want this to work. We're hoping it'll work splendidly."

"We are too," Dylan said, and Rev nodded agreement.

"Okay, third change. We'd like you to hang around here for a day or two. We're hoping the news coverage from the border thing might get us a few last-minute engagements. Probably not a college appearance on such short notice, but maybe a talk-radio spot. We've got a couple rooms booked at the Curada."

"Oh. So—" Dylan looked at his watch.

"The paper comes out around four o'clock. Print edition. I don't know if the story was filed in time for today's paper. If not, we should be able to see something on their website by about that time."

"Right, so we've got a couple hours. Shall we meet you back at the hotel at four?"

"Sure, but—"

"Oh. Right. Well," he looked at Rev, "do you want to ride the buses through Buffalo for a couple hours, see what there is to see, let

Phil have the van? There are buses in Buffalo, yeah?"

"I imagine so. There must be a visitor information center somewhere. Maybe I can drop you off there before I head back to the hotel. Or we can ask here about a cheesecake place," Phil had not missed that, "and I can drop you off there."

"That works," said Rev.

So shortly after four o'clock, Phil knocked on the door of the room in which Rev and Dylan were staying, newspaper in hand.

"Hey," Dylan said, answering the door, "come on in."

"We've got cheesecake!" Rev said. "Would you like Buttercream Delight, Plum Paradise, or Chocolate Monkey?"

"Oh, I—" he looked at the spread on the table.

"We also have Pineapple Sunrise and Fudgeroo." Then, seeing the expression on his face, she added, "We got enough for the first few days of our trip."

Dylan grinned. As if.

"I'll have the Plum Paradise. Though the Pineapple Sunrise looks good too."

"No problem." Rev halved the slices and put them on a plate for him.

"Coffee?" Dylan asked from the kitchenette. He was right about their reservations. Not only were swimming pools likely to be included, the AAC had sprung for suites for much of the trip.

"Yes, please. Thank you." Phil sat at the small table, opened the paper, and started looking for the write-up of their incident. Not on the front page. Not on the second page. Nor the third.

"We didn't make the front page?" Rev asked, joining him at the table. With half of the Buttercream Delight and half of the Fudgeroo.

"Apparently not. Didn't think we would, though." He continued scanning the pages, as Dylan set coffee for three onto the table. And the other half of Pineapple Sunrise.

"Ah. Here it is."

"Back page?"

"'Chief Officer Tom Eggleston approved entry into the United States'," Phil read, "'for two convicted criminals, Chris Reveille and Dylan O'Toole. It is not known at this time why Reveille and O'Toole, who live in Montreal, chose to cross the border at Buffalo.'"

"That's it?" Rev asked, with surprise.

"That's it," he put the paper down, and sighed.

"But it doesn't even say what we were convicted of! And it doesn't even *mention* the tour! Or the consortium. And Dylan made a really good argument, which doesn't exactly happen every day—"

"Hey!"

She grinned. "Why wasn't *that* reported?"

"Well—"

"I can tell you why," Dylan said. "The newspaper's largest advertisers are conservatives." Phil nodded. "And he who pays the piper...."

"But wouldn't they *want* to hear that blasphemers were convicted?"

"Yes," Phil sighed. "But not that they were let into the country." He took a sip of his coffee.

"Geez! We should sue!"

Dylan looked at her with surprise.

"What? When in Rome," she said. "I'm trying to fit in."

He let out a little snort at that improbability.

"We can't sue," Phil said. "What they said isn't untrue."

"No, but it sure as hell is incomplete." She waved her spoon full of Fudgeroo.

"Yes, but it's a newspaper. If *any* of the stories were complete, they'd be books," he said, taking a bite of his Plum Paradise.

"Hm," she said, unconvinced. Clearly thinking about the sports page.

"So I guess this isn't going to land us any last-minute gigs?" Dylan said. "They wouldn't put something more substantial in tomorrow's paper, would they?"

"No, what we see is all we'll get." Phil started to fold up the paper, but Dylan's eye was caught then by the back page of the entertainment section.

"Hey, there's a laser show with Pink Floyd at the planetarium. Anyone in?"

o they left first thing next day. At two o'clock in the afternoon.

"Wow," Rev said, climbing into the passenger seat, "this is high up."

"It is. When we cross bridges, we'll be able to see the water now."

"Yeah. Talk about poor design."

Dylan looked over in confusion.

"The bridges. There's no reason they couldn't be structurally sound and at the same time allow a view of the beautiful. I mean apart from men's inability or unwillingness value beauty."

"Most musicians are men," Dylan countered. "And painters, sculptors—"

"Most we *know* of. Who've succeeded in making a *career* of it. I doubt that says anything about their capacity for pleasure."

"You're probably right," Dylan sighed, and turned his attention to the dashboard.

"No one behind us will be able to see ahead. We should be prepared for lots of rear-end collisions," Rev said then.

"I wonder if minivans really do have more rear-end collisions...."

"And whether the auto industry is suppressing that research...."

"Hey, we have air conditioning," he said.

"Cool," she grinned. He grimaced.

"What's this?" She pushed a button.

"Please state your destination," a fake-cheerful voice said.

Rev was thoughtful for a moment. Then said "Did I ever tell you about my Turing test for Emily?"

"Emily as in Bell's automated interactive customer service program?"

"Yeah. When it first came out, and human telemarketers were so compelled to stick to their script they sounded automated, and were supremely unhelpful because of it—the sticking to their script, not the sounding automated—sometimes I really didn't know when I was talking to a real person and when not."

"So, one day, when you were talking to Emily—to a supremely unhelpful Emily—"

"I told her to fuck off. And she didn't get angry!" Rev said with delight.

Dylan was thoughtful for a moment. Then deactivated the on-board GPS.

"Did you know Fort Wayne has won the All-America City Award three times?" Dylan had his laptop open; they'd switched and Rev was driving.

"That can't be good."

"No," he agreed. "If it were the All-Ameri*can* City Award, then at least...," he continued browsing. "And it's known as the City of Churches."

"That can't be—"

"Hey, we're in time for the Johnny Appleseed Festival!"

"That—could be interesting."

They pulled into the Curada Hotel, where Dorothy had made reservations.

"Care—" Dylan was too late. Rev had opened her door and—

fallen out.

"Shit."

"Long way down?" he asked mildly.

"Oh shut up."

They signed in, found their room, and, since they'd been able to replenish their supply at the Pink Floyd show (who'd've thought?), decided it was time to get silly.

"So this is pretty good, yeah?" Dylan said, once they'd gotten settled and he'd rolled and lit a joint. "Not too beige?"

"This is pretty good," she agreed, taking it from him. "Not too beige."

"We've got a tv, with a remote control, that works," he demonstrated. "We've got air conditioning *and* heat. We've even got a little kitchen."

"But there's no cheesecake in our kitchen," she said sadly.

"That's because somebody ate it all," he exhaled and passed it to her.

"Yeah," she said, drawing in.

"We can get some more," he said brightly.

"Yeah?"

"We've also got room service," he nodded to the phone sitting on the nightstand between the beds.

"Okay, let's get some more cheesecake."

Dylan dialled room service.

"Hi, can we get some more cheesecake?" he said. Rather cheerfully.

"And pizza," Rev said, exhaling.

"And pizza."

"And Doritos."

"And Doritos."

"And Pepsi."

"And Pepsi. Room 309."

He hung up. "There. We're getting more cheesecake."

"Cool. I like it that we can order out for cheesecake."

"It's a beautiful world." He took another toke. And opened the drawer of the nightstand.

"Oh, that has got to go," Rev said, looking at *The Bible* he'd taken out.

"Well we can't just throw it away."

"Sure we can. Give it to me. Two points says I can get it in the garbage can from here."

"We should just put another book in the drawer. *The God Delusion*," he giggled. "Or *Aesop's Fables*."

"*Mother Goose*!" Rev sputtered. "We have to find a bookstore."

"Now? We'll never manage to do that."

"No," she agreed. Sadly.

"Maybe the gift shop will have what we want." Dylan was looking through the laminated folder he'd taken from under the phone.

"There's a gift shop here?" Rev asked.

"And a business center—"

"*They* might have *Mother Goose*."

"A dining room, a swimming pool, a fitness room—"

"Let's go to the fitness room."

"Do you feel the need to get fit?"

"I feel the need to go to the fitness room."

"Not the same thing."

"At all," she agreed.

So they changed into their sweats. Mostly because it seemed the thing to do.

"Ready?" Dylan asked.

"Ready," Rev replied, brimming with good fitness intentions, and led the way into the closet.

"It's always door number three."

"Yeah."

They found the elevator, pressed the buttons, and got in when the doors opened. It was easier that way, they'd discovered.

They both stared at the grid of numbers and letters.

"Do you know what floor the fitness room is on?" Rev finally asked.

"No. Do you?"

"No."

They stared at the grid of numbers and letters a bit longer.

"If you were a fitness room, where would you be?" Dylan asked.

"Near a bunch of fit people. Otherwise I'd be called an unfitness room."

"And where would we find a bunch of fit people?"

"Near a fitness room."

"That wasn't very helpful, was it," she said after several moments.

"No."

"There's a phone," she observed. "That could be helpful."

"But it's an elevator phone. Isn't it just for emergencies? Like when you're stuck?"

"Right. Okay. But. Aren't we stuck?"

"Wow," Rev said, half an hour later when they stepped into the room. "Both sides of the room are set up exactly the same way!"

"That's a mirror."

"Oh."

"First one to do five steps on the treadmill wins," Dylan says.

"Wins what?"

"Nothing. Just wins. That's why so many people watch sports. And then beat each other up when 'their' team doesn't win.'

"Didn't that study actually say that people tend to beat each other up when their team *does* win?"

"Oh yeah." He paused on the way to the treadmill machine. "I wonder what the control group did—the ones whose teams hadn't even played."

"Wouldn't the control group be people who don't 'have' a team?"

"Hm."

"What were we going to do?" Rev said after a moment.

"Five steps on the treadmill." Dylan remembered.

"Oh yeah. I can do that." She walked over to it and was about to board.

"When it's on," he qualified, turning it on.

"Spoilsport."

She stood at an angle to it and got into a rhythmic rocking, forward and back, forward and back, like she was trying to enter a double dutch.

"Can't do it," she gave up and stepped away. "You try."

"Okay. New strategy." He turned it off, stepped on, and *then* turned it on.

"Maybe if you'd grabbed on first," Rev said, looking at him splattered against the wall behind it.

She stepped on, grabbed onto the handlebars, then turned it on. And was almost immediately hanging on for dear life, her feet dangling off the end, her body making the hypotenuse of a triangle.

"Let go!" Dylan cried out as the hypotenuse sagged, perhaps painfully.

"No!" She cried back, confirming the painful part. "Turn it off!"

He hurried to the switch and turned it off.

Rev made various parts of several other polygons before she managed to get off.

"I have an idea," Dylan said. And grinned, momentarily happy with just that realization.

He approached the treadmill, threw one leg over, and sat down. "Remember Pickle?" He and Rev had ridden horses at Dim's farm. It was something Dylan had never done before. And until this moment, something he intended never to do again. He wiggled his bottom a bit and made sure his feet were firmly on the floor on each side, ready to walk along.

"Ready!" he said to Rev. She turned it on.

"Okay, that didn't work." Once again, she managed to state the obvious.

"No," he said from the floor at the end of the treadmill. "I got confused as to which part would be moving."

She suddenly lost interest in their task, or forgot again what it was, and began walking around the gleaming chrome and black leather benches, the free weights, and the various machines. "Do you remember when weight rooms first started showing up in high schools?" she said.

"Yeah. We got ours when I was in grade ten."

"I was in grade eleven." She straddled the inclined bench for sit-ups, thinking maybe she'd do a few. Or at least one. "The wrestling team pushed for it and eventually the principal approved the conversion of an old classroom. Turns out, though," she grabbed onto the top part then swung her feet up. They hit the sides of the bench. Well, one hit the side of the bench. The other swung feebly through the air below the incline.

Having seen that one coming—or rather, having anticipated that at some point in the process she'd simply fall off the bench—Dylan was already on his way over.

"Hold on," he said, then lifted one dead weight foot, and then the other, onto the board.

"It was supposed to be just for the boys," she continued unfazed, hooking her feet under the grip at the top, then lay back. "Well, Jill and I—"

"She was on the track team with you?"

"And field hockey and basketball," she stared at the ceiling. "Anyway, we figured we should be able to use the weight room too. So we did."

"And?"

"Well, the boys who were there when we walked in gave us such a look."

"And you told them off."

"Hell, no," she turned her head to face him. Once she found him. Ignoring the little bit of dizzy that ensued. "We were the brainy dweeb girls. We couldn't do that. So we just ignored them. Turns out that works just as well with men. Well, boys. They were so uncomfortable, they all left. And Jill and I started pumping iron." She put her hands behind her head, ready to begin her sit-ups. "Yup, we were the Gloria Steinems of the Plattsburg High School weight room."

Energized, she sat up quickly—then swayed, unhooked her feet, tumbled off the board, and threw up in the waste basket.

Dylan looked at her, curled up on the floor. "You've come a long way, baby," he said, grinning.

They arrived at the college auditorium the next day, an hour ahead of time, as instructed. Which was, they congratulated each other, amazing. They'd even arrived before Tucker. Who they were supposed to have waited for. Back in Buffalo.

They found a table and two chairs outside the room, as arranged, and started unpacking the two boxes Phil had prepared. Rev's box contained, as promised, the table cloth with its AAC logo, the podium banner, a cashbox, some DVDs, pamphlets, and membership applications. Dylan's box was full of books: the classics—Smith's *Atheism: The Case Against God,* Ruth Hermence Green's *The Born Again Skeptic's Guide to the Bible,* Carl Sagan of course, Ingersoll, Dawkins, Hitchins, O'Hair, and Harris, as well as a series they'd never seen before—reprints of Russell's *Why I am not a Christian* and Warraq's *Why I am not a Muslim,* along with *Why I am not Jew, Why I am not a Jehovah's Witness,* and so on.

"This was a really good idea," Rev said, nodding to the series and picking up what was no doubt the best-seller of the bunch, *Why I am not a Druid.*

Dylan went into the auditorium to put the banner on the podium, and when he returned, Rev had the table set up. They had all its items nicely arranged, just as students started to arrive. And walk right by.

"We have to—"

"Offer free beer?" Dylan suggested.

"That'd do it."

They continued to sit at their table, trying to look inviting. Then they tried for nice, and then harmless. The students continued to walk right by.

Five minutes before they were scheduled to speak, Dylan said, "We're both going in, yeah?"

"But then there won't be anyone at our table. What if they steal all the books?"

"This is a Bible college," he said.

"My point."

"Okay, but they're starving students, Christian or not. So if they don't pay for the books, so what? The bigger point is that they get them, right?"

"Yeah. You're right." She tucked the cashbox into one of the empty boxes sitting under the table, and they headed into the auditorium.

The Dean was waiting at the podium, and when he saw them come up the aisle, he stepped forward and called for attention. When everyone had settled, and Rev and Dylan had found the stairs that got them onto the stage, he introduced them.

"Ladies and gentlemen, welcome to the third special lecture in our Bible Study series. Our guests today are from the American Atheist Consortium, would you please welcome Ms. Chris Reveille and Mr. Dylan O'Toole."

There wasn't any polite applause, but as ex-teachers, they were used to that. Dylan took the mic and launched into their prepared talk.

"Good—" A chunk of bread hit him in the head.

"What the—" Rev stood up.

There were a few boos, then a whole loaf came barrelling through the air. And another. They ducked.

"Well, this is just—" A fish smacked Rev in the face.

"Confusing?" Dylan suggested as he stared at the fish now lying among the loaves of bread.

Another fish flopped through the air, then landed with a slight thud.

Rev picked it up and whipped it back. Or rather, tried to. She discovered it's impossible to whip something slimy.

When a third fish was launched toward the stage, the fur really started to fly. Because Peanut came sailing through the air, neatly intercepting the throw and catching the fish. Someone threw another one. He caught that one too. And grinned.

By the time Tuck arrived, just twenty seconds later, half the student body was throwing fish at Peanut. After all, neither Rev nor Dylan were catching them mid-flight in their mouths.

And the other half, demonstrating that college students today have the attention span of a gnat, had simply lost interest. And were apparently texting their friends to tell them so.

"Sorry I was late," a breathless Tuck said to Rev and Dylan when he got onto the stage. "I—Peanut! Drop it!"

Peanut did so. But then rolled on it. Them, actually, since there were now a dozen fish littering the stage floor.

"Peanut Thaddeus Tucker, you stop that right now!"

Peanut froze, belly up. Then slowly relaxed over onto his side, continuing onto his belly. He lay on the fish. Didn't roll on it, mind you, he just lay on it. In fact, he'd stopped rolling altogether, just as he was told, he seemed to point out. As he surreptitiously spread out to cover as many fish as possible. What?

Apparently the third special lecture was over, since most of the students had left. As had the Dean. So Dylan and Rev took the banner off the podium and also left, followed by Tucker and a reluctant Peanut.

"You put that back!" Tucker said to Peanut, when he turned to make sure Peanut was still in tow and saw a fin protruding from out of his tightly closed mouth.

Peanut looked like he was about to shake his head no, but then decided to put his tail between his legs and his fish back onto the stage.

They exited the auditorium and returned to their table. Which was now empty.

The garbage barrel at the end of the hall, on the other hand, was full.

"Guess we should've seen that coming," Dylan said, as he walked over to inspect the damage.

"Yeah," Rev sighed.

"At least they didn't torch 'em," he said, picking out a few undamaged, unsoiled books.

"At least they didn't torch us."

So the four of them stood in the parking lot beside their vehicles, each mentally reviewing the results of the first engagement of the tour.

"He needs a bath," Rev said. True to form.

"Yes he does," Tucker agreed.

"So—does he even *fit* into a bath tub?"

"Not really."

"So what do you normally do, hose him down outside somewhere?"

"No, he doesn't like that. There's a small lake near where we live. I keep a bar of biodegradable soap in my car and—"

Rev was staring at the decorative pond, complete with fountain, that was in front of the campus church on the other side of the parking lot.

"It's their fault he needs a bath," she said.

Tuck got the soap, and they walked over. Peanut happily leapt into the pond, then trotted around its perimeter. Splish splash splish splash. He tried to pick up one of the many shiny pennies littered on the pond's bottom. Got a noseful and snorted. Tried again. Got another noseful and snorted. Laughed.

"Okay, Sweet Pea, bath time." Tucker stripped to his boxers and got in with him. "It's easier this way," he explained to Rev and Dylan. And proceeded to soap and lather a willing Peanut. Who enthusiastically returned the favour.

"You heard the man," Rev said. And followed suit.

"You miss the lake, don't you," Dylan said a moment later as he waded in to stand beside her.

She looked out across the—pond. "Yeah."

"This isn't the same."

"Not even close," she agreed.

"The lake doesn't have a fountain though."

"No, it doesn't." So, mostly out of boredom, she climbed into the top dish of the fountain. Where the campus security guards could see her and call the local police.

"For what?" she asked. Indignantly. When the police told her she was under arrest.

"Indecent exposure."

"But I don't have any breasts," she pointed to her post-preemptive-bilateral-mastectomied chest.

Well that stopped them. Until then, they'd avoided looking directly at her chest.

"But you're still a woman," the brighter of the two said. "According to Indiana's state laws, it's illegal to—"

"To what, exactly?"

Tucker, in the meantime, had given Peanut a quick rinse, then hustled him out of the fountain and into his car. In case it was also illegal for dogs to be bathed in a public fountain. Unfortunately in his covert rush to do so, he forgot to tell Peanut to shake. Before he got into the car. Okay, that works too, he thought to himself, noting the now opaque quality of the windows.

"Yes, what exactly does the law say?" Dylan was curious. "That it's illegal for women to be shirtless in public or that it's illegal for a woman to bare her breasts in public?"

The senior officer scrunched up his face, then stepped away, turned on his radio, and made a call to the station. They heard nothing but static between his linguistically proficient uh-huhs.

"We've been instructed to take you in, m'am." He nodded to his cohort to cuff her.

"Um, would you please put your shirt back on?"

"You'll get cold," Dylan said, handing it to her and putting on his own as well.

Once at the station, Dylan insisted on being booked along with Rev.

"But you're not under arrest, sir."

"Of course I am. I did exactly what she did. If it's illegal for her, it's also illegal for me, right? I mean, how can it not be, if I did the very same thing?"

The senior officer scrunched up his face again. He was clearly in over his head. So he went ahead and did the paperwork on both of them, put them in the holding cell, then left the room.

"You're from Canada," the bright one who had remained at the desk said with some disgust, apparently just then actually reading the drivers' licenses they'd handed over. "No wonder," he muttered.

"What's that supposed to mean?" Rev asked from her bench in the holding cell.

"Well, you let homosexuals marry," he said. As if the connection were obvious.

She thought about it, for several long moments, then finally had to ask. "And that's relevant how?"

"Well, that and what you did, they're both a disrespect to marriage, aren't they."

"How does two people of the same sex getting married show a lack of respect for the institution?"

"Well, they can't have kids, can they," he snickered.

"Actually, they can, but I assume you mean without IVF."

He looked at her dully.

"I think you should take that as a yes," Dylan offered.

"So, what, you're saying the whole point of marriage, the *only* point of marriage, is to have kids?"

He didn't respond.

"Take that as a yes too?" Rev asked Dylan.

"I would, yes."

"So a woman over sixty shouldn't be allowed to get married?" Rev asked him.

He looked at her as if she was crazy.

"Women over sixty can't have kids," she explained.

"Neither can young men who've had a vasectomy," Dylan said to her.

"Right. So," she raised her voice, "young men who've had a vasectomy shouldn't be allowed to get married either."

"But how would they know?" Dylan asked.

Rev stared at him.

"Not the young men," he grinned. Winced, actually. "The marriage officials. They'd have to have everyone get a fertility test before they granted a marriage license."

"Well, and not just that," Rev said, "people would have to sign something saying they were going to reproduce. Right?" she called out.

The officer had, oddly enough, become uncommunicative.

"It doesn't necessarily follow," she said to him anyway, "but I'm just curious: if you believe that marriage should be reserved for those who have kids, do you also believe that those who have kids should be married? So all these unmarried young women who get pregnant—"

"Should be ashamed of themselves, yes."

"The young men too," Dylan spoke up. "They're also unmarried parents."

"Yeah, but they probably don't even know it half the time," Rev noted.

"Still."

"Still," she agreed. She turned her attention back to the officer. "So basically you disapprove of any sex before marriage."

"No," Dylan corrected her, "just reproductive sex. Before marriage. Though, actually, it'd have to include during marriage too, if it's with someone they're not married too."

"No, wouldn't it be only if it's with someone who's not married? Because if—"

"That'd be adultery," the officer found his tongue again. "Which is a sin."

"But not always, right?" Rev said. "Because adultery includes recreational sex outside marriage. And that would have to be okay, right, because they're not making children?"

Back to uncommunicative mode.

"Okay, so we've shown that gay marriage doesn't disrespect marriage—by showing that marriage isn't only for having kids. Given who's allowed to be married. Or, if it is," she acknowledged Dylan's look, "then not only should gays not be allowed to marry, but also women over a certain age, men who've had a vasectomy or are otherwise infertile, and women who've had a tubal ligation or are otherwise infertile."

"And," Dylan added, "everyone who just doesn't want to have kids."

"Right. And in any case, in that case, gays getting married wouldn't disrespect marriage so much as challenge its purpose. Okay. Now, as for the other half," she raised her voice, you said gay marriage *and* women without shirts—"

"Or women with bare breasts—"

"Right. Which one?" she called out.

"He's not answering you."

"No, he's not."

"Go with women with bare breasts."

"Okay. So women with bare breasts also somehow shows disrespect for marriage. How do you figure that?" she called out. "Hello? Did you want me to do your thinking for you again?"

He glared at her.

"Take that as a yes?"

Dylan nodded agreeably.

"Okay," she thought about it. "Well, given your belief that marriage is all about reproducing, it seems to me that women who bare their breasts would be doing just the opposite of what you say. They'd be showing respect for marriage. I mean, if she's baring her breasts because she's breastfeeding, well, you can't get more about having kids than that, can you?"

He was still uncommunicative.

"And if she's showing her breasts in a sexual way, well, there too, if it's in order to attract a mate—"

Dylan interrupted. "A husband—"

"Right. A husband who will, after the contract's signed, become a mate. Which means they'll have kids. So there again, baring breasts seems to *endorse*, not challenge, the whole reproduction thing. Which you associate with marriage."

"Okay," she summed up, "so we've disproved your claim that gay marriage and bare-breasted women are related because they both disrespect marriage—"

"Actually," Dylan chipped in again, "he's still right about them being related: they both *don't* disrespect marriage."

"Ah, good catch. Okay, so where does that leave us?"

"Waiting to hear how being shirtless is wrong."

"Well, *legally* wrong—"

About ten minutes later, the senior officer returned with his supervisor. Dylan and Rev sat quietly in the holding cell while the three of them conferred by the desk. At one point, the supervisor looked over at Rev. She helpfully flipped up her t-shirt, flashing him her chest. Dylan did the same. The supervisor picked up the phone and made a call.

One of the officers, the bright one, busied himself making coffee while they waited. Dylan and Rev didn't know what they were waiting for. They hoped it was the coffee.

Eventually, the supervisor's supervisor appeared. Rev flashed him her chest immediately. Helpfully. Dylan again followed suit. Unhelpfully.

"Release the man," the supervisor's supervisor said.

The supervisor got the keys from the senior officer and walked to the holding cell.

"No," Dylan said. "I insist. If what she did is illegal, then what I did is illegal. We did the same thing."

"But she's a woman."

"And yet," Dylan said, "I've got the nipples." He flashed his chest again. As did Rev, to enable immediate confirmation of Dylan's point.

The four of them conferred, more loudly, by the desk. The discussion was an incredibly disordered mess of claims about decency, women, the law, public order, decency, Canada, morality, America, and decency.

"So have you figured it out yet?" Rev called out after a few minutes.

They all glared at her.

"Maybe if you could put your finger on exactly why it would be wrong if I *had* breasts, you could figure out if it's wrong now that I don't have breasts. Like, suppose the problem is that women's breasts are sexual."

She suddenly had their attention.

"Okay," she continued, "but if the problem is sexual stuff in public, you'd have to arrest almost every advertisement in the city."

"Well, not the advertisement," Dylan corrected.

"No, not the advertisement. The company responsible for the advertisement."

"Unless it's incorporated. Aren't corporations exempt from that kind of—responsibility for their actions?"

"Hm." Rev saw then that they'd lost them. "Blatantly sexual," she said. And had them again. "Maybe the problem is just with things that are *blatantly* sexual. But breasts aren't always blatantly sexual."

"Which is why many states exempt breasts that are in use at the time as fast food outlets," Dylan pointed out.

"Right. But even apart from that. I mean, even before," she said to Dylan, "I didn't always consider my breasts to be sexual. Most of the time they were just globs of fat attached to my chest."

"You are so poetic," Dylan grinned at her. "At the risk of launching you into one of your—well, at the risk of launching you, perhaps the critical point here is that *men* consider them to be sexual," he offered.

"Right. Good point. So once again it's the *male* view, the *male* experience, that defines reality."

"More precisely, it's the *straight* male view and/or experience."

"Right. But even so. I mean, so what if my breasts *are* sexual—objects. To heterosexual men. How does that lead to a law requiring that they be covered?" She looked pointedly at the four officers of the law who seemed to assume she'd asked a rhetorical question. Always the assumption when one is asked a question one can't answer.

"It helps them not go around all day with a hard-on?" Dylan suggested.

"Right. So laws are made by *and for* heterosexual men."

"Oh lay off, lady! It's for your own protection!"

The supervisor's supervisor glared at the supervisor who glared at the senior officer who glared at the bright one who'd spoken.

"Because otherwise we'd be assaulted all day long by men who have so little control they wouldn't be able to keep their hands off our breasts?" Rev asked.

He nodded. Couldn't help himself.

"Well in that case, the law should be that men are not allowed in the presence of bare-breasted women. Not that bare-breasted women are not allowed in the presence of men."

The bright one laughed. The other three didn't.

The supervisor's supervisor walked over to a cabinet full of very thick books. Anticipating, the supervisor sat down at one of the two computers and started to key in a search. They found the relevant law at about the same time. The supervisor's supervisor glared at the two arresting officers. Then he glared at the supervisor. Then he picked up the phone. Then he looked at his watch and put the phone back down. He muttered something to the supervisor, then left the room. The supervisor muttered something to the senior officer, then left the room. The senior officer glared at the other officer, then turned to Rev and Dylan.

"I'm afraid we're going to have to keep you overnight. The District Attorney will arrive in the morning and a decision will be made at that time."

"A decision regarding—"

"What to do."

"Ah."

At around midnight, they heard Tucker's voice. It roused them from the light doze they'd fallen into as they leaned up against each other.

74

"But I promise. I'll have them back in the morning. There's no point in making them stay here all night."

"You agree to provide escort?"

"Actually, sir, I'm already assigned escort."

There was a silence. In which everyone could hear the backfire.

"Well, you're not doing a very good job, are you?"

"No, sir," Tucker mumbled. "I understood, that is, I thought I was to be on the alert for blasphemies. Religious blasphemies."

At around two o'clock, they were again roused from their uncomfortable dozing as a young man was brought in to share the holding cell. He didn't look too good.

"Hey, are you okay?" Dylan asked him with concern.

The young man gave him a look. Through his black eye, cut lip, and skinned cheekbone.

"Stupid question. Sorry. Do you need medical attention?"

"No." He shifted his weight, and let out a groan as he tried to disappear into the corner he'd claimed.

"What happened?" Rev asked.

"I got beaten up."

Rev shouted out through the cell bars, "That's illegal too now?"

The young man grinned. Then winced.

"You're a male prostitute and one of your customers did this?" Dylan hazarded a guess as he sat down beside him.

"If they don't pay, they're technically not a customer. Are they."

"Hey, I like this guy," Rev grinned at him.

"It was a poser john," Dylan said.

"That happens a lot?" Rev asked.

"Define 'a lot'."

"Oh, I really like this guy. Chris Reveille," she held out her hand.

"Kyle," he shook her hand.

"Dylan O'Toole," Dylan reached out his hand.

"Still Kyle," he shook his hand.

They sat there for a bit, not saying anything.

Then Rev spoke. "You should service women instead. They wouldn't beat you up."

Dylan looked at her.

"Most of them," she qualified.

"But he's gay."

"So? He wouldn't be turned on? Please. You think female prostitutes servicing men are turned on? It's a job. It's using your body to provide a service. No different from what's-his-name-football-guy. Actually, we all use our bodies, some of us even include our brains in the deal, to work for pay."

"I suppose," Dylan conceded, grudgingly.

"Think about it."

Kyle was. Thinking about it.

"There's a huge untapped market out there," Rev continued. "I bet there's *a lot* of women who'd gladly pay for the service. For someone who knows what they're doing, someone who can get the job done."

She turned to Kyle then. "You could probably walk into a bar any Friday night, pass around a few business cards, walk out, and half the bar would walk out after you."

She turned Dylan then. "Why waste your whole night only to end up with some drunken asshole when you could, instead, get exactly, and only, what you came for?"

She turned back to Kyle. "If you're good, I'll bet you could establish a regular clientele. You might never have to walk the streets again."

"Well, if there's that much demand," Dylan said, starting to get on board with the idea, "he could even turn it into a franchise thing. He could recruit and train a whole fleet of—studly men."

"He could call his business that."

"What?"

"Studly Men."

Dylan laughed. Kyle let a smile escape.

"But he's right," she said to Kyle. "You could get all your colleagues off the street. Your studly colleagues."

"Run it so they pay you a percentage of every gig," Dylan sat beside Kyle. "In return for the name and reputation. Set up some policies and procedures—a high-end escort service could help you with that—then recruit, interview, and hire. Provide training and company business cards with their names on as associates."

"Yeah, but I don't know what women—"

"Neither do most straight men."

"You can learn," Dylan said.

"Unlike most straight men."

"Don't worry," Dylan said. "It's all in the hands. That's what most men don't get."

"Well, and vibrators," Rev added. "You'd think they'd get that part. What with their fascination with power tools and all."

After a moment, Rev had another idea. "You could hook up with a hooker. Pay her for her time, ask her to teach you."

"Yeah, that's a good idea."

"Hey, *that's* what you could call your business! Great Hands! Oh, oh," she did Horshach, "and I know just the logo for your business card!"

"Sarah!"

They told Kyle about the woman they'd met on their way to Montreal the year before. She had this really hot design on the gas tank of her Harley. It was a man's cupped hand, his middle finger curled in the most provocative way.

"I can't remember her last name, can you?" she asked Dylan.

"No," he shook his head. "I remember Shaun. And Don. And Monty Python. But—I don't think she told us her last name, did she?"

"You can probably track her down," Rev said to Kyle. "Google the NFB, Studio D, find a list of directors from the 70s. She should be listed. Then check the yellow pages or something for Ontario. Canada," she added.

"Duh."

"Can we take him home?" Rev grinned at Dylan.

In the morning, as promised, the District Attorney arrived. He picked up their file from the desk.

"You've been arrested for indecent exposure," he said to Rev and Dylan, more to address them than to confirm the charge.

"That's right," Rev said. "And yet, so wrong. If women's breasts are genuinely considered indecent, why is Hooters so successful? In fact, don't you all say things like 'She's got a *decent* rack!'?"

"Yeah, but we'd never say that about yours," the bright one, back on shift, snickered.

"No, you wouldn't. And I can't tell you how much that disappoints me."

"Is that the only charge?" the DA asked the senior officer, with some disbelief. And perhaps regret.

"Some women's chests are clearly more or less 'decent' than others," Rev continued. "Same goes for men's chests. In fact, I bet you've got bigger boobs than I ever did," she lobbed at the bright one. "And yet," she turned to the DA, "we don't make *them* illegal. Men's chests," she clarified, "not his boobs. Or men like him."

The DA was—amused.

"You want to charge someone with indecent exposure? Charge every President who approved the use of depleted uranium in the bullets your soldiers use."

"Ah, Rev—" Dylan said, "we've been supplying the uranium."

"Oh yeah. Okay," she turned back to the lawyer, "then charge everyone who drives unnecessarily, for exposing us all to—'

"Rev, we're driving—"

"Oh yeah. Okay," she turned back to the bright one, "you know what I think?" Rev wasn't finished with him yet. "I don't think the issue is decency at all. I think the issue is control. *You* want to say when a woman can and cannot take off her shirt. And you want women to take off their shirts only when they do so for *your* enjoyment. Not their own. Well fuck you."

She turned then to the DA then. "I suspect the spirit of the law is that the crime is exposing one's breasts, not going shirtless per se. No doubt the law was written before bilateral mastectomies. Which means it's likely to be put to the test some time soon, what with the increase in cancer and all. So why don't you let the charge stand? Let's go to trial! Let's have the test case now!"

"You *want* to go to court?"

"Hey, good things happen when we go to court." She gestured vaguely at—she gestured vaguely.

Dylan nodded in affirmation.

"Actually," the DA said, "the *letter* of the law, here in Indiana, specifies breasts. Indecent exposure refers to 'a person who, knowingly or intentionally, in a public place, appears in a state of nudity'—and nudity is defined to include 'the showing of the female breast'—"

"Aha."

"—'*with* the intent to arouse the sexual desires of the person or another person.'"

"Oh. So even if I had breasts—"

"You'd be guilty of public nudity, not indecent exposure," he said. "It's a Class C misdemeanour. You'd be fined $500. Sorry," he added.

"Hm. And if a woman had only one breast, she'd be fined $250?"

The DA smiled. "*That* would be an interesting test case."

He turned then to the senior officer. "Drop the charges," he said, closing the file and handing it to him. "They're free to go."

Once back at their hotel, they made some calls to arrange bail and medical care for Kyle, and then decided they deserved some silly time.

"Isn't it a bit weird to celebrate getting out of jail by doing something illegal?" Dylan asked, as he took his first toke then handed the joint to Rev.

"And yet," she drew in, "so perfectly appropriate," she squeezed the words out.

Woof.

"Did someone just woof at the door?" Rev asked.

Woof.

"I believe so." Dylan got up and opened the door.

"Hey, Peanut!"

Peanut trotted in and plunked himself on the bed. In the cloud of second-hand smoke.

"Should he—"

He grinned and wagged his tail. Breathed deeply. And grinned and wagged his tail again.

There was a knock at the door.

Dylan and Rev looked at each other in alarm. Rev took a long draw on the joint, as if she could finish it right then and there. And that would solve the problem. She exhaled and the cloud of second-hand smoke grew larger. As did Peanut's grin. And tail-wagging. Despite their triptych of silence, Dylan put his finger to his lips. Peanut grinned conspiratorially. And wagged his tail. Rev handed the joint to Dylan. He also took a very long draw. Then rushed into the bathroom stifling a coughing fit.

The person at their door knocked again.

Rev stood on the bed and waved her arms through the smoke. Which made her fall over. Peanut grinned and wagged his tail.

They waited another few minutes, during which no further knocks were heard.

"Tucker must have a room nearby," Dylan whispered.

"Or not. He could have come special with Peanut from a whole other hotel."

"Well, it wouldn't be a half other hotel."

"Probably not. But that's all we ever see. Is half hotels. We always *assume* they're whole hotels."

"Okay, but," Dylan struggled to remember the main point, "if Tucker *did* come from another hotel, even if it is just a half hotel, he'll be frantic. Looking for Peanut. Who's here."

Peanut grinned. And wagged his tail.

Rev picked up the phone. "Hi, could you please tell us what room Tuck—Jon Tucker—is in? Thank you." She put down the receiver.

"Well?"

"204."

"Is that near us?"

"You're asking *me*?"

"Right. Okay, let's think about this. We're in—what room are we in?"

"You're asking *me*?"

"Right."

Dylan moved to the door.

"Don't open the door!" Rev whispered loudly.

"But our room number will be on it."

"Yeah, and so might Tucker!"

"Don't be silly. He wouldn't be on the door. Only Wiley Coyote can actually be *on* a door."

"Our key!" Rev was a genius.

"Yes! Where's our key?"

"You're asking *me*?"

"Right."

After a moment, Rev had another great idea. She'd call the desk. Since it worked so well before. Amazingly enough. As she picked up the receiver, she saw the number on the phone.

"208! We're in Room 208!"

"So Tucker's—"

"Near us!" Such a genius.

"Okay. That's good. Right?"

She thought about that. "Generally speaking or specifically speaking?" she finally said.

"We'll just let Peanut out—where's Peanut?"

Peanut was no longer on the bed. Because he was in their kitchenette. Finishing off their pizza and cheesecake from two nights ago.

"It's okay," Dylan was quick to say to Rev, "we can always get more. Always."

"More."

"Yes."

"Okay."

Dylan led Peanut to their door, agreeing with him that the last slice of pizza could be 'to go'.

After he opened it, he closed it, careful to make sure Peanut was on the other side, and then joined Rev who was now sitting on the bed.

"So. Okay. So. Shall we go to the Johnny Appleseed Festival?" He grinned.

"Geez, they were right about this being the city of churches," she said as they walked past yet another one.

"Left here, I think," Dylan said, consulting the map they'd obtained at the Curada.

Rev turned right.

"No, left as if we're walking forward."

"Oh. Well, that's different. Than if we're walking backwards."

"It is, isn't it."

And since it was all suddenly a little confusing, Rev just followed Dylan. After a few seconds, she stopped.

A few seconds later, Dylan realized this. His first clue was the one-sided conversation he'd been having. When he looked back, he saw her staring at a sign. So he joined her.

"What are we staring at?"

"A sign."

"Good. That's what I thought."

"Are we staring at it for a reason?" he asked after another moment.

"I think so."

"But you can't quite put your finger on that reason, can you."

"Nope."

"Maybe if we keep staring at it—"

"We need a felt pen," she said.

"Ah. Not a can of spray paint?"

"No, I think one of those thick felt pens will do in this case."

"Okay." He looked around. "I don't imagine churches sell felt pens."

"Probably not. They sell salvation."

"Not the same, really, is it?"

"Could be."

"Yes," he considered that, "I suppose it could be."

"What were we doing?" he said after a moment.

"Looking for a store that sells felt pens," she said. Staring at the sign.

"Oh yeah." He looked around again. "There!" He pointed to a corner store.

They headed toward it. And actually arrived. *And* found the door.

"Excellent," Rev said, as she selected a large bag of Doritos. They paid for it and left the store.

While standing outside the store munching on Doritos, she said, "This is wrong."

"Yeah. There was something else—"

"The Johnny Appleseed Festival!"

"Right!"

They walked back the way they came, and when she came to the sign, she stopped again.

"Felt pen!" Dylan was quick.

"I'll stay here this time. Maybe that'll work."

He looked at her. "Your grasp of logical relationship continues to—stun me." He headed back to the corner store. And returned with another large bag of Doritos. And, since they *were* standing in the realm where miracles are believed to happen, a thick black felt pen.

A moment later, the sign read 'The Church is not responsible for accidents occurring on the premises. *God* is.'

A mere fifteen minutes later, they found the Johnny Appleseed Festival. Which was just around the corner.

"Woh," Dylan said. They stood at the edge, one step away from the 19th century. They looked out over the huge park full of bearded men in loose pants, white shirts, vests, and hats, and women in loose dresses, aprons, and bonnets. Some were selling their wares, others were making them.

They stepped into the park, entered the stream of people who had come for the event, and walked along the pathway.

Under the first tent top was a man at a potter's wheel. Dylan and Rev, watched, fascinated, as the lump of clay turned round and round and grew into a six-inch high pot.

"How can round and round, and sideways push," Rev wondered aloud, "make up? Round and round alone doesn't make up. Sideways push alone doesn't make up."

"Sideways push could make up," Dylan begged to differ.

"No it couldn't. It would make sideways mush," she said, making 'mush' rhyme with 'push'. And smiling about that.

"If you pushed from both sides at once," Dylan said, watching the potter carefully. "Or from *all* sides at once."

The potter glanced up. They looked harmless enough.

"Hm," Rev thought about that. "How many sides does a round have?"

"None," Dylan replied. "Or an infinite number," he added.

"Wow. How cool is that. That the two answers to a question can be zero and infinity."

"Very cool. A remarkable question then, isn't it."

"Yeah," Rev said. "What was the question again?"

"How many sides does a round have," the potter said.

"Ah, yes, thanks," Dylan smiled.

"I bet a woman potter invented the dryer," Rev said a moment later. The pot-in-progress swayed for just a moment.

"Except when you open the door, the clothes don't come out."

"No, but if you put the dryer on its back and opened the door, the clothes would probably come up."

"A clothes fountain," Dylan giggled.

When it was clear no clothes would be coming out of the pot, they carried on.

Under the next tent top was a woman working at a spinning wheel. Which was simply way too confusing.

The next tent top featured a woman making candles.

"What kind of person would come up with the idea of putting wax on a string?" Rev wondered aloud.

"The same kind of person who came up with the idea of putting soap on a string?"

"Hm."

They walked on, passing displays of corn brooms and straw baskets, cast iron pots and pans, and carved wooden trinket boxes. And then had to get out of the way as a group of soldiers wearing breeches and blue coats marched by, beating drums and playing pipes. Dylan and Rev stared at them.

At the end of the path was a food court. There were steaming cauldrons attended by men with long ladles. The area was filled with picnic tables, which were full of people eating.

"Hungry?"

"Oh yeah."

They walked around to see what there was, decided on beans and cornbread, and apple cider, made with an antique cider press. They chose a picnic table far from the skewered pig. With the apple in its mouth.

As the eating area was next to the play area, they looked on as kids clambered over a decidedly home-made obstacle course consisting of a pole set between two trestles, railed hurdles like those you see at dog agility circuits, wooden monkey bars, and a rope bridge over piles of straw. Four kids were on a wooden maypole merry-go-round. Another one was on a barrel tied to ropes at each end to make a bucking bronco ride.

"They look starved for play," Rev commented.

"They do, don't they."

"I suppose the multicolored all-in-one plastic thing in the school yard pales by comparison. Oddly enough."

"You know," she said then, "I once used bobbing for apples in class."

"And what was the lesson?"

"Resistance is necessary."

"Brilliant!" he said, gleefully.

"Yeah. My grade ten basics thought so too. Since I'd brought a bag full of really hard, perfectly-sized missiles to class. Oh what fun."

"Ah."

They ate their beans and cornbread and sipped their apple cider.

"Want to try the maze after?" Dylan asked.

"Right," she snorted, looking over at the confusing arrangement of piled hay bales. "I'd never find my way out."

"Still a bit stoned?"

"A bit. Speaking of which, I'm going to get some apple pancakes," Rev said. "Want some?"

"I think they're called flapjacks."

"Why?"

"It sounds more fun than pancakes? Yes, get me some apple flapjacks. I'll get us some dessert."

They stood up, took a few steps, but then had to stop as another group of soldiers went by, this group in kilts playing bagpipes. So not only did they have to stop walking and talking, they had to stop thinking.

Rev returned with apple flapjacks, and Dylan returned with a shopping bag.

"There were apple dumplings," he said in answer to her raised eyebrows, "apple pies, apple tarts, apple betty, apple bread, apple butter, apple jelly, and apple sauce. I got one of everything."

Rev laughed with delight, as she peeked inside. "You didn't!"

"I did. I like apples."

"Hm," she said, as they sat down again. "Do the Irish have potato everything?" she asked, digging into her apple flapjack.

"I believe so," Dylan replied, starting in on his own flapjack. "My grandmother used to make potato pancakes and potato bread. And potato soup."

"And your grandfather?"

"Oh he made potato whiskey."

"Ugh."

"Well, the Irish have another word for it. Same idea though."

"What about potato chips?" Rev said gleefully. "Did the Irish invent Doritos?"

"Actually the potato chip was invented by George Crum. Who was an African American slash Native American."

"You're kidding."

"Am not."

"Really? Okay, who invented Mr. Potato Head?"

He considered. "That would have to've been the American Americans."

After a moment, Rev said, "You know what we haven't seen? Apple dolls."

"What in god's name are apple dolls?" Dylan asked, his fork stopped midway to his mouth.

"You've never seen apple dolls? You make heads out of apples. As they dry up, the heads get all shrunk and wrinkled. And you make the body out of—something. And then you dress them up."

"And you did this as a little girl?"

"I was never a little girl," she scoffed at the idea.

"Hm."

"Geezus, but they like their guns," Rev said as a cannon went off.

"Maybe there's a re-enactment going on."

"A re-enactment of what?"

"The war."

"What war? Did Johnny Appleseed have it off with—Mr. Potato Head?"

Two more cannons went off.

"Hey, we should buy Tucker an apple pie."

"We should indeed!" Dylan agreed. "He's such an apple pie kind of young man, isn't he? What do you think Peanut would like?"

"An apple pie of his own?"

"Dogs don't like apples."

"How do you know that?" she asked him.

"I just know."

"Epistemological justification at its finest."

"It's true, though."

"Well then."

Yet another group of soldiers marched by, this one in beige tunics and breeches.

"You know, I think Santayana was wrong. It's when you remember the past that you're compelled to repeat it."

They bought another apple pie, then carried on. There was a group of musicians on the next pathway, a display of straw baskets of all shapes and sizes, pony rides, a musket show-and-tell, and a storytelling tent.

"We could tell our story," she suggested.

"Or," Dylan was looking down the path, "we could do the pumpkin bowling."

"You're kidding!" Rev looked eagerly in the direction he indicated.

"Or we could enter the scarecrow decorating contest," he nodded to the other side of the path.

"Hell no, I want to smash some pumpkins."

"I thought as much."

Rev was disappointed to discover that pumpkin bowling didn't actually involve smashing pumpkins. The pumpkins were the bowling balls, not the pins. However, quick to adapt, she just ignored the rules. And, being the direct kind of person she was, simply grabbed a bowling pin and smashed a pumpkin with it. People cheered, and her modification of the game caught on. Quickly.

Later that evening, back at the hotel, refreshed by showers and apple somethings, Dylan was stretched on the bed with his laptop, Rev on the couch with hers.

"You're touching base with Dorothy and ordering more books and stuff?"

"I am, yes. And you're—since when do you work on your laptop?"

"I'm not working."

"Ah."

"I'm shopping."

"Since when do you shop on—since when do you shop?"

"Since I can shop on my laptop. If I want to buy a bar of coconut soap, I just go to e-bay and enter 'coconut soap' and voilà! I get a list of people selling coconut soap."

"And is that what you're shopping for? Coconut soap?"

"No, I'm shopping for bumper stickers that say 'Blessed are they that bash their babies' brains out.'"

There was the slightest of pauses. "And you found some—on e-bay?"

"Not exactly. I found a site that lets you make your own. Bumper stickers, t-shirts, mugs, fridge magnets."

"You didn't!" he said and scrambled off the bed to see.

She pointed to the screen, to the bumper sticker bearing 'Blessed are they that taketh and dasheth thy little ones against the stone—Psalms 137:9.' "I thought I'd buy a dozen. One for our van and the rest to sell at our table."

"Cool. Make one with the plunder thing."

He went back to his laptop and opened their book-in-progress file, then read aloud. "'As for the women...ye may take these as plunder for yourselves—Deuteronomy 20:14.'"

"Got it."

"Oh, oh," Dylan cried out, Horshach, "we can put the contradicting ones on mugs. Like 'Israel shall rise again—Jeremiah 31:4' on one side of the mug and 'Israel shall not rise again—Amos 5:2' on the other side."

Rev laughed, typing quickly. "Got any more?" she asked.

"Yeah, lots," he keyed to another place in the manuscript. "Ready?"

"Yup."

"'I am merciful, saith the Lord, and I will not keep anger for ever—Jeremiah 3:12' and 'Ye have kindled a fire in mine anger, which shall burn for ever—Jeremiah 17:4.' That might be too much to fit on a mug."

"Yeah, give me another one."

"'Every living thing shall be meat for you—Genesis 9:3' and—"

"Changed my mind," she sang.

"'These shall ye not eat of—Deuteronomy 14:7.'"

"Got it. Another?"

"'And the Lord spake to Moses face to face—Exodus 33:11' and 'No man hath seen God at any time—John 1:18.'"

"He loves me, he loves me not—another?"

"'They shall seek me early, but they shall not find me—Proverbs 1:28.'"

"Nope, I lied," she knew what was coming. "'Those that seek me early *shall* find me—Proverbs 8:17.' Don't know why I know that one," she anticipated Dylan's surprise.

"You know what else we should add to our table? DVDs of *The Life of Brian* and some copies of *The Hitch-hiker's Guide to the Galaxy.*"

Rev typed into her laptop.

"Wow."

"What?"

"I just entered 'atheist' in e-bay and came up with 2,847 hits."

"Really?"

"Books, DVDs, clothing, jewellery, bumper stickers, buttons—" She burst out laughing then. "Oh we have to get this one: 'Fine, I evolved. You didn't.'"

hen they walked into the Colorado Springs Curada a few days later, several parcels were waiting for them. They put one of each of the new bumper stickers on their van, and transferred everything else into their table boxes. Except for one copy of Barker's *Losing Faith in Faith*, which they put into the nightstand in their room. Set neatly beside *The Bible*.

Next day, Tucker and Peanut met them at the front door of the college building in which their talk was scheduled. Tucker had that all-dressed-up-with-no-place-to-go look. Peanut had his Frisbee.

"I probably shouldn't help you set up," Tucker said apologetically as he opened the door for them, each carrying one of their boxes, "or sit at the table—but maybe I can loiter a discreet distance away."

"Better idea," Dylan replied. "We've decided one of us will stay at the table from now on. You and Peanut could station yourselves at the auditorium entrance in case either one of us needs you."

"Copy that."

Once they set up, arranging and re-arranging their new merchandise with delighted fussiness, Rev opted for the table and Dylan went in to give the talk. Students started arriving. Most slowed as they passed the table, but few stopped. They headed straight for Peanut. Who would be, Rev decided, sitting beside the table next time.

After about five minutes, during which Rev used her black marker to correct the spelling of 'American' on the sign on the auditorium door (don't even ask), the students started streaming out. Dylan followed shortly after.

"They didn't throw anything at you?" Rev asked.

"Nope. I even got past 'Good'."

"Good!"

"Anyone buy anything?"

"No. One person stopped and read one of the mugs, though. She got very upset. Actually wrote down the two references."

"Maybe she'll look them up and see for herself."

"Hm. And then what, I wonder."

They packed up their stuff and headed out to the parking lot, Tucker again eagerly opening the door for them.

"All in all," Dylan said, "I'd say our second engagement was a resounding improvement over our first."

"Or not."

They stared at their van. All four tires were flat. And someone had spray painted over the AAC logo, as well as "There are no gods. Deal with it." And their new bumper stickers. The windows were covered with paint as well. Though that may have just been shoddy work, Rev pointed out.

Once the tow truck had come and gone, taking their van to a tire fixing place, from there to be picked up by a body shop for a new paint job, Tucker gave Rev and Dylan a ride to the downtown of Colorado Springs. They looked in vain for a cheesecake café and a used book store.

"You know why we can't find a used book store?" Rev asked.

"Because people don't use books anymore. Hence, no used books. Hence, no used book store. I could pass the LSAT," he added.

"So maybe our book should be an e-book," Rev said as they trudged on.

"Of course!" Dylan said, stopping in his tracks. "We should check the contract. That might be already in there."

"And," he stopped again, "we should have a podcast!"

"Do you know how to do a podcast?"

"Back when I was on the mothership, we used to cast pods all the time. That's how I got here, remember?"

"Right."

"Besides," he continued, "I used to have that radio show, remember? Can't be that different. We'll run the idea past Phil."

"What about a blog too? We can start making daily entries."

"Excellent!"

"Though," he said, "given the van, do we really want to advertise our presence? No wait," he recovered, "I didn't say that. Given the van."

Two blocks later there was a bookstore. A new book store. Advertising a book signing.

"Who do you think is signing books?" Rev wondered aloud as they walked in.

"The author?"

"Funny guy. Okay, *why* is the author signing books? I mean, his name is right there on the title page."

"It makes it personal."

"Oh please. 'And what's *your* name, luv? Who do I dedicate it to?'"

"It makes it more valuable? When the author becomes famous, the person can sell their autographed book. For thousands of dollars. On eBay!"

"Yeah, but that's kinda begging the question," she said. "*Why* does the autograph make it more valuable?"

"Because people are, by and large, idiots. Who are easily deluded."

"There you go."

She casually picked up a sci-fi paperback from a table at the door. The store was almost empty, though voices were coming from an alcoved room up ahead.

"Hey this might be worth a read," she said, looking at the back cover. "It's a 'day after' thing written by some military insider. Be interesting to see what *he* imagines life'll be like after a nuclear war."

"What, the pages aren't blank?" Dylan grinned, and then started to walk around the store, browsing.

"'A man who's been shaken by a bomb knows what it feels like'," Rev read aloud, trailing after him. "Why wouldn't a woman know?" she asked. "Is he saying women never get shaken by bombs? Because they're never in bombed areas? Or they are, but for some reason, they don't get shaken by them? Or they do, but they nevertheless don't know what it feels like?"

She read on. "Oh please. Listen to how he introduces Gertrude. 'She gossips.' That's it. She gossips."

"Oh, oh," she said, turning the page, "'But if your sister was in trouble and wired for money, the secret was safe with Gertrude.' Only if my sister was in trouble?" Rev asked aloud. "What about me?" She followed Dylan as he wove in and out through the racks and tables, her nose still in the book.

"You know," she said a few moments later, "I don't think this guy even *imagined* the *possibility* that *women* might read his book. Probably thinks we don't know how."

They stopped at a table as Dylan picked up then put down a book. "And apparently it didn't occur to him that someone's *sister*, a *woman*, might have money of her own. Or that she might ask another *woman*, not a man, not her brother, for a loan."

They continued to the next table. "Then of course we have the phrase 'in trouble'. Being pregnant," Rev said to Dylan, "having a human being start to grow inside your body, that's not being 'in trouble'. It's either amazingly wonderful or incredibly devastating. But it's not being 'in trouble'."

Neither of them noticed that they were getting closer to the alcove. Nor that the voices there had stopped.

She read on. "'But if your sister bore a legitimate baby—' I guess we're supposed to assume that being in trouble means not only being pregnant, but also being unmarried. And *that's* what makes the baby illegitimate? Not being in a contractual arrangement with a man? So *men* confer legitimacy on life? My, aren't we a little full of ourselves."

"Oh, for Pete's sake!" she said a moment later and almost threw down the book. Dylan waited. "What precious information would Gertrude, the gossip, spread far and wide? Whether his sister survived the birth? No, apparently that's not important. Whether the baby was healthy? No, apparently that's not important either. She spreads far and wide that the baby's—"

"A boy."

"Right. And weighs almost ten pounds. It's male and it's big. *That's* what's important."

"And *why* is that important?" she asked at the next table. "In what kind of world is it important to be big and male? I'll tell you."

Dylan grinned to himself.

"A world in which food and shelter, and women, are gained by one-on-one physical combat—"

"What, no weapons?" Dylan asked dryly.

"And where there's a positive correlation between maleness and size and capacity for said physical combat—"

"Perhaps a post-nuclear America, where no one knows any martial arts—"

She stopped. Stunned. "So *that's* why all these men want a nuclear war?"

They'd arrived at the alcove. The man at the front had been

reading from the very same book Rev had been reading from. And the audience consisted of about fifteen uniformed soldiers.

They put two and two together.

"See Jane read," Rev waved her copy of the guy's book in the air. And then pointedly did not take it with her as they left.

Next day, they were scheduled to do a radio talk show interview. It would be their first. Since their van wasn't yet ready, Tucker kindly offered to drive them to the station. It was an unimaginative building, prompting Dylan to wonder why concrete didn't come in colors.

"Ready?" Dylan asked Rev as they entered the station.

"Can't be that different from fielding students' questions," she said. Then remembered what had happened last time she fielded students' questions.

"I guess we'll find out."

"Hi, we're Dylan O'Toole and Chris Reveille," Dylan told the receptionist who was casually dressed in jeans, a loose shirt, and hiking boots. "We're scheduled for an interview?"

"Right. Hi. Welcome to Colorado Radio. Ted's expecting you." She picked up her phone and pressed a number.

"Ted? Your guests are here. Will do." She hung up the receiver.

"He'll be here in a minute to take you back."

"Thanks."

They stepped away from the receptionist's desk and looked idly out the window at the mountains in the distance.

"Dylan? Chris?" A dark-haired man, also in jeans and hiking boots, extended his hand. "Hi, I'm Ted."

"Hi," they shook hands.

"Glad you could make it! Find the place okay?"

"We did, yes," Dylan replied.

"This way," Ted led them through to the studio.

"So, have you guys ever been on a radio talk show before?"

"No," Rev said.

"Okay, well, don't worry. I'll introduce you—I got the package from the AAC—then we'll just talk a bit, and then we'll take calls." He made it sound so—easy. "Do you guys want some water or something?"

"That'd be good, thanks," Dylan said, as they sat in the two chairs across from Ted.

Ted set a pitcher and some glasses on the table, then put on his headphones. He listened for a bit, then nodded to himself.

"Okay, we're ready to roll," he said, handing them each a pair of headphones and setting a microphone between them. "Just talk with your regular voices, the mic'll pick it up." Ted looked expectantly at a light on the console before him, and when it went green, he began.

"Good afternoon, you're listening to Ted's Talk Show. We have guests on our show today, Dylan O'Toole and Chris Reveille, two Canadians on tour through our fine country." Dylan and Rev exchanged a look. "Welcome to our show!"

"Thank you," they both replied.

"Dylan, can you tell our listeners what the tour's all about?"

"Sure. It started when we added a quote from *The Bible* to a billboard. Up in Canada. We were arrested for blasphemy, and long story short, the American Atheist Consortium asked if we'd like to go on a speaking tour."

"To tell everyone what happened up in Canada?"

"Not so much that as to make it happen everywhere. Not the arresting part," he was quick to clarify, "but the publicizing what's in *The Bible* part."

"Okay, we've got a caller already. Hi, you're on the air." He punched a button on the console.

"Get those commie fags off the air!"

Ted grinned at them.

"And we've got another caller. Hi, you're on the air."

"We don't need any more Bible freaks, Ted. Tell 'em to go home."

"Can we do that?" Rev asked hopefully. "Go home?"

Dylan looked at her with surprise.

"And we're off!" Ted said cheerfully. "Do you have a response for our listeners?"

"Um, we're not commies or fags?" Dylan suggested.

"Or freaks," Rev added.

"Well—"

"Okay, we might be freaks," Rev conceded. "We might also be homosexuals—cultural homosexuals. Since we both reject gender stereotypes. Though," she said as an afterthought, "given drag, maybe that's not a defining—" She got back on track then, "And we're probably—well, no—I guess we're more socialist than communist—"

"Though one of us seems to be galloping toward capitalism of late—"

"Yeah, without any capital," she said somewhat ruefully. "In theory, though, I still endorse socialism. I think. It's just that unless you've got a really like-minded group of people, in practice, you end up with someone like me, and you," she nodded to Dylan and Ted, "supporting the construction worker who hurt his leg and then refuses to accept a ten dollar an hour telemarketing job because it's beneath him. Or the woman who gets pregnant again and again because living on mother's allowance or whatever is easier than slaving away at a Wendy's. Actually," she added, "I've always thought communism was like forced Christianity—you know, you *have to* be your brother's keeper. Which makes it odd that so many Christians hate Communists...."

"So," Dylan summed up, "we might be freaks, we could be fags, and we sort of used to be commies."

"All of which is irrelevant," Rev said after a moment.

"How so?" Ted asked. Glad to get a word in.

"Well, judging an argument by who makes it is—stupid. The argument should be judged on its own merits. Doesn't matter if a three-year-old makes it or a Nobel Prize winner. If it's based on solid, sufficient evidence, and the conclusion is drawn according to the rules of reason, it's a good argument. End of story."

"And what is your argument?"

Dylan took that one. "I guess our first premise is that if people knew the history of *The Bible* or what was actually in it—"

"Or both—" Rev interjected.

"—they might not be so quick to accord it the authority they do."

"For example?" Ted asked.

"For example, it wasn't written in English. So it needed to be translated. So it wouldn't be surprising if it had at least a few mis-translations. The Hebrew word 'almah', for example, means both 'virgin' and 'young woman'. If Jesus was born to a young woman, well, that's not quite so miraculous as being born to a virgin."

"Not miraculous at all in fact," Rev put in. "Young women all over the world are giving birth to male infants who grow up to think they're gods."

"Another basic thing about the history of *The Bible*," Dylan continued, "is that it had to be copied by hand a lot. The printing press wasn't invented until 1400s. So imagine if a 'not' was left out. Just by mistake. What if Genesis 1*really* ended with 'And God saw everything that he had made, and behold, it was not very good'?" Dylan giggled. Rev snorted. Ted adjusted the volume on the console.

"As for stuff that's actually in *The Bible* that people don't seem to be aware of, did you know that *The Bible* says 'Fools fold their hands and consume their own flesh. Better is a handful with quiet than two handfuls with toil, and a chasing after wind.'"

"And what does that mean?" Ted asked.

"Damned if we know," Rev said.

"And we have another caller. You're on the air."

"So I take it you don't believe in God?"

"What exactly do you mean by 'believe in'?" Rev asked.

"Do you believe in God? That's what I mean!"

"Yes, but 'believe in' isn't really clear, is it? Do you mean do I think gods exist? Or do you mean do I hope a certain god will save me from something?"

"I mean do you believe in God!"

"I do not think gods exist, if that's what you're asking."

"I'm not asking about gods, I'm asking about God. You know, *God!*"

"You think there's just the one? What about Brahma? And Zeus? Hey, if Brahma, Zeus, and God got into a fight, who'd win?"

"You are nuts, lady, I'll tell you that much."

"Back at ya," she said. Cheerfully.

"Dare I ask," Ted asked, "why you don't believe in God? Why you don't think gods exist," he corrected himself.

"Certainly. It's the same as why I don't believe Santa Claus exists. There isn't sufficient evidence or reasoning to support such a belief. The stories, the pictures, and the cookies I left out that were gone in the morning—"

"Most belief in a god is based on insufficient evidence or bad reasoning," Dylan offered.

"Can you give us an example?"

"My daddy was a god-fearing man," the caller was apparently still on the line, "and his daddy before him, and his daddy before him!"

"There you go," said Rev. "Just because there's a tradition of something, doesn't make the something right."

Rev leaned into the microphone. "Just because your daddy and his daddy before him believed something, that doesn't mean it's true."

"Why not?" the caller almost shouted.

"Because your daddy was stupid?"

She continued, to Ted, before he could figure out what to do about his guest calling his caller stupid, "The caller's claim could also illustrate, conveniently enough, the mistake of appealing to an inappropriate authority," she looked back at the microphone, "because your daddy's not exactly an expert on right and wrong. Because your daddy was stupid," she beat him to it. And Ted still hadn't figured out—

"And what makes *you* such an expert on what's right?" the caller oozed—well, he just oozed.

"The issue is more whether I'm an expert on argument—whether this or that conclusion is well-supported—but, as it happens, I'm an expert on what's right too. And, to answer your question, what makes me an expert on what's right is the same thing that makes people experts in other fields. A lot of training. About 4,000 hours, actually."

"You've spent 4,000 hours thinking about what's right," the caller clearly didn't believe *that*.

"Well, when you put it that way—it does seem to have been a waste of time...," she trailed off.

"She has a Master's degree in Philosophy," Dylan said to Ted, "specializing in ethics."

"Oh, a *philosopher*," the caller used a tone he would obviously not use for plumbers or pilots.

Only a little distracted by where pursuit of that fact would lead, Rev rallied. "Which means," she said, "that I understand—but would not necessarily endorse—egoism, relativism, and intuitionism. And I can analyze an ethical issue," she continued, "using various approaches, based on principles, or values, or consequences, or intentions, or rights. Concerning just the latter, for example, I can distinguish between absolute rights and competing rights, and between inalienable rights and acquired rights; I can identify the relationships between rights and duties, rights and privileges, and rights and responsibilities—"

"But isn't a priest or pastor trained in ethics as well?" Ted interrupted.

"I think they're obligated by their faith to take the divine command approach," Rev replied. "'God said.'"

"See the difference?" Dylan said helpfully.

"And concerning the consequence-based approach, for example—"

"You say you're an expert in ethics and yet you broke the laws in your own country," Ted interrupted again.

"And that's a problem because...?"

"Well," Ted chuckled, "I would think a so-called expert in ethics wouldn't break any laws."

"And why would you think that?"

"Well, it's wrong to break the law."

"And why do you think that?"

"Well, it's, you're, breaking the law."

"Yeah...where's the 'wrong' part?"

"Oh put him out of his misery," Dylan grinned.

"Only if you subscribe to a position of legal moralism," Rev explained then, "do you think that the laws of this or that country at this or that time actually define, or determine, right and wrong. It used to be legal to buy and sell people in this fine country, so you're saying it used to be right? And the day the law changed, it suddenly became wrong?"

"Well, yeah," Ted said. Lamely.

"No, it used to be legal and then it became illegal. Not necessarily the same as morally right and wrong."

"But it's not just trust in *The Bible* and belief in gods that we're trying to get people to examine," Dylan tried to steer back a bit. "It's also membership in a religious organization."

"And we've got another caller. Go ahead, you're on the air."

"Look, what you're saying is all very nice, but it's just your opinion."

"Well, yeah," Rev conceded. "But my opinion's better than yours."

"Oh yeah? Who the hell are you?"

"Doesn't matter. We went over that." She turned to Dylan then, "I think we confused things by mentioning my credentials." She turned back to the microphone, "My opinion's better than yours not because of who I am but because of the support my opinion has, relative to yours. *That's* what makes one opinion better than another. It's based on more convincing evidence and/or better reasoning."

"Which you're likely to have because of your credentials," Dylan said, more to Rev than to the caller. "I think a lot of people who dismiss the opinions of scientists, for example," Dylan jumped in, "don't understand how scientists arrive at their opinions. They don't just spout off at the mouth, saying whatever they want to be true."

"For example?" Ted encouraged him to continue.

"For example, how old is Earth? People who use *The Bible* as their evidence say it's around 6,000 years old. People who use the scientific method say it's around 4½ billion years old. And we can't just agree to disagree. We can't just say well, everyone's entitled to their opinion. Because they can't both be right. The Earth cannot be 6,000 years old *and* 4½ billion years old."

"I'm with you," Ted said. "It's got to be one or the other."

"Well, no," Rev inserted. "Both could be wrong."

"Okay, so" —Ted was momentarily confused— "so why should we accept one over the other?" he asked Dylan.

"Excellent question," Dylan said. "Good. We should accept one over the other because of the evidence. The religionists use *The Bible* as their evidence. A book full of impossibilities, contradictions, and—scientists use rock as their evidence."

"Rock." Ted didn't sound convinced of its superiority.

"Yes. They can figure out how long a rock has been around by measuring the isotopes."

"Isotopes."

"Istopes are—it's like—you can tell by looking at a person, a white person, whether they've been out in the sun all day or just a few minutes, yeah?"

"Sure. If they've got a really bad sunburn, they've been out a lot longer than just a few minutes."

"Exactly. That's using the scientific method. You started with certain facts about human skin and the sun and what the sun does to human skin over time, and your observations indicate a certain conclusion. Simplifying, the redder the skin, the longer the person's been out in the sun, yeah?"

"With you," Ted said.

"Okay, measuring how long a rock has been around by its isotopes is kind of like that. Over time, uranium gradually turns into lead—again, I'm simplifying—so if you measure how much uranium a rock has and how much lead it has, you can tell how long it's been around, how far along the process is. The more lead, the longer the rock's been around."

"You're on the air," Ted punched the button on the console.

"Yeah," the caller called out, amazingly enough still on the line, or back on the line, "but, all I wanna know is do you believe in God?"

Rev's head hit the table.

"No," Dylan said. After a moment.

"Why not?"

"Because—let's try this," Dylan suggested. "Do *you* believe in God?"

"Yes sir, I surely do."

"Why?"

"It's in *The Bible*. And that's the word of God, it surely is."

"Okay, see, that's another mistake in reasoning," Rev said. "It's called circular reasoning. You assume to be true exactly you're trying to prove to be true. So you don't actually prove it at all."

"Look lady, I don't know what you're talking about. But I do know there's a God, sure as I'm standing here. Look around you! If there isn't a God, who put the birds in the trees?"

"Who put the birds in the trees?" she mouthed at Dylan.

"They developed," she said aloud. "Over time. From single-celled—from little blobs—invisible little blobs—"

"That God put there," Dylan gave up for the both of them and slumped back in his chair.

"Cheesecake. We need cheesecake," Rev said as they stood outside the station.

"Yeah." They looked up the street to their left and then to their right. As if cheesecake might suddenly appear. Put there by God perhaps. Then Dylan sent back inside the building.

"Hi there," he said to the receptionist. "Do you know if there's any café or something near here that has cheesecake?"

"Actually, yes there is. Calories R Us. Left at the second light. It'll be on your right."

"Great, thanks."

"You know we gotta," Dylan said as they stared at the Double Bacon cheesecake in the display case.

"Yeah. But geez. *Bacon* cheesecake?"

"One piece of the Double Bacon cheesecake," he said to the person waiting behind the display, "and one piece of—"

"Very Vanilla," Rev said. "And Creamy Cranberry," she added. "And Cherry Coco."

"And two coffee, please."

"God, that was exhausting," Rev said once they were sitting at one of the little tables by the window.

"More exhausting than your classes at the university?"

"Well, no." Which was a really depressing realization.

"So?"

She'd taken a bite of the Double Bacon.

"It's—confusing."

He took a bite as well. She waited.

"I like it!"

"You like peanut butter on your pizza."

She pushed that plate toward him and pulled the Very Vanilla to herself.

"Have you noticed how a lot of people use belief in *The Bible* or God as a synonym for all that is right and good?" she asked, once she'd taken a bite. "'Yes, I surely do believe in God' just means, to them, 'Yes, I surely am a good person.'"

He thought about it. "You're right. That is *exactly* how they say it. 'Of course I read *The Bible*' means 'Of course I do the right thing.'"

"That's why I made that mistake!" she said suddenly.

"What mistake?"

"I went right to appeal to inappropriate authority on ethics, but we were considering an epistemological claim."

"So you should've told him his daddy wasn't an expert in epistemology."

She snorted, imagining how well that would have gone over, then picked up the main thread again. "And since there's so much more, and so much less, to *The Bible*, they're really just being imprecise." She took another bite of her Very Vanilla cheesecake. It was good. Very good.

"Right! Like calling us commies and fags," Dylan said. "It doesn't mean anything—or at least it doesn't mean anything about political stance or sexual orientation. It's just a verbal spit."

"Yeah but when someone says to a guy 'You throw like a girl,' they're using *what I am* as an insult. That's a lot more than a verbal spit. Words have meaning."

"Well, maybe not to—"

"Then why don't they ever use 'like a *boy*' as an insult?"

"Hm." Dylan took another bite of his bacon cheesecake as he thought about it. "Maybe words just have emotional meaning. To most people. Not cognitive meaning. So they're really not thinking past the emotional value of what they're saying."

"But why does 'like a girl' have the emotional meaning that 'like a boy' doesn't?"

They looked idly out the window for a while.

"And you know," she said, licking her fork, "'God put them there' *is* the better explanation. Occam's Razor and all that."

The next day, they decided to go on a hike in the Colorado mountains with Tucker and Peanut.

"Any idea about the weather forecast?" they asked at the young man at the main desk in the lobby.

"Some sun, some cloud, some wind, some rain."

"What, no snow?" Rev quipped.

"Well, yeah—if you get to the top." He clearly thought they wouldn't make it that far.

They managed to exit the hotel without the use of canes and waited in the sun (and cloud and wind) for Tucker to pull around front. The paint job on their van was done, but the guy was waiting for the stencil from the AAC to do the lettering.

"Hey," Dylan said, "you got a new paint job too?" Tucker's SUV was all sleek and black.

"Yeah, well, I told the Chief what happened and suggested that a stronger security presence was required. I was just thinking of a larger emblem on the door," he confessed. "It was the Chief's idea to repaint in black."

"Very official-looking," Rev said. Just before Peanut popped his head up through the sun roof, grinning like an idiot, his tongue flopping out the side of his mouth.

They drove out of Colorado Springs to the hiking trail they'd chosen. Tucker had wanted the 'difficult and dangerous hike up Colorado's premier summit' while Rev had voted for the 'wimpy walk along streams and meadows'. They'd agreed on the 'moderate hike to a waterfalls with some gorgeous views on the way'.

He parked his vehicle at the entry point, and they got out. Peanut was the most excited. He was the only one doing one-eighties.

Dylan watched him for a while, smiled, then tried one.

"You look ridiculous," Rev volunteered. Peanut barked. Clearly in agreement.

"And I feel ridiculous," he grinned. And barked back at a delighted Peanut.

They started out then, Tucker and Peanut taking the lead. Dylan and Rev trailed behind.

"You know, it really isn't the better explanation," Dylan picked up where they left off. "'God put them there' introduces more problems than it solves. We just didn't get to that part."

"Good thing," Rev responded. "He'd never've understood the problems."

"You're probably right," Dylan sighed.

"So what are we saying," she said a moment later. "Religious belief is good for those with a low IQ?"

"No, we're just saying it's typical of those with a low IQ. All the research shows that the more education you have and/or the more intelligent you are, the less likely you are to endorse any belief in the supernatural."

They walked on. "But maybe it *is* also good," she said after a few moments. "I mean, if you can't handle the complexities of figuring out what's right and wrong—and let's just focus on that role of religion for the moment—though what I'm saying goes double for its explanatory role, of physical phenomena—"

"Thunder is God bowling."

"Right," she stepped around some boulders on the path. "Okay—what was I saying?"

"That if people can't handle—"

"Right, if they can't handle the complexities of figuring out what's right and wrong, then maybe they *should* just accept someone else's rules. An appeal to authority isn't always inappropriate."

"My daddy told me not to put my hand on the stove."

"Really? You had stoves on the mothership?"

He grinned.

"But you were just a kid," Rev said. "So—"

"So the authority *needs* to be a god," Dylan said excitedly. "Most adults wouldn't accept just someone else's rules. But if the rules were given by a *god*—it would be sort of a face-saving thing—"

"Yes! Hey, that's good," she said after another moment. "It fits. I mean, after all, daddy was a god. From a four-year-old's point of view, daddy *does* know everything."

"And can *do* everything."

They turned a corner. "But daddy also said there was a man with a white beard," she paused for a moment, no doubt recalling pictures of God, "who rode through the sky on a sleigh pulled by reindeer. And kids stop believing in Santa Claus at some point in time. So why—why are religious beliefs off limits to rational inquiry? What's so special about religious belief?"

"Because it's so ingrained in our—"

"So's our belief in Santa Claus."

"Maybe," Dylan was excited again, "maybe it's because *not* believing in Santa Claus is a rite of passage *out of childhood*! Whereas believing in God—"

"No, that doesn't work. You believe in God when you're a kid. So it's not a rite of passage into adulthood."

"No, but it is a sign of—" he waved his hand in a vaguely dismissive way "—get a job, get married, have kids, believe in God—they're all markers of being a fine, upstanding, adult."

"Right!" she agreed. "If you don't believe in God, you're some godless heathen running around—"

"Like a kid without a moral compass."

"Exactly!"

They walked on for a bit, gazing out at the huge sky. They didn't see so much sky living in the forest.

"Too," Rev resumed, "I wonder if the authority being appealed to isn't really so much God as people's parents. I mean, don't most people believe in the god their parents believe in? Which is too coincidental to be the result of rational inquiry."

"And don't most people also vote for the political party their parents vote for?"

"But—don't we rebel against what our parents think? Remember

Jill?"

"Weight room Jill?"

"Yeah. She did the conservative thing when she had a daughter because she wanted her daughter to end up as radical as she really was."

"Did it work?"

"Not really. She figured it out. The daughter."

"And then what was she?"

"Pissed off and confused. Changed her name from Summer to Jane. Had a daughter, named her Susan."

"Who changed her name to what, Daffodil?"

"Switchblade."

"So that's why society goes pendulum?" Dylan asked. After a moment. "From the radical 60s and 70s all about racism, sexism, environmentalism, to the nothing 80s and 90s, back now to oh-let's-recycle-and-drive-hybrids? It's all just kids reacting to, differentiating themselves from, their parents? So any real progress over time as a species is—"

"Hopeless, really."

They walked on for a bit in silence.

"But then why doesn't religious belief also swing back and forth—why haven't we had a whole generation of atheists?"

"Maybe once the teenage rebellion is over, most people—especially those who can't think for themselves—just succumb to the appeal of tradition. And expectations."

"Right. So let's add the appeal of the majority. My guess is fewer people would believe in God if the majority didn't."

Dylan gave her a curious look.

"You know what I mean."

They paused for a particularly stunning view of a distant mountain.

"*That's* what we should've asked that guy!" Dylan suddenly said. Rev waited. "We should've asked why he *doesn't* believe in *Zeus*."

"Yeah, that would have been interesting."

They walked on. "Okay, so maybe most people can't think for themselves," Rev resumed. "And so maybe they're better off adopting the opinions of the majority and accepting authority. Being told what to think. Why is it they're the ones most loudly imposing their opinions on others?"

"Insecurity?"

"Hm."

Half a mile later, she seemed to have changed her mind. "I dunno. You don't have to be Einstein to see that there *can't be* an all-good god overseeing the world. Baby deer burn to death in forest fires."

"What?"

"Rowe's fawn. It's a classic thought experiment to disprove God's existence. The fact that there are pointless, preventable, instances of bad shit happening indicates that there *isn't* some all-knowing, all-good, all-powerful god."

"Free will?"

"Forest fires caused by lightning. Not tossed cigarettes."

"Ah. Right."

"And anyone with a grade six education can read *The Bible* and see that it's full of murder, rape, slavery—"

"To put it mildly—"

"— all approved, if not actually ordered, by God."

They walked on, pausing often to take in their surroundings. The rock formations were unlike anything they'd seen before. And so red.

"And," Dylan said, coming full circle, "maybe Occam's Razor isn't such a good rule. Why should the simplest explanation be the best? Isn't that rather—simplistic?"

"You know, you're right," Rev said, stopping suddenly. "I've never really thought about that. Occam's Rule is presented as well, a rule. In philosophical circles."

"And you never thought about it?" Dylan exaggerated his shock.

"No, I must've missed that one," she grinned, then resumed walking.

"Who was Occam anyway?" he asked idly.

Then bumped into Rev. Who had stopped again.

"A 14th century—Franciscan friar."

Dylan giggled. "Oh that's priceless. And you never—"

"Shut up."

There was an intersection ahead with a sign pointing to a side trail. And a note sitting on the ground weighted down by a rock. "Took the side trail—meet you where it rejoins the main—Tuck and Peanut."

"It probably goes straight up," Dylan said with a bit of envious admiration.

"And then straight down," Rev said with her knee's iliotibial band in mind.

"We were twenty-five once," he sighed.

"Alas, just once," she sighed.

"Yes, but it was for a whole year."

"Not it wasn't. Not really."

"Well, no, not really."

They carried on and in a short while saw Tuck and Peanut ahead, sitting on some rocks where the side trail rejoined the main trail. Both were looking very happy. When Peanut caught sight of Dylan and Rev, he jumped up, and ran to them, wagging his tail.

"Down!" Tucker anticipated. Wisely.

"The waterfalls are around the next turn," Tucker said when they got closer, "but off the trail a bit. Wanted to make sure you guys didn't miss it. It's beautiful."

"You've already been there and back?"

Tucker grinned apologetically.

"How was the side trail?"

"Steep. Scruffy. Cool," he confessed. "How was the main trail?"

"Nice. There was one particularly good view."

"Of the mountain with a sort of double peak? And the little lake?"

"We didn't see the lake from our vantage point," Rev said sadly.

They walked on in silence for another minute or two then came to the waterfalls. Multi-tiered, splitting and rejoining, trickling and thundering, it ended in a curtain at the bottom.

"Oh wow, this *is* beautiful," Rev said. "Let's just sit here for a while."

"Wouldn't it look cool if the whole thing were iridescent?" Dylan said after a bit.

"Yeah! We should have your glasses here! Dylan made glasses with different-colored filters," she explained to Tucker. "When we stayed at a house in Montreal that had a skylight. It was so cool to look at the stars all gold, or all purple—"

"Couldn't you get a filter from a photography store that would do that? Split the colors into the rainbow?" Tucker asked.

"Maybe," Dylan said. "We never thought of a going to a photography store."

"I wonder if there are any animals that see things in iridescent," Dylan mused a moment later. "You know, how some see ultraviolet?"

"I bet Geordi's visor could see things in iridescent," Rev said. And a moment later, she added, grinning, "and I bet we can buy one on eBay."

Soon after the waterfalls, they entered a meandering path through a series of meadows. They'd stopped talking and were just basking in the silence, the breeze, the flowers, and—

"Woh," Dylan stopped when he rounded the next corner. Several elk were lying in a meadow. Rev, Tucker, and Peanut stopped behind him, then slowly and quietly fanned out to get a clear view of—

The biggest one, the one with the antlers, looked up. Noticed Peanut right away. And stared at him.

Peanut looked back, with curiosity.

Alpha stood up. The ones behind him rustled a bit then became still.

Peanut took a small step back.

Alpha reared up on his back legs and hoofed the air.

Peanut tilted his head to one side.

Alpha hoofed the air again.

So Peanut broke into his "Thriller" routine.

"What, are we gonna have a dance-off?" Rev muttered.

"No, that's 'Beat It'," Dylan said quietly. "I doubt Peanut—"

"Actually," Tucker said, equally quietly, "we watched 'Beat It' one night. To see if—"

"So what, we tie Peanut's front paw to Alpha's front hoof?" That was Rev.

Alpha hoofed the air again.

Peanut did his "Thriller" bit again.

And then, no doubt eager to show more of his repertoire, he jumped up, did a 180, then waggled his behind at Alpha.

"You know," Rev said as they watched the retreating elk, Peanut's disappointment clear to all, "I think Peanut's understanding of what just happened is quite different from Alpha's."

"Isn't that always the way?" Dylan sighed.

The way back took longer than the way there. Of course. But they did make it back to the parking lot and, after just two tries on Rev's part, up into Tucker's newly cool black SUV. When Tucker pulled into the Curada lot, he drove right up to the front entrance to let Dylan and

Rev out. He was such an apple pie young man.

Rev opened her door and—did some elaborate stretching and flexing before she made the exit attempt.

"Good idea," Dylan said. With disappointment in his voice.

"Oh shut up," Rev replied.

After a very long, very hot, shower, Rev's muscles regained some of their elasticity. Even so, they decided to stay in for dinner. They invited Tucker and Peanut, and ordered several pizzas from one of the many pizza places. And a local brand of root beer instead of their usual Pepsi.

After pizza, Tucker asked if Peanut could hang out with them. It was a Friday night and there was a band he wanted to check out. "Unless—"

"What's the band?" Dylan asked.

"They're called 'The Noise Makers'."

"I think we'll pass," Dylan said, with Rev's tacit agreement. "We've got a lot of work to do. And hanging out here with Peanut sounds like more fun."

Tucker accepted that, said his good-byes to Peanut, then left.

"We are *so* old," Rev said in the ensuing silence.

"No," Dylan countered, a little defensively, "we just prefer bands with more sophisticated names."

"Right. Like 'The Butthole Surfers'."

Dylan idly turned on the tv, changed the channel a few times with the remote, then said in an announcer voice, "This program contains violence and coarse language and is intended for an immature audience."

Rev smiled, settling into her chair with her root beer. Dylan changed the channel a few more times, then settled onto the bed and started rolling a joint. Peanut stretched out on the bed beside Dylan, rolling luxuriously in a way that suggested he *never* got to lie on the bed—which Dylan knew was simply not the case.

"Isn't it just a little bit sick that we pay people who pretend to be doctors more than we pay people who actually *are* doctors?" Rev commented, paying a little attention to the news program that Dylan had stopped on.

"Way more," Dylan said when he heard the $200,000 figure. Per episode. He exhaled, and Peanut wagged his tail.

"And why is the acting category of the Emmys sex-segregated? Lead Actor and Lead Actress. We don't have separate awards for directors. Or cinematographers, costume designers, editors, composers, or make-up persons," she read the list that was scrolling down the screen.

"Because otherwise the actresses would never win," he passed the joint to her.

"What? Are you saying—"

"Of course not. The award isn't really for the actor, or actress, it's for the character portrayed. My guess is most people can't distinguish the two. I'll bet George Clooney still gets asked what to do by moms whose kid has a fever."

"Okay, yeah, but—" she exhaled, and Peanut wagged his tail, then she passed the joint back to Dylan.

"We award the heroes. And women never get to play hero," he said simply, finishing the joint.

"Ah."

Dylan reached for his laptop then, moving over a bit to give Peanut more room. Rev already had hers open.

"Hey," Dylan said, checking his email, "did you get the message from Phil?"

"No, I'm still deleting messages from people who think I want a larger dick."

"Well, not only did he approve our podcast and blog ideas, he's given us a raise."

"Really? I don't think I've ever gotten a raise before."

"Really?" Dylan moved over a bit more as Peanut stretched out his legs, pushing against him.

"Well, not for having a good idea. I've gotten the kind you get just for being there a long—no, actually, I've never gotten those either...."

"I've had good ideas before," she assured him a moment later, when she remembered what they were talking about. "But then I've been fired for showing up my boss."

Dylan moved over a bit more and—Rev looked up when she heard the thump. Peanut wagged his tail.

"Oh shut up," Dylan said to him, and Rev, as he climbed back onto the bed, with residual giggles.

"Hey," Dylan said a few moments later, having resumed his email tasking, "Phil's already set up a special page for us on the AAC website. Oh wow. It's got our tour schedule, the media package info, a photo of our van—he says all we have to do is log in and start talking."

"I can do that," Rev said.

Peanut wagged his tail.

"Oh shut up," she said to him.

T he next day, they entered Salt Lake City. Rev was at the wheel, and Dylan was online to see what there was to see.

"Did you know Mormons account for only 1.4% of the American population?"

"Really? I thought they were bigger," she said, then amended with greater precision, "more numerous."

"As did I. They seem to get more than 1.4% of the religious publicity."

"Maybe they're just good at that. Aren't they part religion, part chamber of commerce?"

"And Jews are even less," Dylan said with surprise. "Fewer. 1.2%. I had this notion they were ten times that."

"Again," Rev said, "part religion, part chamber of commerce."

"*Atheists* are ten times that!" he said then with even more surprise, continuing to browse through the site he'd found.

"No chamber of commerce."

"And listen to this: a nationwide poll by the University of Minnesota found that Americans distrust atheists more than they distrust Muslims."

"Really?" Rev found that hard to believe. "That must've been pre-9/11."

"Nope. Post Iraq even."

"But—" she was speechless with surprise. Near speechless. "That doesn't make any sense. Why would—"

"Oh, wow, look," Dylan pointed up ahead to the towering church building of spires and turrets. "Temple Square. We should stop there."

Rev found a place to park, not so nearby. The square itself covered 35 acres and consisted not just of the temple, but of an assembly hall, two libraries, a museum, a conference center, a theatre, and gardens. Lots of gardens.

"It's—magnificent," Dylan commented, as they approached the towering structure.

"Yeah, too bad it inspires awe for some god instead of for its architect and the construction guys who built it."

"But that was, no doubt, the intent of the architect."

"Emotional manipulation, pure and simple," she said as she looked around. "If churches were just dull, small buildings, I doubt people would imbue their gods with such grandeur."

"But if they didn't already imbue their gods with such grandeur, they wouldn't have made their churches so—grand."

"But consider the music. Do people enter a church all pious and solemn or do the hymns put them in that mood? And the use of Latin. Men in robes droning on in a language no one understands. It's the spitting image of magicians incanting a spell. No accident, I'm sure. Hey, what's that bubble building over there?" Rev pointed.

"The Tabernacle."

"As in the Mormon Tabernacle Choir?"

"Yup."

They walked toward the building, and saw as they approached that they were just in time for the daily organ recital, so they went inside.

"Oh," Rev let out a breath. "Oh," she said again, staring at the massive, and majestic, pipe organ. "Bach would—wet himself. I have to play it."

He looked at her curiously.

"It's been a life-long dream of mine to play Bach on a harpsichord. He didn't write for the piano, it wasn't invented then. So playing on an organ—an organ such as this—this magnificent beast—" she was walking toward it, attracted like an iron filing to a magnet. "Do you think they'll let me be an impromptu warm-up act?"

"They might. Why not ask and see? Tell them you have your Associate Performer's diploma. From the Conservatory. So you wouldn't hurt it."

"Yeah, that's good. I do, you know," she added.

"I know you do. That's why I said it," he smiled.

"I could tell them I'd just play one of Bach's chorales—'The Sheep Can Safely Chow Down Here' or something."

"Do you know that by heart? I thought you needed the music to play anything beyond 'Happy Birthday'."

"Well, yeah, pretty much," she conceded. "Oh, oh," she said enthusiastically, remembering, "there's another organ classic I can play. By heart," she added.

They spoke to one of the ushers, who handed them off to another usher, and a few minutes later, he was introducing Rev to the assembly.

"Ladies and Gentlemen, we have a special guest today. Ms. Chris Reveille from Canada will play a short piece before our regular program."

There was some applause, and Rev walked from the side toward the organ. Dylan waited in the wing. She nodded a thank you to all the people in the pews, then sat at the organ.

Everyone waited, in pious anticipation, to praise god through his music. She lifted her hands, paused just a moment, then burst out in what could be called singing. "'Ma belle amie, [CHORD! CHORD!] ba da ba boom. You are a child of the sun and the sky and the deep blue sea.'"

In the confused shock that followed, Rev went on to the second line. "'Ma belle amie, [CHORD! CHORD!] ba da ba boom. Le bonjour, le toujour, ba da boom, merci merci.'"

The crowd couldn't help but feel the joy of the old Tee Set pop hit—so they joined in for the next line. "'You were the answer to all my questions—'" Rev looked upward dramatically.

No one could remember the next bit, so she filled it in with a short run on the keys.

"'I want to tell you that I adore you—'" Everyone looked upward. Dramatically.

And another run on the keys.

On the chorus, Dylan entered from the wing and roused the audience to further joy, circling his arms to increase participation. "'Let the bells ring [CHORD! CHORD!], let the birds sing [CHORD! CHORD!]....'" Everyone sung out with glorious enthusiasm.

No one remembered the next bit, and it was more complicated than a run, so they just skipped it.

"'Let the bells ring [CHORD! CHORD!], let the birds sing [CHORD! CHORD!]'" Even more glorious enthusiasm. And then a pause, a searching in memories for—

"'For the man after him waits here!'" Rev wailed out the suddenly remembered next line.

"'For the man after him waits here!'" Everyone joined in for its repeat, then clapped like crazy.

Rev stood up and took a bow. Dylan followed suit, then they quickly left. The building.

"Le bonjour, le toujour, ba da boom, merci merci'?" Dylan looked over at her once they were safely back in the van.

"Pretty good for just five years high school French, eh?" Rev replied.

"The people of Quebec would be—moved."

"Nailed the chords though," she said.

"All four of them," he agreed.

"Someone is waiting for you," the desk clerk at the Curada in Salt Lake City nodded to the side of the lobby where several chairs were arranged in a sitting area. They were expecting Phil's replacement, so they approached the clean-cut young man in a suitcoat, only to hear the woman two chairs down, somebody's grandmother, say "Shame." They turned their attention to her instead. She had grey hair, glasses, and a somewhat amused expression on her face.

"Chris Reveille and Dylan O'Toole?" she asked.

"Yes, and you are—"

"The person you're looking for. I'm with the Atheist Consortium."

"Right, good," Dylan said, reaching out his hand. "And your name is—"

"Faith Abernathy."

They contained their laughter for about two seconds.

"Sorry," Rev said, "it's just—"

"Oh you don't know the half of it," she said. "I've got two sisters. Had two sisters. Hope died. Suicide."

Rev snorted. Dylan jabbed her with his elbow.

"Seriously?" she asked.

The woman nodded. "And Charity is now CEO of a definitely-for-profit corporation."

Dylan paused for just a moment. "You're putting us on," he then said.

"Am not!"

They liked her immediately.

"Even so," Rev said, "I don't think I can call you—Faith."

"Well, my friends call me Chuck."

"Why, because you actually figured out once how much wood a woodchuck could chuck if a woodchuck could chuck wood?" Rev asked dryly.

Faith's jaw dropped. "Yes!"

Dylan looked in amazement from one to the other.

"I was going to add that my middle name is Helen. But *you* can call me Chuck."

"And *you* can call me Rev."

"I'm still Dylan," Dylan said sadly. "So, are you already settled in?" He looked around and saw no luggage.

"Yes, thanks. Actually, I'm Phil's replacement only for—I'm in Salt Lake City for a conference and I said I'd love to introduce you for your talks here. I understand you have a few in the area."

"We do, yes. Well, shall we—have lunch or something?

"Yes, let's."

"Okay, we'll take our stuff up to our room and then meet you—"

"I'll get us a table in the diner."

"Sounds good."

A waiter approached their table as soon as they sat.

"Surprise us," Dylan suggested. "Something local, something different for each of us?" he looked to Faith for approval.

"Perfect," she smiled broadly. "But vegetarian for—"

"All three," Rev spoke up.

"I've never actually been in Utah before," Faith said.

"Oh, where are you from?"

"Texas originally, but I've spent most of my life in Oregon."

"Doing?"

"Teaching. Research. I'm a professor at the university in Portland. Shame on you, again," Faith said, seeing Rev's poorly disguised surprise.

"Yes. You're right. I'm so sorry. God damn it but it runs deep."

"I have a Ph.D. in Psychology. *And* I'm somebody's grandmother. Deal with it," Faith grinned broadly.

The waiter appeared with a pitcher of water and filled their glasses.

"Phil sent me the media package for the tour," Faith continued, "which means I know everything there is to know about you two except," she smiled dryly, "except what color you are. But I know that now."

They looked at her expectantly.

"Dylan's lime green."

He expressed surprise. Since he was wearing a turquoise t-shirt at the time.

"And Rev's red."

"I'm trying to become—more pastel," she muttered apologetically.

"And why is that?"

"I wouldn't say more pastel," Dylan offered. "I'd say more—fuchsia. More fun," he explained to Faith. "Less driven to right the wrongs of the world."

"Ah. Give it time," Faith said with a slight grimace. "Though of course there's the danger that by the time your head and heart get to fun, the rest of you won't be up to it."

"Do you also know what animals we are?" Rev asked after a moment. "Since you've got the Ph.D. in Psych and all," she grinned.

"You're a panther," Helen grinned right back. "An absolute panther. And Dylan's a—" she considered that for a moment. "A bird, I think."

"A parrot?" he asked hopefully. "A Norwegian Blue!" he sputtered.

The waiter arrived then with several plates of food. Among the dishes were french fries with fry sauce, she explained, sweet red punch, funeral potatoes—

"Okay, what are funeral potatoes," Rev had to ask.

"Potatoes, of course," the waiter smiled, "baked with creamed soup, sour cream, and cheddar cheese, topped with buttered breadcrumbs."

"Ah," Dylan said with understanding.

"No," she corrected him, "it's what people around here *take* to a funeral."

"Creating an interesting feedback loop, I'm sure."

She grinned, not correcting him, and left them to their food.

"So what's your research really been about?" Dylan asked, dipping a french fry in what looked like mayonnaise and ketchup. "I don't imagine 'If you were an animal, what would you be?' would get a lot of funding."

"You'd be surprised," Helen said, then answered his question. "I spent quite a few years watching cats play. As I'm sure you know, play is hypothesized to be practice for predation. I'd noticed, even as a child, that cats take an especially great delight in killing things. I wanted to know why. It occurred to me that cats for whom hunting, and killing, wasn't fun didn't survive to reproduce, so basically what you have," she paused, "is self-selection for psychopathic tendencies at species level."

"Cats as a species of psychopaths," Rev said thoughtfully. "It so makes sense."

"Unfortunately, since self-selection works in all species...."

"I'll bet that got funding," Rev took a forkful of funeral potatoes. "If not, it should have."

"It does have rather broad explanatory value, doesn't it," Dylan said as the implications settled in. "So how did you get from cat play to atheism?"

"Well, when you compare religion with evolution, religion actually seems preferable. Because it has a moral component. Evolution is quite Machiavellian, isn't it? And most people prefer the nice guy. Jesus. Which is a good thing, I think, but—"

"But it's comparing apples and oranges," Rev objected. "Evolution is just descriptive, whereas religion is both descriptive as well as prescriptive. The correct comparison would be between evolution and creationism."

"Yes," Faith agreed, "but I don't think a lot of people see it that clearly. And religion is correctly compared with atheism, but even then, atheism per se doesn't have a moral component. It *can*, of course, and most atheists do have a system of ethics, but I don't think religionists see that. So *that's* what we have to emphasize. We have to show that being atheist can include being moral. Which is to explain what brought me to the Atheist Consortium.

"As to what brought me to atheism, I'm certainly well aware of the psychology of religion, more specifically, the psychology of belief, the need to feel part of something bigger than oneself, the fact that it's hard to accept that one is so very unimportant in the grand scheme of things—"

"That there *is* no grand scheme of things—we live, we die, end of story."

"You are such a ray of sunshine, aren't you?" Dylan said, smiling.

"And, on a smaller scale," Faith continued after a moment, "I understand the need to belong to a social group, a club. Going to church on Sunday is just like going to the Legion on Friday or going bowling on Saturday. My guess is that people would still 'go to church' on Sundays even if it didn't involve any religious ritual."

"Though it wouldn't have that self-righteous quality then that separates it from the Legion and bowling."

"Well, perhaps not from the Legion. That's for war veterans, remember. So they've got the I-did-my-duty thing."

"But most people who belong to the Legion today were never even in a war."

"My point."

"Ah."

"It's really quite a lazy sort of life, isn't it," Faith pondered as she picked at her food. "I mean, you do so little for so much. You get that righteous buzz and all you have to do is follow a few commandments. Which are, to boot, negative. Much easier to *not* do something than to have to *do* something."

"I've never thought of that!" Dylan said. "You're quite right! It *is* a lot easier to go through life not stealing than to go through life being generous. For example."

"But," Rev said, "there's 'Love one another as yourself' and 'You are your brother's keeper'."

"Yes," Faith said, "but oddly enough, neither has the status of being one of the commandments. And most people interpret those, I think, in a very general 'Be nice' way. They don't really take them seriously.

"And if you do mess up," Faith continued, dipping a French fry into the fry sauce, "God will forgive you anyway. No, I think it's quite easy to be a Christian."

"Unless you're called to do God's work," Rev suggested. "You know, be a missionary, spread the word, get your heart ripped out and eaten."

"Yes, but isn't it surprising how few are called?" Faith grinned mischievously.

"Indeed."

"Too," Faith continued, "it's a rather passive life. It's atheists, I think, who tend to be more active, more activist. They're the ones who are out there righting wrongs," she smiled at Rev. "If you're religious, you believe it'll all work out in the end, everyone will get what they deserve. If you're an atheist, you know that's not true. Everyone will *not* get what they deserve. The people who get away with making other people's lives hell, well, they do get away with it. Unless someone does something about it.

"It's the atheists who are out there trying to make the world a better place because they know this is all there is. Religious people are okay with it as is, because there's heaven. Almost half of all Americans think Jesus is coming back *in their lifetime. And* that he'll take them to heaven. So global warming? Not to worry. We're running out of water? God will provide. Or it's meant to be.

"In fact," she continued, "maybe this world isn't supposed to be so good, because we're on trial, we're being judged according to how well we can suffer in silence. Any injustice, any problem, well that's God's plan. Things happen for a reason. And that reason has nothing to do with us. With what we may or may not do or have done."

"Well except for Katrina. Didn't that happen because of the gays?"

The waiter had cleared their table, and returned with dessert. Green jello with chunks of carrot and pineapple. And sour cream on the side.

"This isn't cheesecake," Rev said.

"No, it isn't," Dylan agreed.

She returned with coffee and tea.

"What brought me to atheism per se," Faith continued, as she stirred some sugar into her tea, "well, that predated most of my psychology study. I simply thought about it."

Dylan and Rev exchange a look. "We're firm believers," Dylan grinned at his use of the word, "that the way to atheism is just thinking about it. If people just took off their rose-colored glasses—"

"Oh but it's usually not as simple as that. Often those glasses are sewn on. Have been since childhood. So the stitches have long been grown over with new skin. It's more like ripping them out of your face."

"I suppose it is, yes," Dylan casually agreed, stirring cream into his coffee. Rev was silent.

A few minutes later, Dylan saw Tucker and Peanut in the lobby and waved a 'Come in!'

Tucker entered the dining room, Peanut in tow.

"Pull up a chair, want some coffee?"

"No thanks," Tucker looked around anxiously. "I don't think Peanut's allowed—"

"But the room's empty—"

"Still."

"Right. Okay, well, Faith, this is Jon Tucker, he's the one assigned as our escort."

"Pleased to meet you," Faith said.

"And this is Peanut," Dylan introduced him as well. Since he was about to shove his nose into her lap.

"Hello there," Faith said to him. "You're not a cat," she added.

Tucker was puzzled, but Peanut was inordinately pleased that she had made the distinction. He started to do "Thriller".

"You've really gotta teach him another routine," Rev said.

"He knows another routine," Dylan came to his defence. "'Sweet Pea,' remember?"

"You're right though," Tucker said to Rev. "I think he misses it. Since we've been on the road, we haven't been dancing as often as we usually do."

"Surely the Curada has a room you could use. All you need is a portable CD player, right?"

"Yeah—"

"Hey, Peanut," Rev said, "want some green jello?" He thumped his tail. She started to put the dish onto the floor, but Peanut showed her how unnecessary that was.

"Good afternoon," the Chaplain of the college tapped the mic. "I'm pleased to see such a large turn-out for our Bible Enlightenment talk this week, so without further ado, would you please welcome our guest, Mrs. Faith Abernathy." He reached out to shake her hand as she approached the podium. The auditorium was full, but the applause was, of course, merely polite.

"Hello," Faith smiled, her voice amplified a little by the sound system. She was dressed in what she privately called one of her Betty White specials.

"You know, with a name like mine, I've given faith a lot of thought over the years." There were a few laughs.

"And that's been a lot of years," she smiled. There were a few more laughs.

"And I find it surprising that most of us still think there's a god." A few smiles.

"Well, all right, maybe that's not really the surprising part. We still think it's an all-wise and all-good god." The laughter was uncertain.

"But we pray to this god."

"Amen!" The audience had recovered. "We surely do!"

"And yet he's omniscient—he already knows what we're going to —— say."

Some of the Amens were just As.

Dylan and Rev were watching from the side, delighted.

"They don't know what to do with her," Dylan whispered.

Rev nodded and whispered back. "She's like a Trojan horse."

"Yes!" he turned to her. "That's exactly what she is!"

"And it's not like we're going to change his mind," Faith was saying. "Hey, Supreme Being and Ruler of the Universe—this is what *I* think should happen here."

Some mumbling, or perhaps grumbling, started to rise from the audience.

"And now I'd like to introduce our speaker for today, Dylan O'Toole."

About twenty minutes later, Dylan burst out through the double doors of the auditorium. Rev looked at him expectantly from her spot behind the table.

"They're still there!" he said with a mix of surprise and dismay.

"Who's still there?"

"The students. The people who came to hear the talk. I said 'Good' and even 'Afternoon' and they wanted more! So I told them about the billboard thing, and then I talked about what I talked about on the radio show—"

"And now?"

"Faith's filling in for you."

"Me?"

"Yeah. I said you'd be in to talk next," he grinned. "You can talk about what Faith said at lunch," he paced around excitedly. "How atheism needs to—the compatibility of atheism with morality. You can go into all the other approaches, you know, what you talked about on the radio show. You can go over all the other reasons one can have for doing the right thing, show how one doesn't need to believe in God, in the existence of a god, to be a good person."

"Okay, yeah, I can do that," she'd gotten up. "Actually that's a good idea," she said as she considered it further. "Yeah, that's real good!" She trotted toward the doors.

"So," Dylan said as the five of them stood beside their van, untouched thanks to Tucker and Peanut who had been guarding it. Or playing Frisbee, if you'd asked Peanut. "That was a resounding success! I say we all go out to celebrate!"

"Sounds good to me," Faith said. "I rather enjoyed it. And it *did* go well, didn't it?"

"You should've seen the first time. And the second—"

"There's a dessert café downtown a little ways. What?' she said as Dylan stared at her. "I googled."

Back at the hotel, Dylan flopped onto the bed with his laptop, then logged on to touch base with Dorothy and tell Phil what a success their talk with Faith had been.

"Though, actually," Rev said, "it wasn't *that* much of a success. I mean, they didn't throw stuff at us, but they weren't really interested either," she said. "And that's why!"

Dylan looked at her, expectantly.

"It makes religious belief unnecessary. Ethics without gods. *That's* why they're opposed to values education and ethics courses. But if the only reason they're good is to get into heaven," she thought it through, "that's just blatant self-interest. How unchristian.'

"And, actually," Dylan said, "most atheistic societies, Sweden, for example, and Norway, Denmark, are more generous than religious societies like the U.S. and the Middle East. They also have a higher standard of living."

"And what if they knew that?" Rev suggested.

"Well, Sweden's full of commies, isn't it," Dylan anticipated the response. "Uh-oh," he said, returning to his email.

"What?" Rev said from the chair she'd settled into to update their blog.

"There's been a sort of epidemic of billboards undergoing, um, adjustment," he read Phil's email. "Oh, this is good. A billboard near here proclaiming 'The end is nigh' got appended with 'Give or take a couple thousand years'."

Rev laughed.

Dylan scrolled down and read another one out loud. "'Jesus loves you. He just doesn't know how to show it.'"

"Where was that one?" Rev was delighted.

"Someplace called—" There was a knock on the door.

"Tucker?" Dylan said curiously to Rev as he got up off the bed.

"Or Faith maybe."

He opened the door to a pair of uniformed officers.

"Are you Dylan O'Toole?"

"Yes."

"And is a Chris Reveille here with you?" The officer peered into the room.

"Yes, but—"

Tucker and Peanut turned the corner of the hallway at that moment. Seeing the officers, Tucker broke into a trot. And a sweat. That had nothing to do with the trot, of course.

"We've received reports of several defaced billboards in the area, and we'd like to ask you a few questions if we may."

"Certainly," Dylan said. "Come in."

Tucker entered the room too, anxiety on his face. Dylan tried to reassure him with a look, but it didn't work.

"Where were you earlier today?"

Tucker let out a barely concealed sigh of relief.

"We gave a talk at the local Bible college, then went for a bite to eat."

"I can vouch for them," Tucker spoke up. "Jon Tucker, Border Patrol 13621, assigned escort for Mr. O'Toole and Ms. Reveille. They arrived at the college at 3:05 p.m. today—"

Dylan and Rev looked at him in surprise. They didn't know whether to be impressed or appalled.

"—and spoke at 4:00 p.m., or shortly thereafter as a Ms. Faith Abernathy provided a short introduction. Then we all went to Franni's, a dessert café in the downtown area, immediately following. We were there until 7:15, at which time we all returned here."

"You all drove in the same vehicle?"

"Well, no, but—"

"You might want to consult with your colleagues in Richfield, Officer—" Dylan looked at his badge— "Morrison. Billboards there were 'defaced' as well. We can't be in two places at once."

"God can, though," Rev spoke up. "Maybe he did it."

Since they had a cluster of engagements in the area, the next day they were at it again at a Mormon church.

"I see a lot of women in the audience," Faith started off. They cheered. "I have to confess that I used to be upset because none of the disciples were women. But I'm at peace with it now."

"Amen!" Several people called out, in support.

"Because I realized what a sorry lot of gullible schmucks they were, traipsing along after a total stranger, leaving at a moment's notice their families, their jobs—'Come follow me! I'm God! Look, I've made this man walk. He was a cripple before. Really!'"

Silence.

"But woman are the backbone of the family, aren't they?"

And they were back. With applause.

"I saw a lawn sign today that said 'A Christian Family lives here.'"

More applause.

"'We have kept the Christ in Christmas.'"

Stronger applause.

"And missed the sermon on pride," Faith smiled kindly.

Uncertain applause.

"But even so, many people do keep Christ in their lives, all-year long."

The audience rallied.

"We give him money. Why, you people alone give him $13 million a day."

Cheers. Loud cheers. Whistles even.

"$13 million a day! Just what has he been doing with all that money?" Faith asked. Smiling. "And when do you think he'll start paying taxes, for roads and schools and hospitals?"

The applause died quickly, and just a little uncertainly.

"But you know," she smiled kindly, "God works in mysterious ways."

Applause again. But clearly cautious.

"Why is that again, exactly?"

The three of them stepped outside, packed boxes in hand, congratulating each other on how well things were going.

"You know," Rev said to Faith, "it's too bad you're not coming with us. You're—"

"What the—" Dylan was looking across the lot to their van.

They saw as they approached that it had been trashed again. A crestfallen Tucker stepped out from behind it. He was covered in paint.

"I tried—" he began.

"Wow," Rev interrupted, as Peanut also stepped out from behind the van. "He looks like a Jackson Pollock." Peanut turned around obligingly. "A three-dimensional Jackson Pollock."

"Well," Dylan set his box down and circled the van. "No broken windows this time. Or dented fenders."

"No, but—"

"This happened before?" Faith asked. "Oh yes, I remember, Phil told me about it. Oh my." She too circled the van. "I had no idea. I imagined just a little, you know, just a—this is, these people are really angry!"

They all decided to spend the evening in. Tucker and Peanut had gotten cleaned up and were in one of the Curada's empty rooms working on a new dance. Faith had left, after goodbyes all round, to present her paper at the conference she was attending. Dylan and Rev had done their first podcast, Dylan was updating Phil on events and checking in with Dorothy, and Rev had updated their blog and was working on some LSAT questions. They were both paying occasional attention to the movie that was on tv.

"Hey," Dylan said, "we've got a magazine interview tomorrow."

"Yeah? Okay." She reached out to accept the proffered joint.

"And bees see iridescent!" He studied his laptop. "Apparently flowers are iridescent, but only they can see that."

"Really? Do they have visors like Geordi?"

"They'd have to be really little visors."

"I'm sure the replicator could manage that. We could ask Jean-Luc to make a bunch of little visors. For all the bees." She inhaled then passed the joint back.

"No, I think, we're missing something here." Dylan thought a moment. As he took a drag. "Ah. Bees can see iridescent *without* visors. They can do it with just their eyes. With their really little insect eyes."

"Yeah, I guess if anything can see iridescent without a visor, it makes sense that it'd be a bug."

"A bee is not a bug!" Dylan protested.

"Sure it is!"

"Okay, but it's a warm and fuzzy bug." He liked bees. Apparently.

"It's got a stinger!" She protested.

"Yes, well, so do you!"

"I wanna be a bee," he giggled.

"You'd have to wear bright yellow t-shirts and black jeans."

"I could do that."

"Yes," she grinned at him, "I know you could."

They decided then to just watch the almost-over movie since multi-tasking was no longer within their cognitive capacities. But first they called room service for a pizza.

"We're supposed applaud the achievement of literacy?" Rev snorted at the tv. "That's what we've come to? Oh this *is* precious."

"Well she had such a not-a-headstart."

"Yeah, but she had to travel the same distance as an average person achieving genius. Where's the principal knocking on *that* kid's door, telling his or her parents that although he's getting Bs, he's really capable of much more? Where's the person going to bat for *that* kid so Yale or Columbia opens its doors for him or her.

"Oh, oh," she sputtered, eyes on the television, "and she's decided to keep the kid! And we're also supposed to applaud that? Her decision to raise a child? With no job, no money, no co-parents, no knowledge, no skill—"

"She can read and write."

Rev burst out laughing. As did Dylan.

"Do you think they'll come and take away our teacher's certificates?" he asked.

"They already took mine away, remember?"

"Oh, right. Corrupting minors and all that. Good thing 'all that' didn't come up at the border," he said suddenly.

"Yeah. You know, I'd actually forgotten about it? Wow."

"Hm."

There was a knock at the door.

Dylan looked over at Rev in alarm, the smoking joint in his hand.

"Who is it?" he whispered loudly to her.

"How should I know?" she whispered back. Loudly.

He took a long draw. There wasn't much left.

"Maybe it's just Peanut," Rev suggested. "Come for—more giggly?"

"No, he woofs at the door, remember? Besides, he's with Tucker, practicing. Hey, we should go join them! That'd be fun!"

"Maybe Tucker's with him. Here. At the door. On the other side of the door," she struggled for precision. "Tucker can knock," she added.

"That's true." He handed the joint to her and got up off the bed. She took a long draw, finishing it. Then went into the washroom and flushed the butt down the toilet.

"Okay," she said tightly when she returned.

The knock repeated. "Room Service!"

"It's room service!" Dylan said cheerily.

"Yes! Otherwise they wouldn't've said 'Room Service!'" Rev was pleased with herself.

He answered the door then, and a minute later they were watching the tv again, pizza slices in hand.

"The thing is," Dylan said, "she's choosing to be a Mother." He said it with a capital M.

Rev took a bite of her pizza. "And when did parenthood become such a sacrament?"

"When it became a sacrifice?"

"Hm."

Their magazine interview wasn't until the afternoon—Dorothy had kindly agreed not to schedule any morning events, if at all possible— so Dylan and Tucker had a surprise planned for the morning

"But you know I don't do mornings," Rev had protested.

"Trust me, it'll be worth it. You'll want to do this. Even in the morning."

"Okay."

They bundled her, sluggish and stiff, into the front seat of Tucker's SUV, then opened the back for Peanut. For whom mornings were clearly not a problem. Half an hour later, they were at the lake.

"A lake!" Rev cried out when she saw it. "This is Salt Lake?" she asked. Dylan nodded. "It's water!" Dylan nodded. They got out, Rev more carefully than the others, and walked towards it.

"Oh wow, look at it!" It was huge. And so calm. Rippling gently in the breeze, sometimes shimmering, sometimes sparkling, the sight washed over her like the most beautiful music in the world.

Peanut ran to the water's edge, then stopped suddenly. It smelled wrong. Then he noticed the white line on the sand. He gave a sharp bark to Tucker and took off down the beach, nose to the ground. Tucker took in the scene, then sighed.

Fifty meters away, Peanut stopped again. At the huge salt formation sitting like a white boulder almost as large as he was. He gave another sharp bark to Tucker, sat beside the formation, and pointedly raised his paw. Then, because he couldn't contain his joy, he gave a howl of triumph, jumped up, did a one-eighty, wagged his bottom, then sat down again and raised his paw.

"What's he doing?" Rev asked, as the three of them approached.

Tucker looked a little embarrassed.

Dylan suddenly grinned with understanding, then laughed. "He thinks he's just discovered the world's largest stash of crystal meth—or cocaine—or—"

"Salt," Rev said flatly.

Just to be sure, Tucker squatted, put his finger to the line of white powder, then touched it to his tongue. He nodded a sheepish confirmation.

"Hey," Dylan came to Peanut's defence, "it's an easy mistake to make." They had reached the exuberant Peanut, and Dylan went over-the-top with congratulations. Peanut lapped it up.

"Oh come on, isn't he trained to—"

"Salt's probably not in the training kit," Dylan came to his defence. "And he hasn't ever been to the ocean before, right?" Dylan looked at Tucker for confirmation. Tucker nodded. "Let alone a salt lake. And who would expect a ton-huge chunk of salt to be lying on a beach?"

"Right. But a ton-huge chunk of crystal meth, yeah, we find *them* lying on beaches every day."

"You're so mean," Dylan continued to pacify Peanut.

"So now what?" Rev asked Tucker.

"Well—" Tucker couldn't bear to break Peanut's heart. "Good dog!" he said, ruffling his neck.

Peanut was so proud.

"Guard!"

Peanut plopped his ass onto the sand in front of the world's largest chunk of salt, and tried to look mean. Nearly succeeded, but for the tongue lolling out his mouth and his tail thumping at Dylan and Rev.

Tucker jogged back to his vehicle and returned with an evidence bag. And Peanut's Frisbee. He made a big show of collecting some of the salt into the evidence bag, Peanut watching very closely, then tucked it into his pocket.

"Unguard!"

Peanut didn't move. He looked at Tucker with such an intensity—

Tucker sighed, then set the small evidence marker that had been in the bag on top of the salt boulder.

"Okay, good dog, unguard!"

Peanut didn't move.

"Oh, for Pete's sake," Tucker mumbled as he pulled out his cell phone and pretended to make a call. "Border Patrol Jon Tucker 13621 requesting drug squad back-up to Great Salt Lake." Peanut thumped his tail.

"Unguard!" Tuck said to Peanut once more.

Satisfied that protocol had been followed, Peanut leapt out of his position into a swirl of glee, then sprinted after the Frisbee Tucker had thrown as reward.

Tucker drove them to the magazine interview, since their van was still in the shop getting its new paint job.

"This doesn't look like the right place," Rev said as Tucker pulled under the awning of the entrance area of an apartment building. "It looks like just an apartment building."

"An expensive apartment building," Dylan amended, as a uniformed attendant approached their vehicle.

"May I park your vehicle for you, sir?"

"Um, we're not sure we're in the right place," Tucker said. "We're looking for—"

"A Ms. Shevron," Dylan leaned forward from the back seat. "With *City Magazine*."

"Yes, Ms. Shevron is waiting for you inside."

"Oh, okay, thanks," Tucker said as he undid his seatbelt.

"You really don't have to come to this, Tuck. I mean what could go wrong at a magazine interview?"

Rev snorted.

"I know. But the billboards, the van again. I can't afford another—"

"You're doing fine. The billboards had nothing to do with us, and you did all you could with the van."

"Still."

"Okay, let's go then," Rev said cheerily as she opened her door. And fell out.

"Jesus Christ!" she said from the pavement. "It was all of ten minutes!"

Dylan giggled. In his lean and lanky sort of body that never seemed to seize up. And Tucker, well, Tucker just didn't understand. He was twenty-five.

Rev got up and the three of them entered the lobby.

"Hello," a stylish young woman approached them, her manicured hand outstretched. "Dylan and Rev?"

"Yes," Dylan reached out his hand, as did Rev. "And this is Jon Tucker. He's—with us."

"*City Magazine* has its offices in here?" Rev remained unconvinced.

"No, we keep a suite here for our photo shoots."

Rev and Dylan exchanged a puzzled look. "But we're here for—"

"This way, please," she smiled warmly.

She led them into a ground floor suite. It was high-end. Very high-end. So high-end it didn't look lived in.

"This is Maria, our wardrobe person," she nodded at a woman standing beside several racks of clothing. She took one look at Rev and started wildly searching through the racks.

"And Cheri, she'll be doing your make-up." Cheri gave a little finger wave. Rev hated finger waves. Dylan grabbed her hand before it shot out.

"Dave, our camera," Ms. Shevron nodded at him. "And Greg, sound."

"I thought we were just going to talk," Rev said. "As one does in an interview."

"Oh we are. But it *is* a magazine, not a newspaper, so we'll want a few good pictures too."

"Yes, but—" Dylan also tried.

"We thought this living room would reflect well," she waved her hand expansively around the room.

"Reflect what well?" Rev asked.

"Cheri, if you want to get started?"

Tucker quickly took a position at the door, as Cheri herded Dylan and Rev into the spacious bathroom she'd set up with bright lights and several industry-standard make-up kits.

"Is this really necessary?"

"If you don't want to look like—" Cheri caught herself in time. "If you want to look your best, yes."

"We just want to look our—us," Dylan said.

"Oh I'll keep it light. I see you didn't put anything on this morning," she said to Rev, and Dylan muffled a snort, "so that makes my job easier, thanks. Some women get so upset when I have to undo everything they've done."

"Upset?" Rev said. Ominously, Dylan thought.

Maria, in the meantime, had continued rifling through the wardrobe racks, pulling out item after item, holding it up in the direction of Rev and Dylan, then putting it back. With increasing—hysteria.

"We've got our own clothes," Rev said. Helpfully. "We came dressed."

"Yes, of course," Ms. Shevron breezed in, "but we want you to look your best."

"This is our best," Rev said, in her good jeans and t-shirt. Then grinned with what could not be called regret. And certainly not embarrassment.

Dylan, for his part, stuck out his chest. After all, he had his yellow t-shirt on. And his black jeans.

"Look, you've got us in a fake apartment," Rev said, "and you're putting on fake faces and fake clothes. Why don't you just use fake people? I'd like—" she thought for a moment— "I'd like Lori Petty to step in for me."

"Yes!" Dylan agreed. "She'd be a perfect fake you! I loved *Tank Girl*."

"Who do you want for you?" she asked Dylan.

"Mr. Bumble Bee!" he said without hesitation.

"Look, if you're not going to take this seriously—"

Rev glared at her. She was accusing *them* of not taking this seriously?

"I believe we're getting paid for this," Dylan said quietly to Rev.

"A lot?"

Five hours later, when Ms. Shevron deemed they looked presentable, they sat—they were positioned—on the latté leather couch, in front of a really huge, and rather scary, Emily Carr print. Mugs of cold coffee sat on the chrome and glass coffee table next to clearly unread copies of *Hockey Night in Canada* and *Arctic Flora and Fauna*.

"So," Ms. Shevron said, "ready?" She nodded to Dave, who nodded back.

"I'd like to thank you for giving *City Magazine* the opportunity to interview you," she began. "We're really excited to be talking with you about what's been going on. What's *really* been going on," she smiled conspiratorially and leaned in as if she were a long-time confidante about to hear all the juicy tidbits about—

"No you aren't," Rev jumped right in. "You're not interested at all in what's *really* been going on. You're just interested in appearances. So, fine, let's talk about appearances. Let's talk about women, their make-up, and their fashions."

"Excuse me," Dylan said, and as unobtrusively as possible left the set. He motioned to Tucker to join him in the kitchen.

"Let's talk," Rev dove in, "about how women present themselves as sexual beings *as a matter of routine*. About how, even if they're going to the grocery store or to the bank or, of course, to work, they 'put on their face'—they redden their lips and make their skin look younger. They expose their legs, all shaved and waxed, and by wearing heels, make them look longer than they really are. They arch their feet, again with the help of heels. And they emphasize their breasts, they wear bras and tops so just a little bit of cleavage shows. Lips, legs, breasts, all are sexually attracting."

Ms. Shevron made no attempt to redirect Rev. Curiously.

"And all this is part of the woman's morning routine, her 'getting ready'. Well, the phrase begs the question 'Ready for what?' And the answer is, obviously, 'Sex!' And then they get all pissed off when they're treated like sex objects, when they're not taken seriously, when men focus on what they look like instead of what they say."

"Are you suggesting," Ms. Shevron asked, crossing one shapely leg over the other, "that we all walk around in burkas?"

"No, I'm saying—what if men did the same?"

As if on cue, Dylan returned to the room—to the set—with Tucker. Per Dylan's request, Cheri had had her way with them. Dylan had lost about ten years and had gained a sexy, frisky, charm. Tucker was to-die-for in dark-and-handsome. Maria too had gotten in on the action. Dylan had exchanged his yellow t-shirt for a sleek button-down shirt whose several top buttons he hadn't buttoned down, better to show the gold chain drawing attention to his chest, the chain matching the one on his wrist, very visible due to the rolled up sleeves. And Tucker, well, Tucker had apparently sacrificed his black t-shirt—the sleeves had been cut off, turning it into a 'muscle shirt'. Aptly named in his case. Along with his tight jeans, he looked—very good.

"Ooh-la-la," Ms. Shevron cooed, looking at Tucker. He blushed. Then cleared his throat in a manly way. Then crossed his arms across his chest. Then uncrossed them, when he saw Ms. Shevron's eyebrows lift.

"What if men routinely wore make-up to emphasize their chiselled jawlines, their dark, mysterious eyes, what if they cultivated the rough rather than clean-shaven look, even at work, and—"

"I'd say 'Bring it on!'" She hadn't yet turned her attention back to Rev.

"Yes, but would you take them seriously?" Rev asked.

"Oh yes, I could certainly take him—"

"You would listen to what he says, with undivided attention?"

"What*ever* he says—"

"Could he be your boss, the one making all the decisions? "

Ms. Shevron let out a little 'Hardly' snort before she realized— what had just happened.

O regon was next. They had several radio interviews on their schedule, but thanks to Alexander Graham Bell and satellites, none required an in-studio presence. They had planned a leisurely more or less direct route from Utah to Oregon, but Phil had sent an email encouraging them to take a more circuitous route south to Arizona and then up through Nevada. More visibility for their newly-yet-again-painted-and-lettered lime green van, of course, but also, he said, they could stop and see the famous 'Wave'. He'd already taken the liberty of entering them in the lottery—the sandstone rock formation was such a popular site, and degradation was such a possibility, that only 20 people a day were allowed to hike through. Turned out Rev and Dylan were among the chosen few. Go figure.

"'Imagine walking into a humongous vat of cinnamon taffy'," Rev said, slowing to an awes-struck stop as she turned the last corner of the three mile walk that actually took them into the Wave. "Isn't that what that guy said?" She was referring to an article by Hugo Martin they'd found on the internet.

Dylan stood beside her, equally amazed. "Yes! And that's exactly what this looks like! Feels like!"

They didn't say another word for quite some time.

They debated whether or not to continue on to the arch and alcove, but the brochure's cautionary "Only those experienced in slickrock scrambling should attempt to go to the arch and beyond," and the searing heat, dissuaded them.

"It's not because we're old," Rev said.

"Certainly not," Dylan agreed.

"It's because we aren't experienced in slickrock scrambling."

"That's it."

They did, however, go to the 'Dinosaur Dance Floor'.

"What do you think," Dylan asked, looking at the arrangement of what must've been over a thousand indentations. "The Stroll or the Jive? Oh, oh, I know—the Mashed Potato!"

Given the desert conditions—Peanut would have been very thirsty after any hike in the area and some of the campsites had no water—Tucker had already gone on ahead, but Dylan and Rev decided to stay overnight at one of the nearby campsites. Neither of them had seen the stars in the desert before.

"I know this sounds stupid," Rev said as they gazed up, "but I didn't know there were so many."

"And you know what's nice?" Dylan asked. "It's not so freakin' cold." He was referring to the fact that up around Sudbury, the nights when the stars were particularly brilliant were also the nights when the temperature was near 40 below.

After a while, they heard someone bustling about in the next site which had, to that point, been empty. Rev waited with percolating rage for the screech of kids or the scratch of a radio. Playing Britney Spears.

"Come join me," they heard instead, and saw a woman beckoning them with a joint in her hand.

They looked at each other, agreed, picked up their folding half-chairs, and walked over to her site.

"Sharon," she said, by way of introduction, and offered a toke.

She had a Janis Joplin thing going for her.

"Dylan," he said, taking a draw then passing it to Rev.

"Rev."

"So what brings you to the Wave?" Dylan asked her, once he'd exhaled.

"I'm working on my dissertation," she said, "about the association between religion and drugs."

"Really? That sounds interesting," Dylan was intrigued. And not particularly clear about its relation to the Wave.

"Yeah, there's actually a long history. Peyote and shamanism go way back."

"Right, of course."

"And if you think about it—burning bushes, people walking on water—add some shrooms or whatever," she waved her joint, "and it all makes sense."

"It does!" Dylan said. He was surprised the connection had not occurred to him before.

"One theory," Sharon continued, "is that the ark of the covenant just contained the high priest's stash."

"That would explain why no one was allowed to go near it!" he said, delighted at how the pieces fit, then passed the joint to Rev again.

They gazed at the stars for a while.

"God is great, God is good," Sharon inhaled. "God is everything!" she exhaled.

"Well, no he can't be everything," Rev said. "He can't be both good and evil, for example."

"No, he's not evil. How can you say that?"

"I wasn't saying that. Because he doesn't exist. Existence must precede essence? I was just illustrating the fact that he can't be everything. That would involve so many logical contradictions."

"So?" Sharon giggled.

Rev tried again. "Okay, if I say God wants us to be rich and you say God wants us to be poor, how do you decide which of us is right? How do you settle that dispute?"

"Decide! Settle! Dispute! You're so adversarial. God is love. There's no need for any adversity. What's true for me may not be true for you."

"Truth isn't relative!" Rev looked around for a rock to kick. Or knock her over the head with.

"Wait a minute," Dylan said, just catching up. "You believe there's a god? Despite knowing that the miracles were just drug-induced hallucinations?"

"Oh yeah," she beamed. Beamed. "That doesn't really matter, does it? I mean, if that's the way God made things—if he made it so we need drugs in order to see him, that's cool."

"Have you heard of Persinger's studies? He hooked up people's brains to electrodes and whenever he stimulated a certain part of the brain, his subjects reported feeling the presence of God."

"Of course. Same thing. God put that trigger neuron in our brain to make sure we'd be able to feel Him near!"

"And the thing is," Rev was ranting behind the wheel the next morning on their way to Portland, "she's a Ph.D.!"

"Well, not quite—but point taken. However. Which of the premises in the implied argument contains an unjustified assumption?"

She glanced over at him. Wondering how he could be so lucid in the morning.

"Sharon has a Ph.D. Therefore, Sharon is intelligent. Therefore, Sharon should be an atheist," he helpfully articulated the implied argument.

She glanced over at him again. Wondering how he could be so articulate in the morning.

"There's intelligence, and there's intelligence," he said then. Perfectly aware of how very intelligent that observation was. Not to mention lucid. And articulate.

Their entry into Oregon was welcomed. If the billboard at the city limits was any indication: "People who go to church are happier than those who do not" bore the addendum, "And people who take Prozac are happier still."

They checked into the Curada, unpacked their stuff, tucked a copy of Judith Hayes' *The Happy Heretic* beside *The Bible* in the nightstand, then called Tucker to tell him they'd arrived. Their scheduled lecture wasn't until the next day, so once they confirmed the arrangements, per the to-do list Phil had provided, they decided to spend the rest of the day catching up on email, updating their blog, making another podcast, and working on their book.

"I need to go out," Dylan stood up and stretched, "you want anything?"

"Do I want anything," she said slowly, philosophically.

He grinned. "I prepared a new lecture, and I need a prop."

"Sounds intriguing," she said. "Bring back a pizza?"

"Good afternoon," Dylan said, walking onto the stage carrying a big, bright balloon. "We've talked a lot, on this tour, about stuff in *The Bible* that really shouldn't be there, if God wrote it. Contradictions, outright errors, and just truly awful stuff. There are several good books, available at our table of course, if you're curious. We've also put a fair amount of it on our blog."

"Boo."

"But today, I want to talk about stuff that's *not* in Bible. That *should* be. If God's who, or what, you say he is."

"For instance?" someone called out.

"Well," Dylan replied, "dinosaurs."

"Boo."

"DNA. Cancer. Nuclear weapons. Black holes. Helium."

"Helium?"

"Yes. We didn't discover it until 1868, but surely God knew about it long before then," Dylan said, untying the balloon's end. "I mean, he created it, right?" Dylan inhaled, then squeaked out like a chipmunk. "So why didn't he mention it?"

"He mentioned semen and ovum," someone called out.

"No he didn't," Dylan squeaked back.

"Yes he did."

"But microscopes weren't invented yet," his voice was back to normal.

"Yeah, well, God *created helium*. He doesn't need a microscope."

And then they all left.

"Did you know people are playing fast and loose with *The Bible* these days?" Dylan said to Rev that evening, staring at his laptop, his balloon bobbing beside him.

"What do you mean?"

"Today at the lecture, I was talking about how so much stuff that one would expect to be in the Bible isn't. You know, like dinosaurs, DNA, and so forth."

"Right..."

"Well, someone called out that semen and ova are in *The Bible*."

"Can't be. The microscope wasn't invented yet."

"What I said!" he grinned at her. "But they're right. Sort of. According to a version available at the Bible Gateway website, *The*

Bible says—" Dylan took a gulp of what was left in his balloon— "'Oh, that marvel of conception as you stirred together semen and ovum.'"

She giggled at his chipmunk voice. "Really?" She got up to look over his shoulder.

"Yeah. But in the King James Version, that verse is—" he inhaled again, because *The Bible* sounded so much better in chipmunk, "'Hast thou not poured me out as milk, and curdled me like cheese?' And the New International Version has translated the original to something similar: 'Did you not pour me out like milk and curdle me like cheese....'"

"So what version has the semen and ovum?"

"Something called *The Message*. Written by Eugene Peterson."

"Matthew, Mark, Luke, and—Eugene. Yeah, I remember now."

"He says he wrote it straight from the original Greek text."

"Is he an ancient Greek scholar?"

"He has an M.A. in Semitic Languages from Johns Hopkins," he conceded, then handed her the balloon as he continued reading, "but he says he just typed out the pages the way he thought they would have sounded to the Galatians."

Rev inhaled the last of the helium, then squeaked, "I guess that's what they call divine inspiration."

Their next in-person gig was a television interview. In Texas. Phil had suggested they scoot over to North Dakota and then turn south to travel through South Dakota and Nebraska. They were booked in Kansas a bit later, so, he suggested, why not go through Missouri and Arkansas instead. Take the secondary highways, he said. You've got the time.

"So we've been at this for a couple months now," Rev said somewhere in South Dakota. "Do you think we're being noticed?"

"Yes...."

"But?" She rearranged herself in the passenger seat. "But not as much as a bus, travelling at the speed of crawl, through downtowns, stopping every two minutes in front of a crowd of people."

"Yeah. What I think."

She added a minute later, "Maybe we should park at Walmart more often."

A week or so later, after a relatively uneventful drive, which, for reasons they didn't fully appreciate yet, seemed to surprise Phil, they entered Texas. As they approached Dallas, they realized they were a couple hours early, so they stopped in some outlying surburban area to take a walk before dealing with the bustling metropolis.

The first house they passed had an American flag flying from a pole in the yard. So did the second house. The fourth house had a flag flying from the porch. The fifth house had a little one sticking up out of the mailbox. The sixth had one again flying from a flagpole in the yard. A man was sitting on his verandah.

"Excuse me," Rev called out. After all, it had been a relatively uneventful drive. "May I ask why you've put up a large American flag in your front yard?"

"Because I'm American," he said proudly.

"Yes, but you're also a man. You don't have a man flag in your front yard."

He looked at her like she'd escaped. Possibly from the zoo. And since he apparently didn't have a reply, they moved on.

"There's another one," Dylan pointed out. He was such an enabler.

"Excuse me," Rev called out to the person doing yard work at the next flag-flying house. "May I ask why you've got an American flag on your porch?"

"Why? I'll tell you why!" he said, responding as if her question had been a challenge, maybe even a disapproval. Most people had no intellectual curiosity, Rev realized, and so they refused to believe her questions were, often, just that—questions. "I'm proud to be an American!" he said, waving his garden shears at her. "That's why!"

"Name five decisions 'America' made in the last year that you were part of, that you had a say in."

He was silent.

She tried again. "What are you proud of? What have you done to make America America? You go to work every day. Well so does the guy in China. And Sweden. That's not uniquely American. So you may as well fly the Chinese flag or the Swedish flag if that's what you're proclaiming."

"I was born here!" He shook the shears again.

"So you really had nothing to do with it. With being an

American," she added. "It's really just an accident of birth."

"This is a great country!" he shouted.

"I'm sure it is," Rev lied, "and I can see you're happy to live here, but being happy isn't the same as being proud. You can be proud of running a marathon in under four hours. That's an achievement. How is being an American an *achievement*? What did you *do* to become an American? What exactly are you taking credit for?

"And even if you *did* do something," she continued, "why not just put the flag on your fridge? Why are you so concerned that everyone knows about it? Isn't that sort of like bragging?"

"We don't tolerate no disrespect for the flag here, you'd best be moving on," he turned back to the shrubbery.

"Well," the next person said, pleased to engage in conversation with the Canadians, "I practice the American way of life. I hold firm American values."

"And what values are those?"

"Oh, dear, we believe in freedom here!"

"Well, so do we. Let's say. Americans don't have a monopoly on believing in freedom. So if that's all there is to being American, you may as well be Canadian. What values make you *American*?"

"Well, I don't know—"

"I didn't think so."

They walked on.

"You know what I think?" Rev said to the next person. "I think it's a gang colors thing. You're proclaiming your membership in a gang, a tribe. Which is sort of like trying to pick a fight. I mean why else would you shove your gang colors in my face?"

"There is another possibility," Dylan suggested a couple houses later. "Maybe the Home Depot just had a sale on flags."

"That would be so—Canadian."

"We hope you're enjoying Texas?" the show's host said, after he introduced Dylan and Rev as his first guests of the day.

"Well, we're a little puzzled by all the American flags. Outside on people's houses and their lawns—we've even been seeing them sticking up in the middle of the forest, at people's cabins presumably. What an eyesore."

She didn't notice the intake of breath.

"Well," the host replied, "many people fly the flag because they have a son or daughter serving overseas."

Rev hadn't thought about that. She did now. Then said, "And why would they want to advertise such stupidity?"

"Well, it's not stupid," the host was trying to be calm. "Wanting to serve your country—"

"Oh please. Most of the people who enlist wouldn't give their fellow Americans the time of day. I'll bet they never volunteered at a soup kitchen or even gave up their seat on the subway. Suddenly they're willing to—"

"They're fighting for our freedom," the host interjected.

"Yeah? How? How exactly does killing someone in Afghanistan or wherever make that guy—" Rev pointed at random to the one of the techies, of which there were suddenly several, all paying rather close attention to what was going on— "free? He looks pretty free to me already."

The host tried again. "They're bringing democracy to a country that—"

"—they know nothing about. Most of them couldn't even point to it on a map. Every time I see coverage of American soldiers overseas, they're shouting at its residents in English. And then they're angry when the people they're shouting at don't do what they're told. Apparently it doesn't even occur to the soldiers that they speak a different language. What, they think the world speaks *their* language?

How arrogant. Or just stupid.

"Which explains why they *really* go," she continued. "They get suckered in by the ads, about courage, honor, glory. 'I'll do what my country asks me to do,' they say with such self-righteousness. Oh please. Who asked? Name one person who came to you and said, 'Hey, John, could you please go kill that person for me.'

"And then they come back all distraught and messed up because they did just that. Like it's such a horrible surprise. The six weeks of being taught how to load and shoot a gun should've been a clue."

"Well, they thought they'd just be killing—"

"The bad guys? What are they, twelve?"

"But—"

"I get, and admire, the desire to be a hero. It's just that in the context of war, heroism is—" she paused, trying to find the right word, "—manufactured."

No one seemed to understand what she was getting at, so she turned back.

"Look, you sign up to be a soldier, you kill people. At the very least, you hurt them. And they scream, and bleed, when their arms and legs are blown off. Especially the kids. Go figure. Did you think they'd get up and walk away after they'd been shot?" She spoke into the camera. As she'd been instructed.

"And now you want to kill yourself because you can't live with what you did. Or, worse, because you can. You didn't anticipate that? Why the hell not!"

Dylan noticed that a few people in suits had moved in among the growing crowd of techies. As had Tucker.

"How is it you have no idea what happens in war? Wilfrid Owen. 1916. *All Quiet on the Western Front.* 1929. *M.A.S.H.* 1970. *Coming Home, Apocalypse Now.* Late 70s. *Born on the Fourth of July, Casualties of War.* 80s. *In the Valley of Elah*! Every generation comes back and tells us. This is nothing new. Where have you been?

"I'll tell you. With your head in the sand and your hands on your video games, dreaming little boy dreams of being a hero.

"Did you think it wouldn't actually be *you* to pull the trigger? Zimbardo! Milgram! We have done the studies. We *know* what happens when people are put in that situation. And it's not like these studies are hidden or censored. Anyone can go to a library and sign out a book on psychology, a book on group influence, peer pressure, indoctrination, brainwashing, there are lots of them. You can even get one on eBay. For ninety-nine cents."

One of the suited men had started making throat-slitting gestures to the host, who was trying, unsuccessfully of course, to stop Rev. Tucker quietly moved to stand behind the man, ready in case—well, ready.

"And it's not like you had to sign up. If you'd been forced to do it, that would be different. If someone had held a gun to your own kids' heads, that would be different. But you *chose* to go. You chose to subject yourself to military conditioning and now you're crying because it worked. "So if you ask me," she said, fully aware that no one had asked her, "you deserve every sleepless night, every nightmare, every flashback you're now getting. You should have known. That you didn't is your own fault.

No one jumped into the silence that followed.

"And you should have thought about it. *Before* you did it. But you didn't, and now you're a mess. Well good. You should be. That's the price of being a philosophically irresponsible idiot. Not to have thought through the ethics of it—it's a failure of personal responsibility." She looked squarely into the camera again. "Again, what are you, twelve?"

"But if you question the morality," the host pointed out, "you're labelled a bleeding heart. A boyscout. A pussy."

She looked at him. "Since when did ethics become a girl thing? And besides, *so what*? You ignore right and wrong just to avoid being called a pussy? When your loved ones tell you they're enlisting, you don't try to stop them? Because you don't want to appear weak? You should tell them what fools they're being! Tell them it's a suicide mission no matter how it turns out!"

Dylan noticed then that many of the people, actually all of them except the one still slitting his throat, were nodding, silently applauding, or giving a thumbs up.

"And please, enough with the talk about 'psychological injury' and trouble 'transitioning'. Since when is 'transition' a verb?

"And 'post-traumatic-stress-disorder'—give me a break. It's guilt. Nothing more, nothing less. Guilt for having done something monstrously wrong, something cruel, something barely justifiable. And since when is *guilt* a *disorder*?"

"So," Dylan said in the heavy silence that followed, "You wanted to ask us something about our tour—of enlightenment?"

After the interview, they checked into the Curada. When Dylan opened the nightstand drawer—he'd brought in a copy of *Misquoting Jesus*—he found a sheaf of papers that did not look like take-out menus.

"What's that?" Rev asked.

"I don't know. Looks like some sort of report—a psychological assessment of some kind. Left by the previous occupant?"

"Oh yeah? What does it say?"

Dylan read aloud. "'Mr. Morris reports that he was born in Dumas, Texas, but presently lives in Perryton, Texas with his wife of 32 years. He does not remember exactly, but he says he had a previous marriage in the early 50s and has seven or eight children from that union—'" Dylan raised his eyebrows at Rev, then continued. "'Mr. Morris reports that he attained a grade six level of education. With regard to his work history, he says that for most of his life he has driven trucks. Presently, he is a pastor—'" Rev widened her eyes— "'with the Upper Room Outreach Ministry.'"

"You don't need any qualifications to become a pastor?" she said with disbelief. "I mean other than being able to drive a truck?"

"Well, or being able to catch a fish."

That evening, Tucker dropped by with Peanut. "Hey, I've got extra tickets to the game—a friend sent them to me—wanna come?"

"Sure," Dylan said, "it'll be fun."

Rev looked at him curiously. "You're not a football fan."

"This is Texas. Home of the Dallas Cowboys. We have to go," he added, giving her a weird look. Which she, of course, understood. In general terms. And she couldn't wait to find out the specifics.

They had to park some distance from the stadium, and as they joined the multitudes travelling on foot to their Mecca, Rev started to get a sense at just how big football was in Texas.

So she thought. Until, through the doors, past the ticket taker, through the lobby with its hanging pennants, shiny Ford display truck, and many booths selling memorabilia, then up the stairs, and into the stadium proper, she—stopped. Simply stopped. "Wow," she said, staring at the stands, already full of people. Thousands of people. Tens of thousands. "I had no idea." Perhaps millions. "You know, this is why I could never be a rock star."

Dylan waited.

"If I had this many people paying attention to me, I'd feel obligated to say, or do, something—meaningful."

Dylan nodded. He understood.

They had only three seats, so Dylan encouraged Peanut to snuggle in between his legs, with his rump on the cold concrete. He wrapped his arms around him, just because he was just so very big and so very huggable. He was happy. Dylan, that is. Peanut too though. Dylan had become his almost-bestest-friend.

They remained seated as the flag was unfurled.

"That's a big flag," Rev said as it turned out to cover the entire playing field. The cheers of the crowd were deafening.

Tucker looked over at her. The flag was no bigger than it usually was. Suddenly it dawned on him. "You've never been to a football game before?" he said, incredulously.

"Nope."

"Never? You've never been to a game?" He really couldn't believe it.

"Never."

"But—you get football on tv, don't you? I mean, there's football in Canada, isn't there?"

Rev looked at him. "Well, yeah. But we use a frozen penguin instead of a football."

Dylan sputtered into his Pepsi.

"We're—Rev and I, not Canadians as a whole—we're not really into team sports," Dylan explained. Tucker accepted that and turned his attention back to the field.

"Speaking of which," Rev said to Dylan, "I've never understood why the national anthem is played at sports games," Rev said.

"Well it's a perfect opportunity, isn't it," Dylan said. "The masses have already gathered. Why not turn it into a political rally—"

A woman was led—led, Rev noticed with irritation—onto a stage. Catcalls ensued. Rev looked around her in surprise, since the woman wasn't particularly tarty. Not at all tarty, in fact. The woman stepped up to the mic and proceeded to sing the anthem, over the cheering that never seemed to stop.

Then the cheerleaders came onto the field. More catcalls. To say the least. They began their—bump and grind. "Okay, this isn't how I remember cheerleading," she said, watching the not-at-all-subtle pelvic thrusts.

Tucker looked over at her again. "You've *never* been to a game? *Ever?*"

"You know," she said a moment later, thoughtfully, over the cheering that still hadn't subsided, "I don't think people even know what they're cheering. First, nation, then sex, in a minute, athletic prowess—"

"It's all the same," Dylan said.

"How so?" she asked, intrigued. "I get that sports is just symbolic war, so for two of the three you've got the excitement of combat, the anticipation of conquest—Jesus Christ!" she exploded as she got it.

The team took the field then. More cheering. Well, louder cheering.

"And furthermore," Rev managed to say a short while later, a mere two minutes into the game, which is when she officially became bored, "we're all just watching tv here," she said, looking up at the huge screen suspended above the play, which was itself too far away to see. "Why do people pay fifty bucks to come here and watch tv? And scream," she added. Since the cheering still hadn't stopped.

Dylan, bored as well, had been looking up into the stands, and seemed to finally find what he was looking for. He nudged Rev, stood up, and made his way out into the aisle. Peanut wanted to go too, but Dylan, and Tucker, told him to stay. So instead he gazed longingly at Dylan as he left.

"Where are we going?" Rev asked, as she followed him.

"To provide some color commentary," he replied, making a quick dip behind one of the now unattended memorabilia booths to confiscate a bullhorn.

"Saw it there on the way in," he explained.

They went up, and up, and up, and then came out on the very highest level. Dylan saw that he had misjudged somewhat, led them back in behind, walked a bit further along, then came out again.

"Perfect," he said, seeing that it was the unoccupied section he'd spotted from below. He stepped to the railing to watch the game.

Just as the linemen took their three-point stances and presented their asses, Dylan broadcast to the stadium, in his best Eric Idle voice, "Oh give it to me! Yes!"

The linemen quickly straightened and looked up at the stands, whether in embarrassment or in anger, it was hard to tell.

After a few moments, they took their positions again. The quarterback adjusted his position and reached for the ball. "Ooh-la-la!" Dylan called out.

The quarterback pulled back his hand.

"Ooh-la-la?" Rev mouthed at him.

He shrugged. The quarterback resumed his position.

"He likes me, he likes me, he wants to get into my endzone," Dylan sang out.

The quarterback pulled back his hand yet again and this time stepped away. Jumped away, actually. He looked up into the stands. Definitely in anger. The crowd was also looking up and around. Rev calmly stepped in front of Dylan, shielding him from view. After a few fruitless moments, the players once again resumed their positions.

"Such a tight end. I like a tight end."

The players broke from their game once again, and looked up once again, trying to find Dylan. Rev saw several members of Security briskly walking this way and that, conferring on their walkie-talkies, scanning the stands. She continued to stand in front of Dylan, trying to look as concerned as everyone else. The referee decided to proceed, because the crowd was really getting pissed. And because in a minute the players were going to start hitting each other. Just to prove—

It was a short play. "Oh they're piling on! Snuggles all round!"

The players jumped up and off each other like they'd been burned, and the crowd was *really* starting to be pissed. But the referee insisted on continuing.

"He scored!" Dylan cried out. "Ooh slap me on the bottom!"

Peanut, Tucker, and Stadium Security converged on them at about the same time. Peanut, no doubt inspired by what he had seen so far, sprinted ahead and tackled Dylan. After all, he'd just found his almost-bestest-friend! He lay on him, full body, Dylan squirming underneath with delight, giggling, and trying unsuccessfully to avoid Peanut's overactive tongue.

"Peanut—" Tucker called him off, and flashed his badge at Security, hoping to discourage any further involvement on their part.

Peanut got off Dylan, reluctantly. Then did something that looked like a cross between James Brown and the Hokey Pokey. Clearly this was not the first football game *he* had watched.

ennsylvania was next. They figured four days on the road.

"You know, what I don't understand," Rev said from the passenger seat somewhere in Louisiana, "is why they just don't go for the head honcho. Or all the guys in charge. The ones responsible for the war in the first place. I mean, they kill hundreds, thousands of soldiers, but they can't manage to kill the guys in charge?"

"That would break the rules. No doubt made by the guys in—"

"What rules? You mean they have rules? For war? Isn't that sort of—"

"Like having guidelines to ensure that torture is humane."

She looked over at him. He wasn't kidding.

"We are so fucked up."

One of their gigs in Philadelphia was another on-site radio talk show. Another *call-in* radio talk show. And this call-in show went pretty much like all the others they'd had. Two minutes in…

"Look, you can't just say whatever you want!" Rev said with frustration to the caller.

"Sure I can, it's a free world!"

"Where to begin," she murmured. "Okay first, it's not a free world. There are laws constraining our behaviour. Physical laws, at the very least. You are not free to fly. Unaided.

"Second, you keep uttering non sequiturs, which I m tired of identifying. We never get to the main point *because* you keep saying whatever the hell you want. It's like you don't even know what the main point is. Which would explain why you don't know what's relevant and what's not. Either that or you're just not thinking. You don't care if what you say is relevant or not. Well I'm frickin' tired of doing your work for you. So from now on, unless what you say is relevant to what I've said, I'm going to just ignore it."

The caller continued for a good five minutes, during which Rev said not a word. Dylan was astounded. Truly and thoroughly astounded.

But then there was the next caller…

"God told me—"

"Well that's interesting. Because he told *me* something different. Now what? How do we determine who to listen to?"

"If God truly speaks to you—which I doubt—then you should do what He tells you to do. And I'll do what he tells me to do."

"So if he tells you not to eat fish, but pork's okay, and he tells me not to eat pork, but fish is okay, you're okay with that? Or what if he tells you to kill me, and he tells me to kill you. You don't see a problem with that?"

"No, I do not. With God all things are possible."

Rev threw her hands up in the air. "Oh, well, if that's your stance then there's no point in discussing any of this. There's no point in even thinking about any of it.   Ah." It was one of those eureka moments with the two-second delay. Tagged with a 'been there, done that'.

And then there was the warm feeling justification for the existence of God…

"I just know He exists. When I think of the Lord, my Saviour, I get such a warm feeling, it spreads throughout my entire being."

"Yeah," Rev said, "I feel that way when I think of cheesecake."

"And you know," she was saying a few minutes later, "I'm tired of the whole *The Bible* says thing. You are all such hypocrites. If you really believed what *The Bible* says, you'd be hacking off body parts. Both Matthew and Mark say cut your hand off if you sin with it. And who among you is without sin? By hand?" she added.

"Show some respect!"

"No! I will not respect unjustified belief! *You* show some respect! For the minimum level of intelligence that would reveal your cherished beliefs to be nonsense! And for the least bit of courage that would reveal the voice you hear in your head to be your own wishful thinking."

Dylan put his hand over the mic. "A little compassion? Remember how Faith described it, like ripping out—"

"I know. I *know*. I do have compassion. For anyone under twenty-five, but after that, they're dishonest, irresponsible, immature, and/or stupid. Not to mention dangerous."

"How so?" the host interjected, gesturing them both back to the mic.

"Well, consider, for example, the whole transfusion thing. How many kids died because of *that* religious belief? *The Bible*—"

"Actually," Dylan spoke up, "*The Bible* doesn't specifically prohibit blood transfusions, because that particular procedure wasn't 'discovered' until the 17th century. It was tried before that, we have a record of the blood of three boys being put into the Pope's mouth to bring him out of a coma, this was in 1492, but transfusion as we know it wasn't developed until around 1667 CE. And *The Bible* was written before that," he added. Just in case. "The last of it was finished around 100 CE."

"What do you mean, the last of it?" Of course the caller was still on the line. Or maybe it was the next caller. Waiting…

"Well it was written over the course of about 1500 years, by about 40 different people. The parts written by Moses were written about 1300 years before Jesus Christ was born, and the parts written by Paul were written about 100 years after he died.

"But about transfusions—are you still there?"

The caller had gone silent. Possibly surprised by the fact that *The Bible* wasn't written in one sitting by one person with an angel standing over his shoulder.

"What *The Bible* does say," Dylan continued anyway, "is that people should abstain from blood. Acts 15:20. It's talking about ingesting blood—drinking it or eating flesh that contains blood.

"Now the interesting thing isn't whether a transfusion is drinking blood. The interesting thing is John 6:53-56, which has Jesus saying *do* drink blood—specifically, drink *his* blood. That's what the Eucharist is all about—'This is my body, this is my blood…'."

"Yes, but that's just a metaphor," the caller had recovered.

"Actually, no, it's not. Jesus says, 'Whoever eats my flesh and drinks my blood has eternal life, and I will raise him up at the last day. For my flesh is real food and my blood is real drink.' *Real* food and drink. Not *symbolic*.

"Furthermore, if it is just a metaphor, then wouldn't the supposed prohibition also be just a metaphor? Not a command against real transfusions?"

And then there was this caller, the highlight of the show, for Rev at least:

"Yeah, hi, regarding intelligent design versus evolution, I find it ironic that the stupid people are backing intelligent design, and the intelligent people are backing dumbfuck non-design. That's essentially what evolution is: whatever traits lead to increased reproduction, those are the ones that survive.

"And what traits lead to reproduction? Not intelligence, that's for sure," she said. "Intelligent women don't want to have ten kids.

174

They'd rather be doing medical research, making art, studying society. And intelligent men? They're not cruising the bars. They're home with a good book if they're not still in the office. It's stupid women who forget to take the pill or don't get a tubal ligation after one or two. And it's stupid men who don't use a condom or get a vasectomy. And it's stupid brute force that rapes. And those men aren't targeting the intellectuals. So we're evolving all right. Right into propagated species-wide stupidity."

"But isn't evolution all about survival of the fittest?" the host interjected.

"Yeah, fittest to the environment. And that's the curious thing. Because since stupid people, the ones reproducing, don't even know what an 'ecological footprint' is, let alone have the desire to minimize their ecological footprint, we're *not* going to survive."

"Which means maybe evolution is intelligent design after all," Rev concluded for her.

And then to…

"Jesus is our Saviour. You must remember, young lady, that he died for our sins."

"What about me?" Dylan interjected. "Do I have to remember it too?"

"Of course, sir."

They just looked at each other.

"Okay," Rev rallied, "but what exactly does that mean? How can someone die *for* your sins. I mean, suppose Sir Dylan here sins. Let's say he steals something. So if I die—well, I don't get it. Why would I die—how does that change—oh, I die in his place? But who's going to kill him for stealing?"

"God—"

"God's the one who would have killed him? For stealing? I thought he was all-forgiving.

"And wait a minute," she continued, "we were born *after* Jesus died. So it can't be *our* sins he died for. We didn't sin yet. We didn't exist yet.

"And we haven't even touched the notion that God suggests his *son* dies in our place: if his son dies, he'll agree not to kill us for sinning. Wouldn't a loving father just say he won't kill us in the first place?"

And from there to…

"What about Sundays? All you atheists want to take away family time—don't you believe in the sanctity of the family?"

"Um, could you connect the dots for us?" Dylan asked. Politely. "Why is Sunday exclusively family day? And how exactly is family sancti—fied? Sanc—titious?"

"Sanctimonious!" Rev crowed.

"And how exactly are atheists taking away Sundays?" Dylan continued. "I didn't know we could make days disappear. Did you know we could do that?" he asked Rev.

Straight to…

"Are you advocating a world without prayer?"

"*Yes*, we're advocating a world without prayer!" Dylan said. "It's easy to talk to a god that doesn't talk back. But it's more effective to talk to real people."

"Well, no," Rev said, then leaned back in her chair, sighing. "Actually it's not…."

"You know what we need?" Dylan asked, back in their suite at the Curada.

"More helium?" Rev suggested, inhaling what was not helium.

"No, silly. Cheesecake. Let's make our own cheesecake!"

"With helium?"

"No, with cheese and cake. Obviously. And root beer!" he added on a whim. "Let's make a root beer cheesecake!"

"Okay, so we have to go get some cheese and cake. And root beer."

Their phone rang. They both stared at it. They were good at identifying the source of sounds that way.

"Hello?" Rev said into the receiver. After she'd picked it up. And pleased with herself about that.

"Oh. Okay," she said a couple seconds later. "There's a package waiting for us at the desk."

"Oh. Okay. Are we expecting more books? Or bumper stickers—and—stuff?" Dylan narrowed his eyes at her. "What did you order off eBay?"

"You'll see," she grinned. Because she actually remembered what she'd ordered off eBay.

So they got their act together and went down to the main desk, intending to go to a store from there.

Rev looked at the return address, then gave it to Dylan. "It's a gift. Open it."

Dylan unwrapped what looked like a piece of PVC pipe. It even had "PVC pipe" written on it. Tied to one end was a sort of embroidery red-and-orange ropey thing, like the trim one might buy in a fabric store if one were making a dress for one's daughter in order to ensure that she never ever made any friends at school. The other end of the ropey thing was tied to a ring that slid up and down the pipe.

"It's nice," he said, sliding the ring up and down. "What is it?"

"A PVC pipe with a ropey thing tied to it."

"Yes, but—"

"It's a bubble wand. Look." She pointed to the picture on the accompanying pamphlet. It showed someone making amazingly large bubbles.

"Oh, oh, let's do that!" Dylan said excitedly. He feebly waved the wand around. The Curada receptionist was trying not to stare.

"How do we do that?" he said when no bubbles materialized.

"We have to dip it into bubble stuff first. There was a whole page of instructions on the guy's website. The guy who makes these. He's in Florida."

"So let's go to Florida to get his bubble stuff!"

"No, we can make our own. We need—" she took the pamphlet from him and skimmed through it— "dish detergent and baking soda. Or corn syrup."

"Okay, we can probably get that where we get the cheese, cake, and root beer! We're going to make cheesecake *and* magic bubble stuff!" Dylan informed the Curada receptionist. Who muttered something about their having already had some magic stuff.

So half an hour later, they found the open-all-night grocery store that was a block away from the Curada.

"Hi," Dylan said, to the first person he met. "We need some magic bubble stuff." Rev, who had not inhaled quite as much of their usual magic stuff, tugged him away.

They eventually found the dish detergent aisle and stood in front of the fifteen kinds of dish detergent.

"Is this because we dirty a lot of dishes or because we really like clean dishes?" Rev wondered.

"Both of the above?" Dylan had been reading her LSAT questions. "Neither of the above?"

After a few moments, Rev consulted the pamphlet.

"Ivory Clear," she said. "He says that's best."

"Okay! Let's get some Ivory Clear!" Dylan suggested.

As they left the dish detergent aisle, Ivory Clear in hand, Rev was caught by something but couldn't immediately put her finger on it.

She stood beside the mops and sponges for a minute, waiting for it...

"A pail! We'll probably need a pail for the bubble stuff."

"Yes! Brilliant! If we just squirt the Ivory Clear into the air and then throw baking soda at it—" he grinned. Pleased he'd remembered they also needed baking soda.

They selected a bright orange pail, then went in search of the rest of the items on their non-existent list.

"What kind of cheese do we need?" he asked as they stared at cheddar, colby, brie, parmesan, havarti, feta, gouda, and gruyere.

"Brie?" Rev suggested. "It has the right consistency. Sort of."

"Excuse me," Dylan said to someone standing nearby, "do you happen to know what kind of cheese we need to make cheesecake?"

"Certainly," she said. "You need cream cheese."

"Ah. Thanks."

They stared at the cheddar, colby, brie, parmesan, havarti, feta, gouda, and gruyere.

"It's over there," the woman pointed. "In the bright, shiny, foil packages," she added, a gleam in her eye.

They moved to where she was pointing, and Rev selected one of the bright, shiny, foil packages. "Who'd've thought?" she marvelled at the idea that it contained cheese, turning it over in her hands.

"Oh, oh! It has a recipe for cheesecake on it! And it doesn't require cake!" she added with disbelief.

"That can't be right."

"Well, rugby doesn't require rugs."

"It doesn't, no."

"And there aren't any fences in fencing."

"And squash isn't played with a squash!" Dylan blurted out.

Once they finished thinking about squash played with a squash, they actually succeeded in finding all of the ingredients they needed, that were so conveniently listed on the package.

"Root beer!" Dylan practically shouted when they were at the checkout, and went racing back toward the aisles.

"Aisle 4," the cashier called out, having ascertained early on that they both needed help.

On the way home, they bought a pizza and a couple chocolate bars.

"For later," Rev said.

"Right," Dylan said, as Rev opened one immediately.

Once back in their room, Rev eagerly opened the pizza box.

"Ah," she said, breathing in deeply.

"You eat the pizza," Dylan said, "and I'll make the cheesecake."

"No sweeter words—" she smiled broadly at him.

He took their bag of cheesecake ingredients into the kitchenette, while she settled in front of the tv with the pizza. Two slices later, she decided to try to get some work done, so she turned off the tv and opened her laptop. But she needed sustenance.

"Out! Out!" He shooed her from the kitchenette.

"But I want my chocolate bar."

He stared at her.

"My *other* chocolate bar."

"It's gone."

"You ate my chocolate bar!"

"No, I did not. And yet, it's gone. Make an LSAT question out of that!"

One hour, and one LSAT question, later, Dylan called out exuberantly, "I have created a masterpiece to rival your pudding in the middle brownies! Let me present to you," he appeared in front of her with a flourish, "a cheesecake shake!" He handed her one of the two glasses he was carrying.

"Mine's root beer," he said, "yours is chocolate."

She raised her glass to her lips. "This is good."

She took another sip. "This is *really* good!"

He smiled. Inordinately pleased with himself.

In the morning, give or take a couple hours, Dylan mixed a pail of bubble stuff according to the directions and they took the wand and their pail out into the Curada courtyard.

He dipped the wand into the pail and slowly wafted it through the air.

"Woh," he said, as a large iridescent wormhole formed in the air. They both stared at it, wobbling and shimmering in the air. After a few moments it disappeared. Dylan made another. The bubble lengthened to make a six foot long tunnel that looked, again, very much like an iridescent wormhole.

"This is so cool. Way better than regular bubbles," Dylan said, having spent a fair amount of time while they were in Montreal playing with forementioned regular bubbles. "Thank you!" he beamed at her.

"I knew you'd like it as soon as I saw the pictures."

"We should call Tucker and Peanut. He'd go wild chasing these. Peanut, I mean. You know, dogs and butterflies and all." He handed the wand to Rev, who tried her hand at making a few wormholes, and got out his cell phone.

"Hey Tucker. You and Peanut gotta come down to the courtyard. No, no, we're fine. We're playing. With bubbles. You gotta see it. Bring Peanut."

So Tucker and Peanut went down to the courtyard. Peanut bounded toward Dylan and Rev as soon as he saw them, but then stopped short when the shimmering jiggling wormhole registered. He hunkered down, in preparation to—slink behind Tucker. Where he promptly piddled.

T heir next stop was Kansas. On the way, they passed through Ohio and were surprised to see that the state motto was 'With God, all things are possible.'

"So much for the separation of church and state," Dylan observed.

"Yeah, well, the prayer was mandatory in schools back home, in decidedly-unzealous-by-comparison Canada, until just a few—well, until *after* I got fired for refusing to stand for it."

"Was that before or after you were fired for refusing to stand for the anthem?"

"I think—first I was fired for wearing jeans and a sweatshirt, wasn't I? Priorities," she snorted.

As they passed through Illinois, they were delighted to see that all of the crimestopper billboards had been modified: underneath the various mugs of thugs, someone had painted 'God created us in his image.'

A few days later, they arrived at their destination and found the Curada with no problem. They settled in like a veteran rock band with an entourage of two. Tucker and Peanut went for a very long walk, then booked a meeting room for use in the morning to work on their new dance. Dylan put Kick's *Everything You Know about God is*

Wrong into the nightstand, then stretched out on the bed to check their email, make a short podcast, then work on their book. Rev updated their blog, then considered their inventory and decided they needed more mugs. She got a few with Faith's 'They say God works in mysterious ways' backed with 'Why is that again, exactly?' and her own favourite, 'Why did the guardian angel cross the road?' backed with 'To be with his imaginary friend.'

Next day, as they pulled into the lot in front of the building at which they were to speak, they saw a group of youngish people in the distance, just standing around, near a cluster of vehicles, waiting.

Dylan stopped their van.

"Do you think they're waiting for us?" Rev asked. "With guns this time?"

"Actually, it does look like—" Dylan squinted.

"Shit!" Rev said, also squinting. "They *are* carrying guns! I was kidding."

"We're not in Canada anymore."

Tucker had also stopped and gotten out of his SUV. He approached Dylan's open window.

"What do you think?" Dylan asked. The people were openly looking right at them by now.

"I think this might be what the Chief had in mind when he asked if you'd be speaking in Kansas."

"Right. Well, then, we should just turn around and—"

The people waved them in.

"—run away!" Rev supplied.

Then one of them opened his jacket and stuck out his chest at them.

"Is he flashing us? Is that what passes for flashing in Kansas?"

"No, look," Dylan said oddly. "Look at what he's wearing."

"A t-shirt," Rev said. "In December." The possibility fascinated her.

"A *lime green* t-shirt," Dylan clarified.

Everyone in the group had made a show of opening their jackets. And every one of them was wearing a lime green t-shirt.

Tucker had by this time gone back to his SUV and returned to look again at the group with his police-issue binoculars. Peanut looked intently in the same direction. For show mostly.

"It's okay!" he said then, with an odd grin. "They're with us. Looks like."

"Let's see," Dylan took the binoculars from Tuck.

"Oh, Rev, you gotta see this!" he giggled, then passed the binoculars to Rev.

She burst into laughter as well. "What a great idea!"

As they drove toward the group, it let out a cheer. Dylan drove the van right up to where they were standing and parked.

"Hi, you're Dylan and Rev?" a young woman said as they got out. "We're here to protect your van!" She was wearing a lime green t-shirt that said "There are no gods" on the front. Rev walked around her—and let out a gleeful snort as she saw indeed that "Deal with it" was on the back.

"We have got to get a bunch of these!" Rev said to Dylan. "Where did you get them? We can sell them at the table!"

"But—" Dylan was puzzled.

"It's okay," Tucker said from a few feet away, where he'd been speaking with a young man. "They're paintball guns!"

It took a moment before it hit them. "Perfect! You guys are—perfect!"

"We've been following you. Online," the woman explained. "Reading your blog and listening to your podcasts. And of course checking your website."

"So that's how you knew where we'd be and when."

"Yes. Which is how everyone else knows too."

"Ah. Right. Of course."

"We've got groupies!" Rev said to Dylan.

"Looks like!" He grinned as they took in the motley crew of, presumably, college students, most of whom were now talking to Tucker and fawning over Peanut. Some were in camouflage, some had the young republican look, some had piercings and tattoos, some looked ready to krump. Altogether a delightful group of groupies.

"So," Tucker walked over to Dylan and Rev, "you're good to go?"

"Indeed we are!"

"Um, you go ahead," Rev said to Dylan. "I'm going to stay here."

He looked at her. "I doubt they have an extra."

"Oh." Busted.

"And they surely don't have two." He grinned at her.

Shortly after Dylan and Rev went in to set up their table and give their talk, they came back out. The crowd let out a cheer.

"Done already?" Tucker asked as they approached, Rev and Dylan carrying their two table boxes.

"The auditorium was empty. We waited, but no one showed up," Dylan said. "How about here?"

"A few cars pulled in, took in the situation, and left."

"You know what's going to happen next time, don't you."

Tucker nodded.

"These things are loaded with *latex* paint, right?"

Next time turned out to be two days later. They were still in Kansas.

As soon as they arrived at their destination, three cars pulled into the lot and parked some distance away from the van and its circle of lime green t-shirted, paintball gun wielding defenders. Several people got out, dressed head to toe in what looked like painters' smocks. Or bedsheets.

"Okay, didn't expect that," Tucker said, looking carefully through his binoculars. Peanut set his Frisbee into the back of the open SUV and sat by Tucker's side. For show mostly.

"What?"

Tucker passed the binoculars to Dylan who passed them to Rev.

"Hm."

The figures approached the van, many of them with both hands visible, supplicating. A few hands weren't visible, Tucker noted. One of the paintball gun brandishing youths fired a warning shot onto the pavement at the first figure's feet. The oncoming group paused for just a moment and then resumed approaching the van. Suggesting very much the night of the living dead at this point.

Suddenly Peanut let out a weird bark, flew through the air, and tackled one of the figures, bringing him to the ground. A gun clattered out of his smock and skid across the pavement.

"Everyone down!" Tucker yelled in a voice that achieved instant compliance, sprinted the short distance, picked up the gun, then turned to face the rest of the smocked figures who had taken flight and were running back to their cars. With impressive speed, given their attire.

He pocketed the gun, then went to assist a growling Peanut who had continued to pin the man to the ground. Since he was *not* his almost-bestest-friend. Tucker pulled the man to his feet, led him to his SUV, and handcuffed him to the vehicle's frame. Peanut did his James Brown-Hokey Pokey touchdown dance.

Dylan rushed up beside Tucker then, the rest of the brigade close behind. Rev was still on the ground. "How did Peanut know?"

"Well, he did do some explosives sniffing training before we got into the drug attachment—"

"Ah."

"But he failed."

"Oh."

"My guess is he's just been around enough real guns to know the difference between the smell of metal and the smell of plastic," he nodded to the paintball guns.

"What a hero," one of the young people said, crouching and flinging her arms around Peanut's neck. The others moved in to provide similar congratulations. Peanut beamed.

"Well, actually," Tucker confessed, "it's probably just that he didn't want the gun to go off. The noise scares him," he explained.

"Me too," Dylan said to Peanut, scratching his ears fondly.

Dylan, and Rev, who had by this time managed to get back up, started to get their boxes out of the van.

"Wait," he said then. "Let's check—before we unload."

"Good idea."

They left their boxes in the back of their van, went into the building, found the auditorium, and opened the doors. Empty.

So, since everyone was still in the parking lot, or more precisely, in the grassy area beside the parking lot, mostly playing Frisbee with Peanut, who was almost literally beside himself with so many enthusiastic throwers, Dylan and Rev decided the AAC should treat everyone to beer and pizza.

"Okay, first," Dylan stood up at one of the several tables they'd commandeered in the corner of the local university pub, "thank you all for showing up both times. That was so great. Really. But you'll put the word out that we'll have no more paintball defence brigades?"

The students groaned.

"It's too dangerous!" Dylan insisted.

"But we didn't even get to—"

"Hey!" Tucker said sharply, making even Dylan and Rev turn with attention. "If you have a gun, that doesn't mean you have to shoot it. If you can't resist that pull, you shouldn't be carrying. Even if it is just a paintball gun."

There were a few grumbles.

"We'd much rather repaint our van, every time if we have to, than lose one of you," Dylan added. "Now," he raised his mug, "a toast to—a god-free life!"

There were cheers and clanking mugs, and someone turned on the karaoke machine. Three young women went up and did a song neither Dylan nor Rev recognized. Because they were so very old.

Once the pizza had been served, Rev called out to the happily noisy table. "Okay, so whose very bright idea was the t-shirts?"

"That was Ell. Mary Ellen," someone said, pointing to the pierced and tattooed person descending from the stage, as two others ascended.

"Hey, Ell," Rev said, "pull up your chair here. We gotta talk." Rev made room so they could hear each other amid the noise and subsequent karaoke performance. "We'd like to buy a bunch of your shirts. All sizes. Add them to the stuff we sell at our table."

"Really? That'd be great. I'll need a few days—"

"You know," Dylan said, shuffling his chair closer in order to be heard, slice of pizza in hand. "I think we can do better than that. Why not make them available for purchase right on our website? We can make you rich!" he said to Ell.

"Really?" Her eyes widened. "I mean, not the 'rich' part—well, kinda—I mean, it'd be nice not to have to work at Hefty Burgers during the year—you know, so I could concentrate more on my studies. 'Course, then I'd have to work on the t-shirts instead—"

"You could hire some help. Turn it into a little business. If it turns out there's a demand—"

"Yeah, you could hire us!" the two women who'd been on stage with her said. "Then we could quit our shit jobs too!"

"I'll send Phil an email—he's our AAC liaison. I can't imagine him saying no, but—"

"Give me his address, and I'll send him a complimentary shirt tonight," Ell said, reaching for a napkin.

"Are you studying business by any chance?" Dylan asked, impressed with her entrepreneurial sense.

"No, archaeology. Pen!" she shouted to the table at large. And six came flying through the air.

"Her dad runs the local church," one of the young women explained. "He does that kind of thing all the time."

"Interesting," Rev said. "That explains—that explains."

"And you guys too," Ell said to Dylan and Rev as she was pulled onto the small dance floor. "Don't leave without a getting a t-shirt from me!"

A little while later, several of the students encouraged Dylan to do something with the karaoke. They must've known. About Rev's—association—with it. So he went up, sat on the stool off to the side of the stage, and selected a song.

The raucous guitar of the Stones' "Satisfaction" blared out. On cue, Dylan opened his mouth and—spoke. As if at a poetry reading. "'I can't get no'," he said gently, thoughtfully, "'satisfaction.'" The crowd giggled.

"'I can't get no'," he repeated with *such* sensitivity, "'satisfaction.'" They giggled more loudly. He went on, about how he'd tried. And tried. And tried.

When the verse started, Tucker jumped onto the stage and launched into his best Mick Jagger imitation, which was very good indeed. "'When I'm drivin' in my car....'" The crowd cheered as he strutted across the stage. Mick's strut in Tucker's body was, after all, definitely something to cheer about.

Peanut then joined him, perhaps thinking he was to be taught another new dance. He strutted behind Tucker, following his every movement. It was almost picture-perfect. And the crowd cheered some more.

When the chorus came, Dylan did his coffee house poetry reading thing again, exercising great restraint, Rev saw, and the contrast was choke-on-your-beer uproarious. "'Oh no, no, no,'" he lamented, and Rev saw one young man laughing so hard he had tears in his eyes.

Then Tucker belted out the second part of the chorus, weaving in and out of Dylan's soulful delivery. It was brilliant. The students went wild. And everyone just had to join in with the next verse. And Tucker smiled.

They got a very late start the next afternoon, but managed to make it into Missouri before deciding they'd driven enough for the day.

"So," Dylan said, from his spot on the bed in their Curada suite, "we'd better give Phil the heads up. To increase the budget for paint jobs."

"We could just start parking in underground garages or taking public transit," Rev said, happily eating cheesecake—Boonville didn't have a dessert café, but it did have a Walmart, and Walmart carried Sara Lee.

"But," she noted Dylan's look, "that would defeat the purpose." After all, parking at Walmart *had* drawn attention. Though mostly of the disapproving looks variety.

"Hey," Dylan said a moment later, "Steve's Body Shop in Sioux Falls sent us a coupon for a free paint job. Ditto Bob's Body Shop in Wilmington."

"Guess the word is out already," she said. "They were probably texting the world as it happened."

"Well, maybe not *as* it—yeah, they probably were."

Rev had started to roll a joint.

"And Mike's Body Shop," Dylan continued to read their email. "He says he's already got the lime green paint and he's contacted the AAC for the stencil."

"Why don't we just tell Phil to post the stencil on our site," Rev suggested. "Surely it can be downloaded."

"And Phil says he's posted the stencil on our site. It can be downloaded," he grinned over at her. "And—oh," he said, with delight.

"What?"

"A coupon for a free massage," Dylan reached over to take the offered joint. "From Candy's Body Shop. Oh," he said a moment later, with disappointment, "it's for Tucker."

It took them a moment. Given.

"Do you think—wait—" Rev tried again. "Does that mean—"

Dylan was busy tapping his keys.

"She didn't even ask about the tour," Rev said. "What would she have published?"

"Something titled 'Atheists Refuse to Cooperate'," Dylan said, tapping away.

"No," Rev got up—and fell out of the chair. She too had let loose in the bar last night. With great satisfaction.

"No," he hastened to add, "I'm just thinking aloud. Remember that reporter at the border?"

"Oh yeah—"

"Estée Lauder will want a word with you," he smiled as he kept searching.

"Yeah," Rev snorted, "and Maybelline will want a word with you."

There was a knock on the door.

"Right now?" Dylan said, taking a quick puff then handing the joint back to Rev. Who scooted into the bathroom just in case.

"Hey, Tucker!" Dylan said, loudly, when he answered the door. Peanut bounded in and went straight to the bathroom. He pointedly sat at the closed door. Tucker noticed and looked at Dylan for explanation.

"Rev's in there. Guess he wants to say hi," he said lamely.

194

"Can Peanut hang out with you guys again tonight?"

"Sure, no problem, checking out another band?"

"Yeah," Tucker said distractedly, staring at Peanut who was still sitting at the closed bathroom door. Even though Rev had come out, closing the door behind her.

"Hey, Tucker," Dylan distracted him, though that wasn't his intent, that would have been too—thoughtful, "you've got a coupon for a massage from Candy's Body Shop."

"What?" Tucker was completely lost.

"Yeah, we got a bunch of coupons for paint jobs today in our email. Phil set up a 'Contact' on the tour's webpage, and he ends up forwarding most of the messages to us. And we got a coupon from Candy's Body Shop. For a free massage. But it's specially addressed to you."

"Oh." Tucker was blushing. "The make-up person at the interview. Cheri? She tried to set me up with her younger sister. Candace. But I said no," Tucker hastened to add. "I guess—"

"Cheri probably got some pictures from Dave and showed them to Candace," Rev said, in an amazing display and articulation of linear reasoning. Given.

"Ah. That could explain it. We were wondering—well, we were afraid something got published."

"Something bad," Rev said.

"Something very bad," Dylan confirmed. "From the interview." he added. "Because that's the only time you were there. With us. Visibly."

Tucker looked from one to the other again.

"No, I don't think so. I told Cheri I wasn't interested."

"Right. Okay then!" Dylan abruptly turned away from the door.

"See ya!" Rev said.

"Okay, well, thanks," Tucker said. "See ya later, Sweet—Pea," he said to the closed door.

Peanut thumped his tail. He was still sitting at the bathroom door. Rev opened the door, retrieved the joint, relit it, took a drag, and handed it to Dylan.

"Do you think he smelled anything?" Dylan asked.

"He can smell tuna and chocolate, remember? And metal."

"Not Peanut. Tucker." He handed the joint back to Rev.

"And salt. Oh." Her brain had caught up. "Maybe he has no sense of smell. Which would be ironic. In an Alanis Morissette kind of way. Given."

"Hm. Though even if he *did* have a sense of smell, he would still be—nosedeaf? scentblind?—as far as Peanut's concerned."

Peanut, who had been following the joint back and forth, wagging his tail, got up and started doing "Thriller".

"We should teach him another dance," Rev commented.

"He knows another dance. 'Sweet Pea'."

"Yeah, but *another* 'nother dance."

"Oh. Yeah! Good idea!" Dylan got up and stood beside Peanut. "What other dance should we teach him?"

Rev gave it some thought. "Disco. We should teach him that Travolta one." She got up—and fell down.

"It doesn't go like that," he said, looking down at her.

She glowered at him.

"Oh, oh!" Dylan got his bag out of the closet and started rummaging through it. He pulled out a flashlight, stood on the bed, and turned it on and off.

"What are you doing?"

"I'm being the disco ball."

"Oh. Good. Okay." She'd gotten up. "And I can—"

"We need music."

"I can sing!"

196

"No you can't!"

"Maybe it'll be on tv. You know, on one of the music channels." Rev turned on the tv and started flipping through the channels with the remote. "Oh, oh, there's someone playing the piano. Maybe he's playing Travolta."

"That's not Travolta. That's—that's Sun Ra!" They watched the great jazz musician for a while.

"You know," Dylan said at one point, immensely impressed, "he could just be making it up as he goes along."

"Or worse," Rev commented, not so impressed, "it could be planned this way."

"Hey," Rev said when it was over, as if it had triggered her next thought, "we can teach Peanut to do Achy Breaky. By the chipmunks."

"But we don't have any helium."

"Oh yeah."

So they sat down and finished the joint.

"*That's* what 'spaced out' means," Rev said a while later. Quite a while later. "The time between what your brain does and your awareness of it is *spaced out*. There's more space between," she was excited with her insight. "So you can see that you're not in control. Of what your brain does. Of your thoughts. It's just like what's-his-name says. 'I' do not think. 'I' just become aware of my thoughts," she paused. "I bet he was stoned when he came up with his theory of consciousness. Hey do we have any Doritos left?"

Dylan looked toward the kitchenette, where Peanut was sitting amid three open and now empty family size bags. Which had been on the counter.

"No."

"Any cheesecake?"

"Probably. Unless Peanut can open the fridge."

"We can do that!"

"What?"

"Teach Peanut to open the fridge!"

"That's not a dance."

"No."

"Pizza is what we really need. We should go out and get some pizza."

"Okay, but we should leave Peanut here."

They looked at him, now lying belly up on the couch, idly waving his paws and wagging his tail.

"Yeah."

hortly after they crossed into Tennessee, having gone through Illinois, Indiana, and then Kentucky, into "the pretty Blue Ridge mountains topped with mist", Dylan had read off his laptop, they picked up a tailgating pick-up truck.

"What do you think," Rev asked. She was at the wheel, and Dylan was casting anxious glances to the rear view mirror on the passenger door. "Just a bad driver?"

"I don't think so. He's got four, no five, 'REPENT!' stickers on the front bumper."

Rev picked up a little speed. The battered blue pick-up picked up a little speed. Rev slowed down. The pick-up didn't.

"Rev!" Dylan called out as the truck came within a few inches.

Rev sped up again. "But the faster we're going, the worse the impact!"

"No, the greater difference our speeds, the worse the impact!"

"Really?" she paused to think about that. "Okay, but if he keeps going faster to come closer, and I keep going faster to match speeds, where's the end of it?"

"Can't you pull over?"

"Have you looked out your window lately?" she asked, with a certain degree of panic in her voice. "Past the mirror?"

"Oh. That's quite a drop. You think he intends to just push us over?"

"Actually that hadn't occurred to me—until now!" she practically screamed at him.

"Okay, okay, so—should we outrun him?"

"So you want me to go faster?"

"I don't know, you're already going pretty fast," he grabbed the dashboard as she negotiated the sudden curve. Mostly away from the drop.

"Maybe there's a rest stop, you know, a look-out view thing—I could pull over," she suggested. "But could we get out in time? I mean, that might just—"

"If we're far enough ahead—" he thought out loud. "We should undo our—no, that would be stupid," he said grabbing the dashboard again. "Second thought, we've—you've been sitting too long—"

"Okay, what if—"

A siren suddenly whined and they saw a sleek black SUV speeding toward the pick-up, police lights flashing from its roof.

"Is that Tucker?" Rev asked, not wanting to take her eyes off the road in front of her.

"I can't tell."

"Woof! Woo-waar-umpf, woo-waar-umpf!"

"Yes! To the rescue!" Dylan shouted with glee.

"Slow your vehicle!" Tucker had pulled up behind the pick-up and was speaking through—

"Is that from our football game? Did he confiscate your megaphone?"

"I didn't know his vehicle was decked out with a siren and flashing lights," Dylan said. As if he'd been missing some fun.

"Woo-waar-umpf!!"

"We knew it was decked out with Peanut though. What the hell is he saying?"

"What do you think?"

"Right."

"Slow you vehicle! This is Patrol 13621 requesting you to slow your vehicle!"

The pick-up slowed.

"Should we stop?"

"I think—that might complicate things. Let's keep going, and wait for him—in Gatlinburg somewhere," Dylan said, seeing the sign that indicated it was just a few miles away.

"Okay," she looked out the rear view mirror to see the pick-up pull over with Tucker right behind him.

A few minutes later, they arrived in Gatlinburg.

"Look!" Dylan pointed with disbelief. There was a crowd of lime green t-shirted people standing amid an assortment of vehicles in a small parking lot. They were waving Dylan and Rev into the lot. Rev obliged.

"What happened?" someone asked as they got out of their van.

"Are we too late? We heard the siren!"

"Are you okay?" someone else spoke up.

"We are," Dylan said, looking at the group of about ten people, all looking, as was the case with the defence brigade, like college students. "Someone was tail-gating us, maybe intending—"

"Oh, that couldn't've been him."

"Him who?" Rev asked.

"The guy who was planning to drive into you guys head-on."

"How very—Islamic."

"What guy?" Dylan asked.

"There's a guy saying all over the internet—"

"Well, not all over, in the chatroom—"

"Yeah, I went into the chatroom, the 'Stop the Tour' chatroom, as a spy—I'm a good girl—"

"I'm sure you are," Rev said, "but—"

"No, that's my handle. My alias. I'm 'agoodgirl'."

"Ah," Dylan said, realizing then that she was spelling it as one word.

"There's a 'Stop the Tour' chatroom?" Rev asked, struggling to catch up.

"Yeah," she said. "You guys don't know about it?"

"No!"

"Oh. Well, there is. Anyway, I went into the chatroom and there was this guy bragging about how he was going to drive into you head-on as soon as you entered Tennessee. We decided to come here and act as a convoy. You know, so he couldn't do that."

"Bloody hell! Well, first of all, thank you," Dylan said. "Second of all—"

"Is that a Lamborghini?" Rev said.

A young man grinned at her, nodding.

"Wow," she said, as she started walking toward it.

"Rev—"

"What?"

Tucker's SUV pulled into the lot.

"Oh."

He got out, Peanut close behind, and approached the group.

"You're okay?" he asked.

"Yeah, you?"

"Yeah."

"Thank you for—we didn't know you could do that," Rev said. "I mean, you're not really—"

"No, not really. But—"

"He didn't know that."

Tucker nodded past them to the gathering. "So what's with the—"

"Apparently there's some guy, they found out about him in some chatroom, online, there's some guy who's planning to drive into us head-on."

"Oh. That's bad."

"Yeah, we think so too," Rev grinned at him.

"I just mean—"

"And," Dylan picked up the explanation, "these good people here got together to act as a convoy. To escort us, safely, through their fine state."

They started cheering.

"Oh. Well—"

"So we thought we'd put them under your supervision," Dylan grinned at Tucker.

"Right. Okay," he said, not missing a step. "Jon Tucker, Border Patrol," he addressed the group raising his voice slightly, "and Escort for the tour. Listen up. When you convoy, if it's a two-lane highway, there should be one vehicle in front and one vehicle behind. It's important that you keep a safe distance from the vehicle for which you're providing escort. That'd be the van," he said, nodding to it. "When the highway becomes four-lane, or three lanes," he continued, "with two lanes in the direction of travel, you must change formation. Ideal is—" he looked out and counted the vehicles present— "one in front, one behind, and four alongside, the inner two driving in closer formation."

"I can be point," a young man spoke up. "I'm Mario. I've got a fast car," he nodded to the gold Lamborghini, and smiled at Rev, "so I can be point. I can go ahead to see if there's any suspicious vehicles oncoming. And then call back if—"

"There will be no speeding," Tucker said. "Do not speed. If you speed, I will pull you over—" Mario muffled a snort— "and ticket you. Understood?"

"Of course," he said, then deadpanned, "I would never speed. Speeding's bad." At which Rev muffled a snort.

"Did you already put a book in here?" Dylan asked that evening when he opened the nightstand drawer in their Chattanooga Curada suite.

"No, why?" Rev called out from brushing her teeth.

"Cady Stanton's *The Woman's Bible* is in here."

"Really?" Rev came out to see. "Well, that's interesting."

"It is, yes."

Late the next morning, they got their act together and headed out to the college at which they were scheduled to appear. Rev stared at the couple exiting the Curada just ahead of them.

"Why do so many men mistake a woman's elbow for a steering wheel?"

"Wrong question. They mistake everything for a steering wheel."

"Hm."

They drove to the campus per directions provided by the ever-reliable Dorothy, then wandered around for a while, but couldn't find where exactly they were supposed to speak. The buildings had no names, and there were no signs announcing their talk. So they entered one at random, then turned to what looked like an administrative office on their right. They opened the glass door, walked in, and waited while the secretary behind the counter dealt with the person at the counter. Dylan stepped to the side to peruse the notices on a bulletin board. Rev stayed close to the counter. A woman entered the office, got her mail from the grid of boxes set into the wall, then left. Another woman entered, nodded at Dylan and Rev slightly, got her mail, left a file on the counter, then left. Then a man swooped in, attaché case in one hand, bundle of stuff in the other.

"Would you take care of this for me, luv?" He handed Rev a sheaf of indecipherable notes, possibly requisitions and book orders, then turned immediately to Dylan. "Hello, sir, can I help you?"

Dylan saw Rev drop the lot into the trash can. He grinned, then said to the man, "Maybe—when you can tell your arse from a teapot."

Five minutes later, following the directions they'd been given, they found the building at which they were scheduled to speak. Dylan burst through the doors of some sort of lounge just as the chaplain was saying that their guests had obviously decided not to show.

"I'm sorry," Dylan said, "we couldn't find the right building."

"There were no signs or anything," Rev added pointedly, from just behind him.

The chaplain not so graciously gave the lectern to Dylan, who launched into his talk about *The Bible*. Rev left to set up at the table they'd passed near the entrance.

"If *The Bible* is the word of God, or at least divinely inspired," Dylan was saying, ten minutes into his talk, "you'd think it would get its facts right."

"It does," one of the dozen or so people present said.

"Well, no, it doesn't. You've got your Bible with you? Of course. Okay go to Genesis 2—"

The chaplain interrupted. "Thank you, Mr. O'Toole, I'm afraid our time's up."

The silence was, as they say, deafening. Suspicion rose like smoke from a sacrificial lamb. They may have been uneducated, but they weren't stupid.

The young man who had spoken caught up to Dylan at their table.

"Excuse me, could you—what were the references you were going to give me?"

Rev handed Dylan a sheet of paper, which happened to be the AAC's reading list, with the membership form at the bottom. Dylan jotted down the chapter and verse, "2:16 says Adam would die on the day he ate the apple, but he didn't."

"Well, yeah, but he's not talking about literal death—"

"Okay," Dylan persisted, "Jeremiah 36:30," he added it to the sheet of paper, "says Jehoiakim wouldn't have a son. But he did. 2Kings 24:6. And you can't tell me he didn't mean literally a son," he smiled at the young man, then continued, writing as he spoke. "Genesis 46:3. God promises Jacob that he'd return from Egypt. But he didn't. He died in Egypt. Genesis 49." Dylan continued, "Nebuchadnezzar was to have captured and destroyed Tyre. That's what Ezekiel says. But he didn't. Alexander the Great did."

The young man looked a little distraught by the time Dylan was done, but he took the piece of paper away with him nevertheless.

"You think it's going to make any difference?" Rev asked.

"It might."

A few days later, they were on the road again, heading to Virginia. Their departure from Tennessee was accompanied by an ever-changing assortment of cars, all of which seemed to be part of their newly acquired convoy, rather than a suicide-assassination plot. Their passage through North Carolina was similarly accompanied.

"You know," Rev said from the passenger seat, thinking about the recent events, "if people like that have been appointed executors of God's will, that's just one more reason not to believe."

"You know," Rev said again, fifty miles later and seemingly out of nowhere, but Dylan knew better, since they'd just passed yet another billboard of a certain kind, "it's a little ironic that so many Christians proclaim family values—because God is the quintessential dead beat dad."

"Quintessential," Dylan liked the word.

"He left almost 2,000 years ago, said he'd be back real soon. Uh-huh. He never calls, he never writes, and child support?" Rev snorted. Dylan grinned. Imagining another billboard adjustment in their future. "How many of us don't even have enough to eat? 'Cheque's in the mail.' Sure it is."

About a hundred miles later, they switched and Rev took the wheel.

Dylan got out his laptop.

"Remember you asked whether we were being noticed?" he said a few minutes later.

"Yeah...."

"Well apparently Dorothy and Phil *haven't* been forwarding most of the emails to us. The ones sent through the tour's website. We're up to several thousand a day."

"Wow."

"They've hired extra help to handle the replies," he said, continuing to read Phil's message.

"They're replying to each one individually?"

"Apparently."

"Cool."

"Except for the ones they're still sending to us for a reply."

"And do we have any of those today?"

"We do." Dylan clicked open the first one. "Leo from Maryland wants to know what it's like to hunt caribou."

In Virginia, they would be staying at someone's house. That of a Mr. and Mrs. Jim Smith.

"Can't be right," Rev said, as Dylan double-checked their arrangements on his laptop. "Her being one of the nameless women...."

"Ah," Dylan said, at first not understanding. He navigated, consulting the directions Dorothy had sent, and fifteen minutes later, during which he engaged in some fast and furious internet searching that set off Rev's radar, they were knocking on the Smiths' front door.

"Hello," the woman who answered the door gushed, "you must be Dylan and Rev."

"Yes, we are," Dylan said. "And you are—"

"Jim, they're here!" she called into the house, and a small boy peaked from around a corner. "Timmy, say hello to our guests, Mr. and—" she faltered. "Ms.—" Rev let her stall. "Say hello, Timmy."

"Hello."

"Hello."

"Hello."

"Hello."

"Hello!" A man bellowed—bellowed—as he rounded the corner. "Please come in! How was the drive? June, why don't you get us all some of that fine tea you just made."

"Yes, of course," she said, sweetly, and bustled off to her kitchen. *Her* kitchen. You just knew. Dylan and Rev exchanged a look, gave each other the slightest shrug, and followed Jim and Timmy into the living room.

"So," Dylan said, as they settled onto the couch that was covered with a flowered throw, "Mr. Seton, how long have you been with the AAC?"

"Jim," the man said with flustered confusion, then repeated—insisted, actually—"Jim *Smith.* And I'm with the Defense Department."

"You're not members of the American Atheist Consortium?"

"Oh goodness no, we go to the Methodist church," June said as she returned with a tea tray.

It took them a minute. Well, just a few seconds, actually.

"Why?" Rev asked.

"Excuse me?"

"Why do you go to the Methodist church?"

"Oh, I don't know," she smiled, pouring the tea. "I guess it's because the Methodist church is closer."

Rev looked up sharply.

"We went to the Presbyterian church once, remember dear?" she said pleasantly to her husband. "But we didn't like it as much."

Rev opened her mouth to ask—

"The people didn't seem as friendly."

"The people didn't seem as friendly," Rev repeated. Faith was right. Church, with its various doctrines of torture, forced pregnancy, and what have you was just a freakin' social club. Unbelievable.

"So, Jim," Dylan said, "what do you do in the Defense Department?"

"Well, I used to run the APD program."

"Anti-Personnel Devices?" Rev asked, switching her attention immediately. "Like guns and bombs? So you kill people," she stated flatly.

June gasped. Such language! "Timmy, why don't you go into the den and watch tv?"

The little boy got up from the couch and obediently went into the den.

"*The Simpsons* is on," Dylan said. Cheerfully. And a little wistfully.

"Yes, sometimes it's necessary to take lives," Jim resumed, stiffly.

"Where do you take them?" Rev asked.

"I beg your pardon?"

"You said it was necessary to take lives. I'm wondering where you take them."

He looked at her in irritation.

"We target the buildings," he said. A little defensively.

"But not the people in them."

"No."

"That's clever."

June smiled at her clever husband. He did not smile back.

"Our goal, of course, is surgically clean strikes—"

"Surgically clean? Oh please."

He looked at her.

"But sometimes when we exchange warheads—"

"Exchange warheads? Sounds like Christmas. Do you guys have a secret Santa and everything?"

"They've got a Christmas tree farm," Dylan said. "Isn't that what you call where all the missiles are lined up in their silos ready for— exchange?" He looked at Jim.

Who was determined to continue. "But now I work on the bus which provides the supporting vehicle to house and operate the payload."

"You use buses? Like, one of those yellow school buses? Or is it more like a greyhound?"

"No, it's not really a bus—"

"Surprise," she said dryly.

"What happens is the main rocket motor pushes what's called a bus into a free-fall," he said, "a precisely determined suborbital flight path. After the boost phase, the bus manoeuvres," his enthusiasm increased as he continued, "using small on-board rocket motors and a computerised guidance system. It delivers a re-entry vehicle containing a warhead, which is released on the specified trajectory. The vehicle then manoeuvres to a different trajectory, releasing another warhead, repeating the process for all warheads."

"And are those warheads, are they the ones that have 'more bang for the buck'?" Rev asked. "Tell me, do you use your 'vertical erector launcher'?"

"What's the 'thrust-to-weight ratio'?" Dylan added. "Do you achieve a 'soft lay down'? 'Deep penetration'? With or without 'penetration aids'?"

Their stay in Virginia was cut short when Dorothy emailed them to say that both their talks had been cancelled. No surprise for Virginia Military Institute, but—

"Ah," Dylan said, googling away from the passenger seat, "*Liberty University* trains *Champions for Christ.*"

"That was the one in Lynchburg?" Rev asked. "You'd think they'd've changed their name by now."

"Hm." He put his laptop away and looked out the window. Their next stop was in Georgia, but they were looping up through Washington and West Virginia, at Phil's request.

"Maybe some of the language is to protect themselves," Dylan said, coming back to their conversation with Mr. June Seton.

Rev waited for further explanation.

"Do you think a country that conscripts fifteen-year-olds is going to have qualms about putting a munitions cache in a school? So of course they have to" —he winced at the 'have to'— "bomb the school."

Rev thought about that. It was perfectly plausible. And yet— "I don't know. It's almost like these guys *want* a war. A *nuclear* war."

"Well, it would be fulfilling God's prophecy."

"So might an asteroid strike. More importantly, there's a difference between prophecy and command. I think they just want to prove their belief is justified. They just want to be able to say 'Told you so!'"

"Hm."

"Remember what he said when I asked how he reconciled what he did with *The Bible*? The part that says 'Thou shalt not kill'?"

"'If God didn't approve, he wouldn't enable me to do it,'" Dylan quoted him. "So much for free will," he sighed.

"And, therefore, moral responsibility," Rev added.

"And yet they have the nerve to go to church," she added a few miles later.

"They might not see that as a contradiction," Dylan commented.

Rev glanced over at him.

"Remember your neighbour back home who refuses to recycle—and yet who votes green? What did she say when you asked her about that?"

"She said she votes green to balance it all out," Rev snorted.

A couple days later, after an uneventful drive, they arrived at Lake Murray. Dylan had arranged to rent a house right on the lake. Which wasn't even frozen. Despite it being February.

"And we can stay here for a whole week?" Rev said, having claimed one of the chairs on the dock as soon as they'd pulled into the driveway. She was staring out at the water. "Even though the lake is—solid brown?" she added, looking out with a mix of curiosity and distaste.

"A whole week," Dylan said, pulling up another chair to sit beside her.

Peanut bounded up, Tucker having pulled in behind them almost immediately, and dispensed with sitting in a chair. He jumped right into the lake. It was, after all, a huge mud puddle.

Tucker gave him one look, sighed, smiled, then pulled up a third chair.

"There's an outside tap and hose," Dylan said.

Tucker nodded acknowledgement, and thanks, and popped open a couple bottles of Pepsi he'd brought with him from his SUV. He passed them to Dylan and Rev, opened the third for himself, and then all three of them just sat and watched Peanut frolic in the muddy water.

"Thanks for letting us stay here with you," Tucker said, once he'd finished half of his clearly-needed drink.

"No problem. There's room. No point in you and Peanut staying in a hotel while we're here. You guys can stay with us in California too. I've arranged for us to housesit a ranch house. So there'll be lots of room for Peanut," he grinned, knowing there'd *always* be room for Peanut.

"You know," Rev said, still looking out at the water, "a ranch house isn't actually on a ranch."

"It isn't?"

"No."

"Oh." Clearly Dylan had been looking forward to living on a ranch. "Still."

"That'd be great, thanks," Tucker said.

"So we go to California from here?" Rev asked. It had been a while since she looked at their itinerary. Dylan was taking care of their route and accommodations.

"Well, sort of."

"What, by way of Wisconsin?" she took a slug of her Pepsi.

"Minnesota."

Rev stared at him for a moment in disbelief. "This time of year?!"

"Yeah, this *is* turning more into a road trip than a speaking tour. Especially now that so many colleges are cancelling. But," he sighed, "that's part of the point, right? To travel across the country in our 'atheist bus'—"

"Yeah, yeah."

"A few more months and we'll be home."

"Home," she sighed, looking out at the water again.

Peanut jumped out of the water then and onto the dock. And, of course, as dogs *must* do, he shook. And shook.

"Where did you say that hose was?"

The next day, Dylan and Rev decided to start out early, relatively speaking, and do a walkaround on their way to the address they'd been given for their afternoon radio talk show. Tucker had finally finished his report to the Chief, detailing the Tennessee highway incident and the convoy development, and was spending a quiet day in the rec room working with Peanut on their new dance.

There was a bait store at the end of the street. Several chairs were in front, all of them occupied. Just as they passed by, a man heaved himself out of one of the chairs, grunting with exhaustion.

"Hard day's work?" Rev asked.

He smiled.

"You know, hard work doesn't necessarily imply virtue."

Dylan poked her and they moved along.

"What? I hate it when people do that."

"Do what?"

"Grunt and groan as if they've put in a hard day's work when really they're just out of shape."

They walked on, and on, consulting the piece of paper on which they'd written an address and directions, and several turns later, found themselves in what was, essentially, a trailer park. Well, not really a park. A dirt trail wove in and out among about fifty mobile homes, none of which looked capable of mobility. Beside each trailer there seemed to be a car wreck and an ATV.

"See?" Rev said, as an ATV roared to life nearby, and someone drove past them, only to stop just two trailers down. After the driver gunned its engine a few times, no doubt to convince himself he still had a penis. "He couldn't've walked that distance? Bet he has one of those lawn mowers you sit on."

Dylan looked around in vain for grass. "I don't think—"

"Used to be you *pushed* your lawn mower. Or at least walked along behind it."

A kid on a dirt bike screamed past them leaving a headache-inducing fume trail.

"And what happened to bicycles?"

They passed another trailer, in silence, since a man was using a loud-by-default power washer on the small porch attached to the trailer.

"You know, pretty soon the malls will be filled with people in motorized chairs. Not just amputees and ninety-five year olds, but everyone who's too fat and out of shape to walk from one end to the other."

"Hm." Dylan had stopped a few trailers further ahead.

"This is it?" Rev said, looking at the trailer. "Can't be. Maybe it's a trap," she added. "We should've brought Tucker."

Dylan noticed the hidden camera mounted just above the doorway. He stared at it curiously for a moment, then just as he was about to strike a pose, or three, a spry old man stepped out in a caricature of caution, silver hair erupting with a mind of its own from his head. He looked to the right and to the left, then asked quietly, conspiratorially, "You're Dylan and Rev?"

"Yes…," Dylan said.

"Well, come on in!" he whooped, extending his hand. "I'm Godless Gus."

It turned out Godless Gus, who was Augustus Connolly, was an independent. He ran a daily show and broadcast it over the internet. Had quite a following.

"Did ya ever see that movie with Christian Slater?"

"*Pump Up the Volume*?" Rev asked. "Yes! I loved it! 'I like the idea that a voice can just go somewhere uninvited and just kinda hang out like a dirty thought in a nice clean mind...,'" she quoted Slater's character.

"Exactly!" Gus stared at her. "Well then, ya'll remember the whole pirate radio thing—had quite an influence on me."

He made room, somehow, in his studio, which was essentially his entire trailer, for the three of them to sit so they could pass the laptop around, depending on who was talking.

"Or we could just keep the camera on you," Dylan suggested, casually brushing some sort of ant-like bug off the arm of the chair he sat in. "The mic'll still pick up our voices."

"Nah, my audience is tired o' me mug. Wanta give 'em a shot of some young things for a change."

Rev grinned at Dylan. And hoped she didn't fall out of her chair when she tried to get up.

"Beer?" Gus went to his small fridge.

"Sure, thanks," Dylan said for the two of them.

Gus popped open three cans, passed two to Dylan and Rev, sat down again, and without further ado, opened the show. He cued his intro music, and both Dylan and Rev snorted beer out their noses. It was "What a Friend We Have in Jesus"—by the Chipmunks.

As the first verse faded out, Godless Gus boomed into the mic, "If we're all children of God," he said, "then I'm the Son of God!" He cranked up the reverb on that last bit.

Dylan and Rev, barely recovered from their beer snorts, broke into broad smiles. This was going to be fun.

"Caller number one," Gus flipped a switch, "how has atheism changed *your* life?"

"*My* will be done!" the first caller shouted.

"Caller number two," Gus called out. "We always start this way," he said off-mic to Dylan and Rev.

"I discovered the life of the mind, Gus. I'm reading a book a day now. Can't get enough. You'd be *amazed* at what's out there "

"Caller number three, how did it change your life?"

"How did it *change* my life? It *gave* me my life. No more always putting others first. No more self-sacrifice, no more being a martyr. For the first time, I'm asking for stuff. I never used to. I'd always wait for someone to offer it to me. And if they didn't, well, I figured I wasn't worthy of it. Well FUCK THAT!"

"All rightey," Gus said then, "we have some special guests today, but ya gotta wait for 'em, 'cause first I'm goin' ta read the letter I mentioned yesterday. Found it on the internet. It's been kickin' around for a long while, but damn it's good. And some of ya might not a heard it before. Apparently it was originally sent in ta Dr. Laura, unsigned, and 'tis a shame the author's still unknown. It may be for the best, we don't know, but whoever ya are, if ya're listenin', GOOD ON YA!! All right, here it is.

"'Dear Dr. Laura: Thank you for doing so much to educate people regarding God's Law. I have learned a great deal from your show, and try to share that knowledge with as many people as I can. I do need some advice from you, however, regarding some of the specific laws and how to follow them.

"'I would like to sell my daughter into slavery, as sanctioned in Exodus 21:7. In this day and age, what do you think would be a fair price for her?'"

Rev couldn't stifle her snort of delight.

"'When I burn a bull on the altar as a sacrifice,'" Gus continued, "'I know it creates a pleasing odour for the Lord—Leviticus 1:9. The problem is my neighbours. They claim the odour is not pleasing to them. Should I smite them?'"

Gus grinned. Clearly delighted with the thought smiting his neighbours.

"'My uncle has a farm. He violates Leviticus 19:19 by planting two different crops in the same field, as does his wife by wearing garments made of two different kinds of thread, cotton and polyester. He also tends to curse and blaspheme a lot. Is it really necessary that we go to all the trouble of getting the whole town together to stone them? Leviticus 24:10-16. Couldn't we just burn them to death at a private family affair, like we do with people who sleep with their in-laws? Leviticus 20:14.'"

Dylan laughed out loud at that one.

"'I have a neighbour who insists on working on the Sabbath. Exodus 35:2 clearly states he should be put to death. Am I morally obligated to kill him myself, or should I ask the police to do it?

"'I know that I am allowed no contact with a woman while she is in her period of menstrual uncleanliness—Leviticus 15: 19-24. The problem is how do I tell? I have tried asking, but most women take offense.'"

Rev snorted again.

"'Leviticus 25:44 states that I may possess slaves, both male and female, provided they are purchased from neighbouring nations. A friend of mine claims that this applies to Mexicans, but not Canadians. Can you clarify? Why can't I own Canadians?'

"Speaking of Canadians," Gus put the letter aside and continued with the show, "guess who we have here today for our show? Dylan O'Toole and Chris Reveille!!" he shouted with exuberance and cued an over-the-top applause track.

Dylan grinned silly at Rev.

"So how are ya?"

"We're fine, thank you," Dylan said.

"So very fine," Rev added. This was so not going to be like their other radio interviews.

"We've all been followin' ya tour, ya got a website, and a blog, and a podcast, so we're pretty up-ta-date about what's been goin' on. But tell me. D'ya need any more paint?" Gus guffawed.

"No, we're good to go," Dylan said, brushing at the arm of his chair again. "Actually several auto body shops have been sending us coupons. And it's much appreciated!"

"So what's been the hardest thing on this tour?" Gus asked then.

"Oh—I don't know," Dylan looked at Rev.

"I do."

Dylan grinned. She would.

"Dealing with people's unwillingness or inability to reason. To think about things. I simply do not understand how people can be so okay with not having reasons for what they think and do. On what grounds can they possibly expect others to pay any attention to them?"

"Maybe they don't," Gus suggested.

"Well they get angry enough when—"

"So that can't be right," he easily conceded.

"Maybe they just assume they have some sort of innate authority. Maybe that's a habit that develops when people become parents. They don't feel the need to explain themselves to their kids."

"And most people by far are parents," Gus agreed.

"And maybe it's a male thing," Dylan suggested. "Men are granted more authority just because. We've proved that time and time again."

"So, what, it's just women without kids who see this need to have reasons, to have evidence, to have support for our opinions? That doesn't seem right."

"Maybe they just expect ta be trusted."

"Yeah, but you have to justify trust. People have to have a reason to trust you—"

"And there ya go, thinkin' about it," Gus grinned. "*I think*," he grinned again, "that part of the problem is we've become a society that glorifies emotion. I was watchin' *American Idol* or some such the other day and it hit me like a ton of manure how *emotional* all the contestants are. They go on and on about how excited they are ta be on the show, they cry when they say how all their lives they've wanted this, they cry when they're told they're movin' on ta the next week—"

"Or *not* moving on to the next week—" Rev inserted.

"And the thing of it is, the more emotional they are, the more they win! Saw one contestant, acted like an adult about the whole thing, instead of jumpin' up and down like a six-year-old, and she was booted off first time out.

"And most of the emotion is in the wantin'," Gus continued. "'I tried *really hard*, I want this *so bad*,'" he imitated the contestants. "Well, then," Gus said, "I guess ya should get it. After all, wantin' is all there is to gettin'.'"

"All experience supports it," Dylan dryly noted.

"You know, you're right," Rev said, "I remember watching the Olympics once and the commentator kept emphasizing that the guy who won must've been the one who *wanted* it the most. Not that he must've trained the hardest—"

"Or took the most steroids," Dylan inserted.

"As if passion, strength of emotion—I think we see the same thing with this 'We support our troops' nonsense. I don't know if you've noticed it."

Dylan and Rev nodded their heads decisively. "We have the same thing back home. In fact, *This Hour has 22 Minutes* did a spoof on it a while ago. It was brilliant."

"What's *22 Minutes*?"

"You don't get that here? Of, of course not. Pity. It's sort of Canada's *The Daily Show*. You'd love it."

"Ah. I'll have to look into it. It's probably on the net somewhere. Anyway," Gus continued, "everyone's tripping over themselves to express support for our troops. But *what kind* of support? Do they send money? No. Do they mean they agree with the goal? Maybe, maybe not. It's just an empty emotional thing. A feel-good, I'm-part-of-the-team, I'm-a-supportive-kind-of-person thing. Nothing is said about *how* we support them or, better, *why* we support them. We just *support* them. And we say it with such *heartfelt* emotion.

"But why is emotion glorified," Gus concluded, "that's the intriguing question. When did emotion become a virtue?"

"When thinking became too much effort," Rev suggested.

"Yah, but I think there's more to it than that," Gus said. "It's become fashionable to express your opinion. Which is fine, so far as it goes. But ya see YouTube or any of a hundred other sites. The comments are nothin' more than 'I like it' or 'I don't like it'—where are the frickin' reasons??" He boomed out into the mic. "What can ya do with 'I like it' and 'I don't like it'? I wanta know *why* ya like it and don't like it!"

"Maybe people don't know how to touch-type anymore," Dylan offered.

Rev turned to him. That was an interesting thought.

"So typing anything more than 'I like it' is physically exhausting," he explained, "and will take forever."

"That would explain," she commented, "the increasing use of those damn smiley faces and anagrams. Amalgams?"

"Acronyms," Dylan supplied.

"Yeah. LOL."

"Perspicuity."

"Ya might have a point," Gus picked up, momentarily distracted by the perspicuity. "If ya're just usin' two fingers—"

"Or two thumbs—on the teeny little keys of your smartphone—"

"I dunno," Rev seemed to change her mind then, "I don't think writing with pen and paper would make a difference. People would still—LOL."

"Yeah, probably," Dylan conceded.

"But consider also," Gus wasn't ready to let go, "the immediacy of email. The speed with which email messages are sent maybe makes people think the messages they send have ta be as immediate, as quickly composed."

"Good point" Rev said. "Even the size of the box on the screen probably unconsciously limits us. To short messages."

"Twitter," Dylan said. "Now there's a medium that encourages extended thought."

"Pretty soon we'll be talking to each other in just emoticons."

"Well, we used to," Dylan noted, "didn't we. Before we came down from the trees."

"Hm. Back to the idea of all that matters it that you try your best," Rev said, "that excuses people from really learning anything. Or at least excelling at anything. I'm a fan of *So You Think You Can Dance* but I have to say I'm so sick and tired of hearing things like 'I trained a whole year for this. And I didn't even make it into the top 20!' Oh please. A whole year. Elite dancers take ten, fifteen years to get there."

"Yeah," Dylan said, "but they make it look easy. People are just suckered in by that. It's the same in sports. Unless you try a triple axel, you don't know—"

"Yeah, but these people, the people we're talking about, they're likely to try, fail, and then say something like 'I can't do it'—as if it's got nothing to do with them, as if they just don't have the magic body for it. They have *no idea*—"

"And then they say somethin' like 'It's not fair!'" Gus added.

"Yes! What conception of fairness are they using?" Rev asked.

"The 'You deserve a break today' conception," Dylan answered. "The 'I have rights' conception."

"But," Gus said then, "if all that matters is that ya try hard and want it really bad, then not only is there no point in learnin', as you said, there's no point in knowin', in *thinkin'!* So we come full circle."

"Yeah," Rev said, noticing the bug crawling along the back of Dylan's chair, "but if people don't think, if they don't have reasons for what they do, if they just do what they do without awareness, they're no different from—" she reached out her hand and flattened the thing.

"I'll do the talk today," Rev said as they were setting up. There was an unusually large and enthusiastic turnout, so they figured the college must have sent invitations to the congregations of every church in the district. "I have an idea."

"Do I want to know what it is?"

"It doesn't involve fish."

"Okay then."

The Dean of the college walked onto the stage and waited for the crowd to become quiet. "I am so pleased to see you all here," he said, and the audience cheered. Rev wondered, briefly, what exactly they were cheering—his pleasure or their own presence. "You make Georgia proud!"

"Alleluia! Amen!"

Oh my, Rev thought to herself.

"And although I would love to stay here and speak to all you fine people, we do have a guest today who will do that. Let me introduce," he glanced at Rev waiting in the wings then at his notes, "Ms. Chris Reveille from the AAC." Ah. He didn't know what AAC stood for.

Perfect.

Rev took the podium.

"Good afternoon," she said.

"Good afternoon," the audience shouted back.

Rev smiled to herself. Devilishly.

"I was walking about yesterday, shortly after I arrived, and I happened to notice the billboard on the highway out of town, the one that asks 'And what will you promise to Jesus?'"

"Amen!"

"Well," she said, "I promise to Jesus—"

"Amen! Alleluia!!"

"To follow his commands—"

"Alleluia! Yahoo!" Yahoo?

"To look after the earth as His steward—"

"Alleluia! Praise the Lord!"

"To sell my pick-up, with which I have never *ever* picked up *anything*—"

There were a few fewer Alleluias. Dylan grinned from the doorway.

"Because it is *such* a contributor to global warming."

There were a few mumbles in the audience.

"And I promise to Jesus—"

"Alleluia! Praise the Lord!"

"To treat my body as a temple of the Lord, to stop power washing my trailer and use instead a pail of water and a rag—"

"Alleluia." Just the one. Without the exclamation point.

"Because I am such a *lard* ass, and I could *certainly* use the exercise—"

At this point, several people heaved themselves out of their seats and lumbered toward the door.

"Alleluia?" Rev asked, hopefully.

A relatively pleasant week later, during which Peanut had discovered the existence of muskrats, and tried to do something about it, they packed up their stuff and left their lake house. Shortly after they reached the highway, a couple cars showed up as escort. The drivers wore lime green t-shirts and waved to Dylan and Rev as they took up positions in front and behind their van.

"'There's a reason atheists don't fly planes into buildings,'" Rev laughed as she read the bumper sticker on the vehicle in front of them.

Over the next few days, they made their slow and winding way through Alabama, Mississippi, and Arkansas. Dylan was content to let their van do the talking, Rev—not so much.

"Do you believe in God?" Rev asked their waitress at their first truck stop.

"Oh I don't know, I guess," she shrugged and took their order. "I haven't really thought about it."

Then, when she brought their coffee, Rev said, "I think you're a lousy waiter."

"Why?" she was surprised, and a little upset.

"Oh I don't know," Rev shrugged and took a sip of her coffee. "I haven't really thought about it.

"That was cruel," Dylan said when she left their table.

"I was testing the bug hypothesis."

"Hm."

The exchange was somewhat similar, and yet significantly different, at the next truck stop.

"Do you believe in God?" Rev asked the waitress.

"I do."

"Why?"

"Oh I guess I feel in my heart of hearts there must be a god," the waitress said warmly.

"And I guess I feel in my heart of hearts you're a bitch."

After the third stop— "Oh, well then, I believe I should spit on you. No reason." —Dylan suggested she had enough data for a conclusion.

"You know," she said thoughtfully, after they'd made another switch and Rev was in the passenger seat, feet up on the dash, "I think we should stop calling God 'God'. We should give him a name instead. An individual name. Like Vishnu or Zeus. Or George. Maybe then people would be more likely to at least see the need to compare, and therefore evaluate."

And so at truck stop number four, Rev changed her research protocol.

"Do you believe in God?"

"Yes, I do."

"Which one?"

"What do you mean?"

"Well, there are several. Which god do *you* believe in?"

Although that trial had to be scrapped as 'Incomplete', the next was more successful.

"I believe in the Lord, Jesus Christ our Saviour," the waitress said with certainty.

"And why do you believe in that one instead of Shiva, for example?"

She seemed to think it was a rhetorical question. At least, she didn't see the need to answer it.

Which amazed Rev. "Even when the belief is clearly for X over Y...."

At truck stop number six, the exchange went a little differently.

"Why do you believe in Jesus?" Rev asked the waitress, nodding to the cross she wore around her neck.

"Oh," she put her hand on the cross, "I'm not really Christian. I really don't believe in all that stuff. It's just my grandmother gave me this."

"I see. And if she had given you a nice little gold-plated swastika, you'd be wearing that?"

And at stop number seven, the truck stop portion of their tour took a turn. A man and woman sitting at one of the tables got up as soon as they walked through the door.

"I just want to say that we've been following you on the internet," the woman said, standing directly in front of them, "and as a mother, I'm appalled that people like you would ever have been allowed in the classroom."

Both Rev and Dylan were silent.

"Well?" the woman demanded.

"You lost me at 'as a mother'," Rev said. "Are you suggesting that having replicated yourself gives you some authority? Some expertise? That when your egg was fertilized, you somehow gained several IQ points or a wealth of knowledge? Must've been some sperm."

Her husband had the idiocy to smile proudly at that.

Shortly after they crossed into Oklahoma, they got a call from Phil informing them that a last-minute booking had been made for them in Oklahoma City, so they headed to the Curada. Dorothy, with her customary efficiency, had already made a reservation for them.

"Hey," Rev had opened the nightstand drawer back in their room, "did you put *The Woman's Bible* in here? And take out the King James Version?"

"No, I thought we agreed to leave the Bibles there. As evidence. And wasn't *The Woman's Bible* in the nightstand before— somewhere?"

"Oh, I bet I know what's happening," she held up a take-out menu. "This is a take-out menu for the local cheesecake place. It's the cleaning staff. In the conservatory. With the candlestick."

"Ah."

"I'll bet they've formed an underground movement, like the billboard thing. And—" she broke off, "you know, it makes perfect sense."

"What, exactly. Makes perfect sense."

"Well, women are more religious than men. So once they realize they've been suckered, they're more vehement atheists than men."

"And why is that? I mean why is it that women are more religious than men?"

"Well," she started unpacking her stuff, "stereotyping still has it that women are the emotional ones, men the rational ones. That's one. And we've established that religion tends to be more of an emotional thing than a rational thing. Two, religious authority figures tend to be male. And women are raised to be subservient to males or at least to regard males as authorities—yes, still," she anticipated Dylan's objection. "'Father knows best.' Remember Mrs.—June Seton? So it's easy for them to accept God, the Father, as an authority and subordinate themselves to him. Men, on the other hand, are encouraged to *be* the authority; they're also encouraged to compete with other men. So to accept God, for example, as an authority and subordinate themselves to him would not be easy—in fact, it would be emasculating."

"Which is why," Dylan got on board, "the macho Promise Keepers came to be. And why they didn't last very long," he added.

"And—"

"You've got more?"

"I've always got more," she grinned. "Except for the war element—men are okay with claiming religious belief when it's associated with war—religion is very much about morality. That's three. Ethics is a girl thing, remember? *Women* are the designated moral guardians—young women are the gatekeepers when it comes to pre-marital sex, wives are referred to by their husbands as 'their better half', 'better' referring to some quality of moral goodness, and mothers are assumed to have the primary responsibility of teaching their children right from wrong."

"Yes!" Dylan agreed with enthusiasm. "I didn't get a chance to say this on our show in Texas," he gave her a lop-sided grin because they both knew why, "but I too have noticed that when a man introduces the matter of morality—which I have done on many occasion, and my penis has *not* fallen off—I've been accused of going soft or being weak. Decidedly unmanly things."

"And yet," he said a few moments later, unpacking his laptop, "it seems to be the men who've been our most vocal opponents on this tour."

"Yeah, well, the key word there is 'opponents'."

"Ah. Maybe."

Dylan stretched out on the bed and began to take care of all the business stuff, checking in with Dorothy and Phil, going through their email, and planning their route, and Rev set up in the chair to update their blog. After a few minutes, Dylan flipped on the tv and reached for their stash to roll a joint, just as someone knocked at their door. He tucked it under the pillow.

Rev got up to answer the door. Peanut bounded in.

"Heading off to another band?" Dylan asked Tucker, giving Peanut a warm snugly welcome.

"Yeah. And—I hate to keep asking, he could just stay in our room, but he seems really happy to spend time with you guys." Dylan and Rev exchanged a look. "Whenever I pick him up, he can't stop wagging his tail."

"He's probably just so happy to see you, Tuck."

"No, I don't think so. I mean even once we're back in our room. He just lies on the couch in his own little world, wagging his tail."

Rev stifled a snort.

"It's like he's remembering what fun he had, or something. Can dogs do that? Remember like that?"

"I suppose it's possible," Dylan said with a straight face. "But whatever, really, we're happy to have him. No point in him being alone all evening when he can be here with us." Peanut was burrowing his head under Dylan's pillow.

"He probably smells the mint they leave there," Tucker said, noticing Peanut's behaviour.

"Yeah...Rev already ate it," Dylan gently redirected Peanut's nose.

"It was very good," Rev said.

"Okay, well, thanks," Tucker said after a moment. "I won't be too late," he said, more to Peanut than to Dylan and Rev.

Once they were sure Tucker had left, Dylan rescued their stash. Peanut wagged his tail. The two of them settled onto the bed, and Rev claimed her chair once again, stretching her feet out onto the footstool.

"What if," Rev asked, idly watching the news she had turned on, "what if for just one year, the media reported 90% of the time what *women* were doing instead of, as is now the case, what men are doing? Not because what women do is better," she hastened to add, "or more newsworthy, but just to see how it would change our outlook, our world view."

"Hm," Dylan took a draw on their joint then passed it over to Rev.

"The news might be more boring," she took the joint and answered her own question, "but then, hey, what does that say?"

"It would likely involve a lot less death and destruction," Dylan suggested.

"And it probably would have less to do with money. No more financial reports."

"And no more sports reports. The obsession with winning—" he clarified, reaching out to take back the joint.

Peanut stretched and rolled over and—Dylan reached out too late. Amazingly enough, Peanut's legs were under him and he was standing neatly beside the bed. He grinned. Then climbed back onto the bed beside Dylan and lay down again. Then rolled over off the bed onto his feet. Grinned again. Climbed back onto the bed, lay down, jiggled a bit to get into the right spot, and rolled over onto his feet. Grinned.

"How many times do you think he's going to do that?" Rev asked, as fascinated with the discovery as Peanut.

Next day, they went to the rodeo. It was the thing to do in Oklahoma. Apparently.

Just as when they went to the football game, they had to park some distance away. They passed several booths on the way to the arena, and Dylan stopped to buy a cowboy hat. A turquoise cowboy hat. He bought a red one for Rev, but since she refused to wear it, he put it on Peanut instead. He looked good in red.

The closer they got, the stronger the smell of animals. Peanut started to become a little antsy, making Dylan wonder exactly what scent signals he was picking up, and Tucker had to tighten his grip on his leash.

They made their way through the lobby with its various booths and into the crowded stands. After a few moments, they found some empty space halfway up, Dylan and Rev squeezing together in one row, Peanut and Tucker in the row just behind them. Peanut was still quite excited, and although he sat down, as Tucker told him to, he kept squiggling and looking around. Eventually he settled down. And rested his chin on Dylan's head. Dylan grinned and tried to keep his head very still.

As soon as the announcer proclaimed that something was going to happen—what exactly, they couldn't make out, since the announcement was nothing but garble—there was a commotion in their aisle and a teenager came rushing up, followed by a rather large and somewhat apoplectic man. The teenager flung himself down next to Rev, who scrunched over to Dylan to make a bit more room.

"You will do as I say," the man shouted at the teenager, grabbing his arm, "so help me God!"

"Go to hell," the teenager said, not even looking at him, and shrugging out of his hold.

"I will not have you talk to me that way!" the man was red in the face. "I am your father, and I swear, as God is my witness—"

"You're going to kill him?" Rev asked. "'Anyone who curses their father or mother is to be put to death.' Leviticus 20:9. Hey, I'm getting good at this," she said to Dylan. "Go ahead," she turned back to the man, encouraging him, "all will be forgiven. Mark…"

"3:28," Dylan supplied. "Though actually," he added, "it doesn't say the parents have to kill him."

"Oh. We'll do it," she offered cheerily.

The man glared at her, then at his son, then at Tucker who'd started to get up, just in case, then stomped away when the announcer made another indecipherable announcement.

"Good one," the boy said, staring straight ahead.

"Well, anyone who calls on God twice in a row—what was he so angry about?" Rev asked.

"He wants me to do calves."

They had no idea what he meant. Well, they did, but thought surely it must be wrong.

"I'll do poles, I like poles, and the horses like it, I'll even do barrels, but—"

"Poles, is that the horse slalom thing?" Dylan asked.

The kid looked at him.

"We're from Canada," Rev explained. "We don't have horses in Canada."

He looked at her.

"Okay, we have horses, but only in Alberta."

He didn't buy that either.

"Okay we have horses in Ontario, but not where we live."

Still no.

"Okay we have horses where we live, but—"

"I rode a horse once," Dylan interrupted. "It was a horse with a name," he bragged. "His name was Pickle. P-I-C-K- "

"Yeah, pole bending is the horse slalom thing."

"-LE."

"And why don't you want to do—calves?"

He simply nodded to the arena. A cute little calf had just run in, moving as fast as its new little legs could carry it. Suddenly it was yanked off its feet by a rope around its neck. Its body arched back into a full somersault before it slammed down onto its head. The cowboy who had thrown the noose ran toward the little calf, picked it up like it was a sack of potatoes, then threw it back down onto the ground. He quickly looped some rope around its legs once, twice, then knotted and tightened it, threw his hands back, then stood up in victory, leaving the little calf heaving in terror at his feet. The crowd cheered. Dylan and Rev were—stunned.

His time, 10.2 seconds, appeared on the score board suspended over the arena. A pixelated bull bucked beside it.

The boy nodded to the board. "And I bet you think they buck like that because—"

"Because they don't like anything on their back?" Dylan managed to say, hopefully, still staring in horror at the calf. "Like horses when you put a saddle—"

"It's because of the bucking strap. They put a strap around where it's sensitive, and pull it real tight."

The crowd's non-stop cheering escalated as the calf was dragged by its neck across the dirt out of the arena.

"Surely they must know it's in pain—" Rev winced. "I mean, how could it be any clearer—"

As soon as the words were out of her mouth, the boy glanced at her, then got up and took the stairs down two at a time. Rev and Dylan, and Tucker and Peanut, quickly followed him, to the backstage area where they soon found themselves in a maze of passageways. At a fork, Tucker and Peanut went one way, the way Peanut was insistently leading Tucker, and Dylan and Rev went the other.

At the end of the passageway Peanut and Tucker had taken, around the corner, lay the little calf, discarded in a heap. Peanut approached, sniffed it, then gave it a gentle lick. When he gave it another, the calf opened its eyes. It took a moment to focus on the big, black, shaggy creature that was standing over him, wagging his tail, but when it did, it gave a weak little tail wag in return. Peanut licked its muzzle once more, but then the calf shuddered, and went still. Peanut let out a whimper.

"I'm sorry, Pea," Tucker said, then stepped forward to close its eyes.

Then commotion in the next passageway and the raised voices of Dylan and Rev sent them both running.

"I'll teach you not to be such a wuss," the man said, raising his hand to the boy. Tucker didn't hesitate. He grabbed the man's arm and twisted it behind his back. The man stumbled and fell onto the ground. In a flash, the boy went down beside him, the coil of rope he'd had clipped to his belt in his hand. He quickly secured his father's elbows behind his back, looped the rope around his neck, down his chest, through his—sensitive area, around his feet, and back up to his elbows. The boy pulled the rope tight, ignoring the scream, as he'd no doubt been taught, tied a final knot, then sprang to his feet, hands held high.

"Eight seconds," Tucker said, checking his watch.

The boy gave him a grim smile, which Tucker returned.

The man was still screaming and struggling, but the more he struggled, the tighter the rope became, which made him struggle, buck actually, and scream even more.

Rev spoke then. "Run away?"

Next afternoon, over a breakfast of hot coffee and cold pizza, Rev was busy making a lengthy blog entry about the rodeo, and Dylan was once again checking their email. It had been steadily increasing in volume as the tour proceeded.

"We've got money," he said after a few moments.

"Yes we do," Rev agreed absently. "You've got some, and I've got some, so we've—"

"No, I mean someone's made a payment to us through PayPal. Five thousand dollars."

"Five thousand dollars?" Rev looked up then. "What for?"

Dylan tapped away. "Bloody hell. It's from Kyle! He says it's our cut."

"No," Rev said in disbelief, setting her laptop aside and joining Dylan on the bed to look.

> *Hi Rev and Dylan,*
>
> *So it's working. This is your cut. I'm paying you 5%. Hope that's okay. If it weren't for you, I'd still be on the streets. This is way better. You were right, Rev. I'm also sending you some of my business cards. Not because I think you need the service. Ha-ha. But because Sarah did a great job.*
>
> *Thanks again.*
>
> *Hope you're well.*
>
> *Kyle, Proprietor*
> *Great Hands*

"Wow. Five thousand is five percent?" Rev was stunned.

"Who'd've thought?" Dylan agreed.

"Well, good for him!"

A few minutes later, Dylan casually asked, "Would you mind spending a couple extra weeks in California?"

"Um, no?"

"What I said!"

"What?"

Dylan angled his laptop so Rev could see the response he'd just typed.

"Apparently, Minnesota has cancelled," he explained. "And Phil sees no point in driving north in winter."

"No argument there. Who'd see us in a white-out?"

"And he says they can't reschedule the tv thing in California, so...oh."

"What?"

"Apparently Head Office has decided that although they will continue to pay gas and associated travel expenses to keep the van on the road, since we don't have any more gigs—"

"We don't have *any* more gigs?"

"Everyone's cancelled," Dylan said, also with some surprise. "Except the tv thing in California and something in Massachusetts."

"Wow. Guess it was just a matter of time. What with the 'Stop the Tour' thing, remember?"

"I suppose. Anyway, he wants to know if we can handle our accommodations."

"Well, we've got the housesit in California, and you've arranged something similar in Myrtle Beach, right? But geez, that leaves a lot of Curada nights in between. And up to Massachusetts."

"It does, but—" he returned to the PayPal screen and turned it toward her, essentially waving Kyle's cheque in the air.

"Oh. Good one," she chuckled.

Next day, they drove to the college at which they were scheduled to talk, Tucker and Peanut in tow. It would be their last talk, they now realized, which was a shame, since their table was now fully stocked with books, DVDs, bumper stickers, mugs, magnets, and Ell's bright lime green t-shirts.

Sadly, not one item was purchased. By those who had come for the talk. Those who provided escort—there were several groupies in the parking lot—received a discount on anything they wanted.

"I'd like to tell you today about Dionysus," Dylan said, once he'd stepped up to the podium on which he'd carefully hung the AAC banner, for the last time. "Dionysus is an ancient god, who was born of a virgin several millennia ago, on December 25. He travelled around, teaching and performing miracles, such as turning water into wine. He was later crucified, but he rose from the dead.

"Attis, another god, was also born of a virgin on December 25. He was considered our saviour, and three days after he died, for us, he was resurrected.

"Mithra, another ancient god, was also born of a virgin. Also on December 25. Six hundred years before Christ. He was visited by wise men at his birth. His first followers were shepherds—he had twelve of them. He was also crucified, and then he ascended into heaven.

"Quexalcote was also born of a virgin, five hundred and eighty-seven years before Christ. He spent forty days fasting and resisting temptation, he was crucified, along with two thieves, and he was resurrected three days later.

"Horus, yet another god, was also born of a virgin. Horus walked on water, was crucified, and then resurrected three days later.

"Now," Dylan said, pausing for effect, "is all this just coincidence or what?"

"How'd your lecture go?" Rev asked when he came out of the auditorium.

"I told them about Dionysus, Attis, Mithra, Quexalcote, Horus—"

"Yeah? And?"

He gave an odd grin. "They said I was making it up."

s they made their way across to California over the next week or so, they were accompanied by an ever-changing convoy of vehicles, all with lime green t-shirted drivers. And the interesting thing, they both noted, was that their escorts became more mixed in terms of age. Many vehicles were driven by older couples, perhaps snowbirds from the cold, cold north. Several truckers, clearly on the job, also became part of the convoy for a time.

"This is so cool," Rev said, nodding a thank you to a new escort that appeared and passed them in order to fill the recently-emptied position ahead of them. She eagerly waited to see a bumper sticker, and was not disappointed: 'Worship me or I will torture you forever. Have a nice day.'

As soon as they crossed into California, they headed for the nearest beach.

"I need to see water," Rev said. "The desert is so—"

"Very much like a beach," Dylan commented. "Vast expanses of sand."

"Yeah. Well. Except for a certain notable absence," she said. "The water you poured into a dish and swirled around when we were in Arizona didn't do it."

They pulled into a parking lot, got out, and went to the ocean's edge.

"I'm surprised it's so clean," Dylan spoke eventually. "Being so close to the city."

"Yeah, well, there's invisible dirty."

"Still.

"I'm surprised it's not all city," Rev said, looking around at the relatively unpeopled area. "You know, like in Toronto. If Ontario were the size of California, you'd have to travel out of state to get to any place like this."

So they spent a couple hours just walking and sitting and walking. And watching Peanut running and splashing and running.

In their Curada suite later that evening, they comfortably settled into their well-established routine. Dylan was on the bed with his laptop, checking their mail, planning their near future, and humming "Hotel California." Rev was in a chair, feet up, updating their blog.

"What to do in California…," Dylan mumbled to himself.

"Lots, I imagine," Rev said idly as she rolled a joint. Peanut watched her, wagging his tail. Tucker had already found something to do in California.

"Yeah, and that's just the—woh. We've got a meeting. With a movie producer."

"Really? Well, we are in LA. Is it the guy we met back at the trial? We never heard from him again."

"No, it's a Steve Mather," Dylan took a puff from the offered joint, "from Mather Films. Go figure," he added dryly.

"Phil and Dorothy set it up?"

"No, our book publisher did." Dylan looked up. "Have you been sending stuff?"

"No, not yet."

"Maybe they've been following the tour. You know, like our escorts. So they know—"

"We were shot at. And chased. And car crashed. No wonder Hollywood's interested."

"We weren't car-crashed," he handed the joint back to her.

"Well we would have been if that head-on guy had shown up. On the wrong side of the road."

"You mean the right side of the road."

"Well, that depends, doesn't it," she took a long inhale.

"Depends on what you mean? Surely meaning is independent of intent. Because words are—"

"No, it depends on whether you're a passenger in a very long train that's moving with a constant velocity in one direction or an observer sitting on an embankment watching the train go by, and there's a flash of lightning," she finished. Somewhat inconclusively.

"Must it be a very long train?" Dylan asked. After a moment.

"No, because if it's a short train, bandits can trap it in a tunnel."

"Right." Dylan thought for a moment. Perhaps about that.

"Unless there's a fat man on the bridge," Rev added.

"Then the bandits can't trap it in a tunnel?"

"Not unless it's to save the five people who are tied to the track."

"I see. And is one of them a neurosurgeon who can cure the train conductor?"

"Yes. Maybe. It depends."

Peanut wagged his tail.

They decided to head to San Francisco for a few days, and while there, they went to the famous Pier 39.

"This is nice," Rev said, as they wandered through along the walkways. "An outdoor shopping mall. What a concept."

Tucker looked at her oddly.

"Wouldn't work so well where we live," she explained. "The polar bears would wreck the place."

He nodded politely, though Dylan rolled his eyes.

A little later, on Tuck's call, they stopped at a new age store that sold candles, incense, crystals, and so on.

"I'm surprised you're into this stuff," Dylan said, as Tucker wandered through the store. "I'm not. My sister is. I want to buy her a gift. She loves this stuff." He was looking at a display of healing stones.

"You know it's a bunch of hokum, right?" Rev asked.

"Well, yeah. I guess. But my sister believes it," Tucker said. "And if it works, what does it matter?"

Rev didn't answer. Dylan turned to look at her. She had opened her mouth, but then had closed it. Without saying anything. He was about to put out his hand and feel her forehead, but then saw that it was crinkled with thought.

Tucker selected some healing crystals that were 'from ethical mines', Rev noted. Apparently, when crystals are mined non-violently they preserve their natural psychic energies and healing properties. She also discovered, while wandering behind Tucker, that blue tourmaline can be used to activate the throat chakra and the third eye, facilitating access to the higher levels.

"You could buy her some CDs," Dylan said. He'd found the music section of the store. "Music has been proven to have a calming effect." With just a slight emphasis on the 'proven'.

"Well, not hip hop," Rev offered, as both she and Tucker joined him.

"No, that's been proven to have just the opposite effect. Raises the blood pressure and—"

"Really?" Tucker asked, intrigued.

"Yeah. Something to do with both the tempo and the frequencies, I think. Some music elicits the release of serotonin, some the release of dopamine...."

Tucker chose a CD featuring flutes, birds, and a babbling brook, and they headed to the check-out.

"So does this stuff really work?" Rev asked the cashier.

"Oh yes!" she replied warmly. "I know it does!"

Rev waited until they had left the store. "So many people have such low standards of knowledge. They say 'I know' at the drop of a hat. Intelligent people—"

"Such as yourself—" Dylan interjected, smiling.

"Such as myself," she agreed, "have much higher standards and so they, we—*I*—come off, ironically, as not knowing nearly as much. As stupid people. Because more often than not—more often than stupid people—*I* say 'I don't know'."

"But do they have lower standards of knowledge or just different standards of knowledge," Dylan asked, as they continued along the pier, Peanut leading them toward—something. "After all, they're using their intuition or gut feeling where you use reason."

"Yeah, well, so-called 'gut feeling' *is* a lower standard, isn't it?"

"Hm. Maybe that's why—have you noticed how many tv shows feature someone who solves crimes or mysteries or what have you not by the careful and tedious collection and analysis of evidence, but by *feeling*?"

"You know you're right!" she replied after a moment. "For every *Bones* there's a dozen shows like *The Medium* or *The Listener* or whatever. Probably because they appeal to people's desire to have the easy way validated."

"Remember *The X-Files*?" Dylan asked. "That's where it first started. Agent Scully versus Mulder. And," Dylan said with emphasis, "the voice of reason was given to the *female* character."

"Yeah," Rev replied. "Frankly, that's always surprised me."

"Well, maybe it's not so surprising," Dylan said a moment later. "If male trumps female, then the message is that intuition trumps reason."

"Hm. Or maybe it just gives the man lots of opportunities to insist that the woman just trust him."

"But *is* it the easier way?" Dylan came back to the main thread of their conversation. "You hear people talk about how hard it is to believe, to have faith—"

"Well, it's only hard in the face of conflicting evidence."

"Which would explain why believers don't want to hear conflicting evidence."

They exchanged a 'been there done that' look, then Rev left to find a washroom.

"She's very opinionated, isn't she," Tucker said to Dylan while they waited at the shoreline. Looking at the multitudes of sea lions Peanut had obviously been aware of all along. When he barked at them, they barked back.

"Well," Dylan said, not unkindly, "that's what happens when you think a lot about a lot of stuff."

"Yeah, but you think a lot too, and—"

Dylan thought about that for a moment. "She cares more than I do," he said then. "About a lot of stuff," he added.

Tucker thought about that for a minute, then simply nodded.

A couple days later, they were on their way to see the famous redwood trees. Tucker agreed whole-heartedly with the idea. He had never seen redwoods either. And Peanut would love to go hiking again.

An hour into the drive, Rev said, "You know what's wrong with it? Tucker's 'If it works, what does it matter?' question," she clarified. "The whole placebo effect. It *matters* if you choose the placebo *instead of* rather than *in addition to.*"

"And it matters if believing something without evidence

becomes a habit," she added a few miles later.

They'd planned to stay overnight somewhere so they could begin their hike through the redwoods in the early morning, as was strongly recommended on many of the websites Dylan had visited.

They discovered why. Redwoods in the morning fog were absolutely majestic. The sun filtered through and it was simply—magical. Like towering turrets in a fairy forest. It left them speechless. They walked quietly on the path for a good hour, stopping occasionally to marvel at what they saw—lots and lots of ferns, fluorescent moss, crimson trilliums, and, particularly intriguing, 'inside-out' flowers.

It wasn't until they reached a waterfalls that they felt they could speak. Tucker wanted to do a side trail; Dylan and Rev were content to sit at the falls while he did so.

"You know," Dylan said, once they'd made themselves comfortable, "I think your bug hypothesis is correct. And that's our problem. We've been assuming, all along, that people's belief in god, or religion, is considered. But now that I think about it, I'll wager most people haven't thought about whether they believe in god for more than five minutes."

"That's—appalling."

"Well, if it's any comfort, they probably haven't thought about *any* belief for more than five minutes."

"That's even more appalling. I—"

"Yes, well, I think it's safe to assume that *you've* thought about *every* belief—and probably just every*thing*—more than most people."

"Then why aren't people lining up to ask my advice?" she said wryly. Then snorted.

But Dylan took the question seriously. "Because people don't value thought. Probably because they don't recognize it. They don't recognize it when it's occurring and they don't recognize its results. Or the results of its absence," he added.

"Oh, that's good," Rev said after a moment. "That's really good. And really disturbing. How can people not value thought? How can they not think? About, well, everything. *Especially* about whether you believe there's some omnipotent entity out there. That has a lot of consequences for how you live your life! For example, I was raised Roman Catholic. So were you, right? So you know it's a mortal sin if you break one of the Ten Commandments. Not a venial sin. A mortal sin. So if you disobey your parents, for example, you burn in hell for ever. I believed that. So of course I obeyed my parents. I did everything they said. And nothing they didn't say."

Dylan was silent.

"And so, also of course, when I was old enough to think about it, I did. And for more than five minutes. Because being Roman Catholic also means believing the Pope is infallible. Which means you can't use contraception. Or get an abortion. Or end your life when you're done. So how can people spend just five minutes thinking about whether or they're going to 'be' Roman Catholic?"

"I don't think it's a question of choice. For them. People are 'born' Roman Catholic. Or Presbyterian. Or Jewish, or Muslim. End of story."

"But that's nonsense! That's like saying you were born—Republican. You can't be *born* believing anything."

"Maybe another mistake we keep making," Dylan said, "is assuming that people connect what they do with what they believe. That most people live according to their beliefs, their opinions."

She turned to look at him. "They don't? Well what's the point then in thinking about—ah." She returned her gaze to the cascading water. "So, what, they say 'I think x', 'I believe y', but then just do what they want? Regardless of the implications of x and y?'

Dylan nodded. "It's easier that way. Figuring out what you *should* do is a lot harder than figuring out what you *want* to do. I don't have to tell you that. Ditto for figuring out what's logical and rational—rather than what's simply appealing."

"God, what careless, irresponsible lives." She looked out into the distance. To the mountains. "Because what they say has—consequences. When my parents said—wait a minute, *you're saying they probably didn't even think about it?*"

She was silent for a long time. Waiting for the anger, the rage, to pass.

"Why didn't they?" she said finally. And then, "Why did I? Why *do* I—take it seriously? That's the problem, right? When my parents, or the priest, or *The Bible* says this or that, I take it seriously. After all, words have meaning, they—*mean* something.

"Okay, so if their belief isn't genuine," she followed the thought where it led, "if they don't really mean 'I believe in God'—*that's* why the phrase is so imprecise!" The 'aha' stunned her. "Because it doesn't *mean* anything! It doesn't mean 'I believe there's an omnipotent entity out there who at any moment can do absolutely anything' or 'I believe there's an all-knowing, all-wise, all-good entity looking after me, and everyone in the world, all the time'. If they said it *that* way, with some precision, they might *not* believe it. They might think about it at any rate. But 'I believe in God' is so—meaningless!"

It took another long silence, but she got there. "So if people don't genuinely believe any of this, even potentially, why do they want to talk about it? Why do they call in to talk shows? Why do radio stations even *have* talk shows?"

"I think those are two different questions," Dylan said. "As for why do radio stations have talk shows—entertainment." Dylan watched her carefully, though surreptitiously.

"We were just entertainment?" She was pissed. Royally pissed. Understandably. All that work—

"And bait. For advertising dollars." Might as well get it all out now. "But as for the other question, I don't know. Maybe it's also entertaining for the people who call in. Or maybe they need to voice their opinion no matter now unconsidered. Maybe they need to convince others to agree with them because otherwise they might just be wrong."

"Truth by consensus. Reminds me of that Larson cartoon. The surgeons standing over an operating table? 'Okay, how many of us believe the heart has four chambers?'"

"Despite all that," Dylan said, eventually, "we still might have made a difference. You don't know how many people heard what we said and took it seriously."

"Yeah," she said not too enthusiastically, "I do. About the same number of students who heard what I said and took it seriously."

After another long silence, Dylan continued. "You know, it's not just you. There are other people who take it seriously. The Inquisition, the Crusades, the Salem witch trials. Every religious war since—well, every religious war."

"I'm not so sure. I bet half the guys who went on the Crusades went for the party. War is part frat party, part road trip."

"Actually, the Crusades—that's good," he broke off, considering what she'd said. "That's exactly what war is. Or it's exactly what many young men who sign up think it is."

"Add to that the badge of masculinity—they should actually have a badge, like in Cubs and Scouts."

"Well, they do, don't they. They have several."

"Yeah but none with the male symbol on it. No Badge of Masculinity."

"That does explain the resistance to women being part of it: if women can do it, it's not a man thing anymore."

"Plus," she continued, "I bet they went, and go, partly because they haven't got anything better to do. Same as in demonstrations. Sure, there are the true believers, but there's always a bunch of assholes who are there just for the action."

"Broadly speaking," he punned. "Though for many it's a job. Haven't you noticed that recruitment centers down here are often right beside the employment offices? Joining the army is a way to support your family."

"Or get away from it. The wife and kids and all that."

"Or a way to get an education if you can't afford tuition."

"Is anyone who works from sixteen and saves all their money really unable to afford tuition?"

"Here, yeah. Isn't tuition in the States something like ten times what it is in Canada? And minimum wage is about the same, isn't it?"

"Really? I didn't know that. I mean I knew Yale and Harvard were expensive, but just your local no-name university? That would explain a lot."

"Including how to end war."

Rev looked at him, puzzled.

"Reduce tuition fees and you remove at least one of the incentives. Improve other employment options and you remove another. No soldiers, no war."

"Nah, you'll always have soldiers. I mean really, who'd apply for a job that involves killing and the possibility of being killed just to avoid schlepping burgers at Wendys. There's gotta be more to it than that. And the promise of honor and glory. I think a lot of men like war. Plain and simple. They like the noise. I once suggested to my neighbour that dirt bikes use electric motors, like some of the stealth fishing boats on the lake. He laughed at me and said the whole point of dirt bikes was to drive around making a lot of noise. Then demonstrated for days."

"That would explain why they take off the mufflers. I always thought it was a strip-down-the-bike-for-the-aerodynamics racing thing."

"And they like the action," Rev continued. "Especially if it's violent. A lot of men genuinely like to fight."

"Your other neighbour."

She grimaced.

"And, of course, they like the proof of manhood."

"However false."

"Yeah, remember Gwynne Dyer's book? Where he said that the bar is moved according to how many soldiers they need, and typically anyone with relatively minimal intelligence and physical fitness can 'pass' boot camp?"

"Hm."

They looked out at the waterfalls.

"What were we talking about?" Rev said after a moment.

"Taking religion seriously."

"Oh yeah."

Tucker and Peanut returned just then, which was probably just as well since they both felt quite done with the matter. Maybe even with the tour. They walked back to the parking lot. Except for Peanut. Who ran. Ahead, then back to his bestest-friend-ever, then ahead, then back...

"Do you have to piddle?" Tucker asked Peanut as he opened the door of his SUV. Peanut considered the question, then purposefully walked back to the trail entrance and although it seemed somehow wrong, he piddled on one of the massive redwoods. And appeared tickled to do so. Perhaps because for once in his life he felt like a Chihuahua.

Dylan had arranged to have their ranch house housesit ready a few days early, so next day, they headed back to Los Angeles. The morning after they'd settled in, Tucker took Peanut to the vet. He'd been favouring his tail, even yelping occasionally when he wagged it.

"So, how did your visit to the vet go?" Dylan asked in the afternoon. "What did he say? Is Peanut okay?"

"He said it was just sprained. And gave me a referral to a dog therapist."

Rev snorted. "Only in California," she said.

"Well, he figured it was from excessive lateral movement. And he thought we should figure out why he wags his tail so much."

"He's happy?" Rev suggested. Then added, "Can we come?"

So the day after that, they all got into Tucker's SUV, Rev in the front seat, Dylan, as usual, in the back with Peanut. They found the address with no problem, and as they pulled into the parking lot, Rev said casually, "I bet the dog therapist's a border collie. They always think they're so smart." Dylan grinned at her.

They got out and approached the building, which only then did they really notice.

"This is so cool," Dylan said, stopping to give it a good look. The building had been designed to look like a car. "So very cool," he said as he stepped forward then to open the door, an actual door of a restored Chevy. The waiting room was full of car seats. Which were full of dogs obviously expecting to go for a car ride. So they were happy dogs. Except the one that was throwing up.

Rev pointed, grinning, to the fan in the corner, in front of which sat two beagles, their ears blowing in the wind, grins plastered on their drooling faces.

Tucker and Peanut went to reception to check in. When Peanut put his paws on the counter, he was every inch as tall as Tucker, standing beside him. They sat down to wait then, Peanut glancing upward, no doubt expecting a sun roof through which to put his head.

After a few minutes, a perky border collie trotted into the waiting area from around the corner, went right up one of the beagles, and barked at it. The beagle got up and followed the collie to the back.

"Yeah," Dylan said to Rev, anticipating, "but she's probably just the assistant."

When Tucker and Peanut were summoned, Dylan and Rev said they'd wait outside.

"So," the middle-aged woman said to Tucker, when they'd settled themselves in her consulting room, "I understand Peanut has sprained his tail by wagging it too hard. Or too often," she consulted the file.

Tucker didn't say anything.

"We prefer to treat the cause, not the symptom, so the question is," she said, tonelessly, "Why do you think your dog is happy so much of the time?"

Rev and Dylan, who had crept under her open window, fought hard to stifle their fits of giggles. As they quickly crawled away.

Next day, they decided to do a walkaround. As they were standing outside a used record store, looking at the wonderful display in the window and lamenting the lost art of album covers, someone stopped beside them, pulled out his cell phone, dialled, then began to speak.

"Simon, Todd here."

There was a moment's silence.

"Well, we wouldn't have this problem if you'd done your job in the first place," the man, Todd, said angrily into his phone.

There was another moment of silence during which Todd was not the only one to seethe.

"No, I don't want to start over! We don't have time to start over!"

The angry conversation continued for a good minute.

"Oh don't give me that. If you had concerns at the beginning, you should have said so!"

"Maybe he knew you would just yell at him," Rev said.

The man looked oddly at her, then said with ice, "This is a private conversation!"

"Then you should have it in private."

"Look lady" —Dylan winced— "it's none of your business!"

"The hell it isn't," Rev said. "You've made it my business. Standing right beside me and speaking loudly enough for me to hear."

"Oh why don't you just shut the fuck up."

"No, you shut the fuck up."

His eyes widened.

"You want to hit me, don't you!?" she taunted. "For someone who so likes to hear himself talk, it's surprising you can't use words instead of fists to resolve a conflict."

"Listen lady—I think—"

"I know this will be hard for you to understand," she cut him off, "seeing as you're a man, but we don't really care what you think. Even if we'd asked. Which we didn't."

"I'm getting really angry here—"

"Oh well then. I'll stop immediately. Can't have a man angry, can we? Everyone," she turned and addressed the gathering crowd, "bow down now. This man is angry. He is to get his way. His right. Of way."

She turned to him, virtually scuffing her hooves in the dirt.

He snapped his phone shut and stomped away. And somewhere Simon was no doubt smiling.

A couple days later, they had their meeting with the movie producer.

"Hi, come on in, Rev and Dylan, right?"

"Yes." They stepped into the office they'd been led to by a smartly dressed young man from reception, who then discreetly disappeared.

"Steve Mather." The man reached out to shake their hands. "So glad you could take this meeting," he gestured to a couple of plush chairs in his chrome and glass office.

"Can I get you anything? Iced tea? A soda?"

"Iced tea would be nice, thanks," Dylan said.

"Sweetener? Lemon?"

"Lemon for me," Dylan said.

"Plain for me, thanks," Rev added.

Steve pushed a button on his phone. "Three iced tea, Jules. One with lemon, one plain, and one for me, thanks."

"So how's your visit to California been so far?" Steve said, clearly making small talk as they waited for the iced tea to arrive.

"Good, thanks."

"Have you taken any of the studio tours yet? Universal has a good one."

"No, we went to see the redwoods," Rev said.

Steve seemed confused. He didn't recognize the name.

"The trees?"

"Oh," Steve laughed.

Dylan and Rev looked at each other.

The young man, Jules presumably, entered Steve's office with three glasses of iced tea on a tray. He distributed them, then left.

"So," Steve jumped right in. "We've been following your tour and, to be frank, we think it's blockbuster material." He smiled at them.

"Okay...."

"I mean, you guys were detained at the border, you're sort of under house arrest, you got shot at—"

Dylan and Rev exchange a look.

"And we're promoting atheism, or at least an examination of religionism," Dylan suggested.

"Yeah, yeah," Steve brushed that away, "but then there was that car chase—"

"Yeah," Rev said, getting on board quickly, "and maybe in the movie we can be strung up with weights attached to our feet—"

"Yeah," Dylan added excitedly, "or we could be lashed onto a wheel and our limbs smashed to bits as it turns—"

"Or strapped into a chair full of spikes—"

"Yeah, yeah," Steve protested, "but we want to keep it real."

And then the TV show happened. It was a roundtable thing rather like Bill Maher's *Politically Incorrect*. Along with Dylan and Rev, there were to be high-ups from three different religions.

"The Pope, do you think?" Rev wondered aloud to Dylan, when they received the details from Dorothy. "Wouldn't that be cool?"

Dylan grinned at the idea of Rev versus The Pope. He wouldn't stand a chance.

They showed up at the studio and managed to 'pass' wardrobe and make-up without incident. They had a brief conversation with the host, Ann, who was warm and enthusiastic, and then they were led to a spot off-set to await their introduction. Tucker and Peanut were allowed to be in the audience once Tuck explained that yes indeed Peanut was a working dog. Peanut barked. For emphasis. Let's say.

A few minutes later, the show began.

"Welcome everyone," Ann said to the studio audience. Which was a dark sea of sober colors polka-dotted with lime green. "Today on our show we have Chris Reveille and Dylan O'Toole, of the infamous 'Blasphemy Tour'." The audience erupted into cheers. The lime green part of it. Ann smiled a welcome at them as they entered from the wing. They nodded to her, and to the audience, then took their seats.

"And we also have—"

"So a priest, a rabbi, and a minister walk onto the set," Dylan said under his breath to Rev as a priest, a minister, and a rabbi walked onto the set.

"—Father Angelo, Reverend Beech, and Rabbi Stein."

"Welcome to you all. I'd like to start off by talking about faith because our government keeps telling us about faith-based initiatives, and I have to say, *I'd* like to see some evidence-based initiatives."

"But the two are not incompatible," the minister spoke.

"Not necessarily," Dylan jumped right in, "but since faith is by definition unsupported belief, if you have reason to believe something, if you have evidence, you don't need faith."

"Yes, but we have evidence," the rabbi said. "That's *why* we believe."

"Then why invoke faith? Why don't you put your evidence on the table, and I'll put mine on the table, and we'll just see whose is the strongest?"

Ann laughed. The audience cheered. The lime green part of it.

"By invoking faith," Dylan continued, "you're exempting your claim not only from comparison to other claims, but from any evaluation at all. 'I have faith in X' is a real show-stopper. What can anyone say to that besides 'Yes, well, you're an idiot'?"

In the gasp that followed, Rev jumped in. "Okay, I'll bite. *Why* do you believe? Why do you believe in a god as the creator of the universe and not, for instance, a purple platypus that lives up in the sky?"

"Well, because that's ridiculous," the minister said, dismissively. "To believe in a purple platypus doesn't make—"

"It doesn't make sense? What does it matter if it makes sense or not? I can list a thousand things you believe that don't make sense. So, again, why don't you believe that The Great Big Purple Platypus created the world?"

"Look up," he smiled kindly.

"Back at ya."

"God is incorporeal," he explained patiently.

"So is The Great Big Purple Platypus."

"I *know* he exists. He's spoken to me," he said fervently.

"So has my Great Big Purple Platypus," she said with equal fervour. "And the things it says, my god!"

"You must be hallucinating," someone called out from the audience.

"Back at ya."

"There are historical documents," the rabbi said, and both the priest and minister nodded.

She waved to a guy standing off-set. He brought in a small hand-written notebook and gave it to her. Dylan expressed surprise. Usually he was the one ready with props.

"This is a book," she said, "*The Great Big Book of the Great Big Purple Platypus*. Written by George," she opened the first page, "inspired by the Platypus. And here," she thumbed through, "on page ten, it says 'The Great Big Purple Platypus doth indeed exist. In a multitude of wondrous purple.'"

The audience erupted with applause. The lime green part of it.

In the caught-off-balance silence of the other speakers that followed, Dylan jumped in. "You want to talk about historical documents? Okay. Good. Maybe you can answer a few questions for me. Why is there no mention of Jesus in the Christian documents, the

Christian documents, that were written before the gospels? The gospels were written some 50 years after he supposedly existed. Doesn't it seem a bit odd to you that that's the first we hear of him? Wouldn't you think people would write about the Lord, their Saviour, when everything was fresh in their minds?

"And what was Jesus doing when he was a teenager? And in his 20s? Did he join a gang or something? There's a twenty-year gap in his life in *The Bible*. We see him at twelve, all smartypants with the elders in the Temple, and then suddenly he shows up at thirty, turning water into wine."

"Maybe he was on one long bender," Rev suggested.

"And why have some Christian documents been suppressed? Documents that are just as authentic as those in *The Bible*? The Acts of John, for example, and The Acts of Peter. There's one that describes Jesus making toys out of thin air. And turning children into goats."

"*That's* what he was doing when he was a teenager," Rev inserted.

"Look," the priest interrupted, "the fact of the matter is that it just isn't true that—"

"The fact of the matter? Just isn't true? So now you're invoking *knowledge*? You can prove God exists then?"

"Certainly," he smiled. Suffer the little children. "Our theologians have been proving God's existence for ages! For example, everything must come from somewhere—"

"Who says so?" Rev interjected.

"Well—logic, I guess—"

"Reason?"

"Yes—okay—reason," he said cautiously. "God is the something that created everything," he finished uncertainly.

"And who created God?" she asked.

"No one," he replied. "He's the First Cause."

"So you suspend the very logic that got you to God in order to explain God: everything has to have a cause, therefore God—but then suddenly everything *doesn't* have to have a cause, therefore God!"

"Is that a problem?" he asked with irritation.

"It's inconsistent, it's illogical!"

"God is exempt from the paltry human rules of logic," he said. "He transcends reason!"

"But it's not *him* that's transcending it, it's *you*! *You're* the one who's saying 'Now I'll use logic, now I won't.' So your 'proof' is invalid."

"But as *I* said," the minister obviously felt he wasn't getting enough air time, "and Kierkegaard will back me up on this—it doesn't *have* to be. Logical. Reasonable."

"Then why not believe in The Purple Platypus instead?"

"Excuse me?"

"Why isn't The Purple Platypus the being that created everything including itself? Unless you invoke reason, there's no reason to have faith in your god instead of mine. And if you *do* invoke reason, you've got to go all the way. You can't pick and choose when it suits you and when it doesn't."

"Well, I suppose God could take the form of a purple platypus— but there's no support for the existence of any 'purple platypus'. Whereas we have reason to believe—"

"Okay, I think we're going in circles here," Ann stepped in. Tried to step in.

"So you're going to use your reason again? You seem to use it when it pleases you and toss it out when it leads to an unfavourable conclusion."

"*The Bible*—" the priest said.

"The Dead Sea Scrolls—" the rabbi said.

"Relics—" the priest said.

"*The Bible*?" Dylan said. "What about the contradictions in *The Bible*?"

"I beg your pardon?"

"How do you decide which stories to believe—when there are two?"

"Such as?"

"Genesis, for starters. There are two versions about the creation of man and woman. Which do you believe and why?"

"And what about the Apocrypha," Rev added. "There's one version that says God has no gender. Why do you believe the 'He' version instead?

"And we've been reading some of the war stories in *The Bible*," Rev continued "Apparently some guy named Adino killed 800 men in a single battle. Abishai and Jashobeam each killed 300. Who were these guys? Even if that battle lasted a full 24 hours, that's at least 12 people killed per hour. Which is one guy every five minutes. Now I've never killed a person, with just knives and swords and shit, but it can't be that easy. One guy every five minutes for 24 hours straight?"

"In another battle," Dylan took over, they were like a tag team, "the Israelites killed 120,000 people in one day. During World War II, he Germans *and* their allies, using heavy tanks, artillery, mortars, machine guns, hand grenades, landmines, fighter planes, and bombs, managed to kill only 176,000 people. Over a period of six weeks."

"So inquiring minds have to ask," Rev said, "when these guys went fishing, did they ever catch anything? How big?" The audience erupted with applause. The lime green part of it.

"Another thing," Dylan said, "God's obviously rounding off to the nearest thousand, and I have to tell you, that lack of attention to detail bothers me."

"And yet," the minister said smugly, "*The Bible* continues to appear on bestseller lists."

"Even though," Dylan interjected, "the plot is repetitious, the characters are unlikeable, the dialogue, unrealistic, and the tone, juvenile."

"And much of it just fucking doesn't make sense!" someone called out.

"'Then the Lord said to Moses,'" someone else shouted, "'take the blasphemer outside and let the entire community stone him to death!'"

Tucker stood up immediately. Peanut barked. For emphasis. Let's say.

"'Turn the other cheek!'" someone else shouted. Then stood. In a lime green t-shirt.

"'Suffer not a witch to live!'" A grey-suited man stood. And faced the lime green t-shirt.

"'Love thy brother!'" Another lime green t-shirted person stood. Then added belatedly, "And sister! Sister too!" he emphasized.

"'Slay the infidel wherever ye find him!'" A respectably-dressed woman stood.

"'Allah forgives all!'"

"'Don't worry, be happy!'" Dylan turned to Rev in surprise, having had that last one blasted into his ear.

"'I am the walrus!'"

Fearing a riot, Ann determined that a commercial break was needed. The dark-robed threesome left the set, and Dylan and Rev stood up to stretch. In their jeans and signature t-shirts.

"You know," Rev said to Dylan during the break, "if wardrobe had put them all in sweats—"

"Or clown suits—" Dylan knew where she was going.

"—what they're saying wouldn't seem quite so convincing."

Three ads later—beer, toilet paper, and breath fresheners— "All to the set!" rang out.

"And relics?" Rev continued their rebuttal, "Please. Two words. Carbon dating."

"And as for personal experiences of revelation," Dylan offered, "two other words. Psychology and neurobiology. The experiences can be explained as other phenomena. And in any case, due to their subjective nature they can't be confirmed by independent investigation."

They dispensed as quickly with the argument from design. "Earlids," Dylan said. "Don't have 'em."

To the best possible universe argument, Rev simply snorted. And then sneezed.

"Bless you!" someone from the audience called out.

"Thank you!" she called back. "I'd hate to lose my soul out my nose. Good thing God's available to see to that!"

The priest was the first to recover. "But don't you see?" he leaned in. "With no sense of right or wrong—"

"Theists don't have a monopoly on morality," Rev said. "Ethics do not have to depend on a god."

"Well without God, how would you know what's right and wrong?"

"*We* would determine that!"

"On what basis?"

"How about justice? 'It is good to treat everyone fairly.'"

"And what's to stop someone from being bad?"

"What stops them now—the fear of God's punishment?"

"Well—"

"Do you mean to say that the only reason you're good is because you want to get to heaven? I thought Christians were all about doing for *others*."

"Can you sit there and tell me right now what's just?"

"Of course not," Rev admitted. "It's not that easy. If you want easy, go back to your catechism."

"So your argument for faith is just that we need God?" Dylan asked. "You're not giving us any proof—"

"We need God, therefore he exists. Let me try that." She turned to Dylan. "What do we need? Let me think. Ah. An unlimited supply of cold pizza and cheesecake."

"Nothing happened," she said after a moment.

"I think you have to scrunch up your face a bit. Try harder."

She scrunched up her face. Closed her eyes even. Then opened them. "Did it work?"

"Who are we to presume, to demand that God prove himself!" The rabbi was enraged.

"God doesn't need proof!" So was the minister.

"Then neither does The Purple Platypus, and it's His will that all theists die!"

"Those who need proof are weak in spirit!" The priest spoke up.

"But strong in mind!" The audience was getting involved again.

"To just sit around and have faith is—why don't *we* just *figure out* what's in our best interests?" Dylan suggested. "Look at all the remarkable—dare I say miraculous—things we've done. Can you name one feat of God's in the last thousand years that rivals the electrical outlet? Or extra-strength Tylenol?"

"But all the electrical outlets and Tylenol in the world won't save us."

"From what?" Dylan asked.

"And God will?" Rev asked at the same time. "I'll put my money on my reason any time. Maybe not electrical outlets. Maybe, instead, a method of re-oxygenating the oceans, or a worldwide ban on all nuclear weapons, or—" she broke off suddenly.

"It's your faith versus my reason," she said then. "My reason tells me that if I jump off a cliff attached to a hang-glider that is built to a specific design, I'll land safely at the bottom. Your faith tells you to trust in God: jump off the same cliff without the glider—*He'll* save you, right? Because he transcends reason, logic, the knowledge we have gained by scientific inquiry. Am I correct?"

"Yes."

"Then let's do it." The audience cheered. The lime green part.

Dylan leaned in to whisper to her. "Aren't you afraid of heights?"

"Oh yeah."

"Okay," she turned back to the threesome. "Change in plan. You jump. Faith. I don't. Gravity."

Next day, they left California and headed to Myrtle Beach, where they had another housesit. Once they got out of the maze of Los Angeles, losing Tucker a little in the process, they settled in for the long drive from one ocean to the other through desert—a fact that amused Dylan for some reason.

"Hey, guess what?" Dylan was in the passenger seat with his laptop open, as Rev had taken the first shift behind the wheel. "We're in *Who's Who in Hell*!"

"There's a *Who's Who in Hell*?"

"Looks like."

"Cool."

An hour later, he spoke again. "You'll want to hear this, I think," he said soberly. He had thought something like this would happen. But hadn't said anything.

"What?"

"'Christians throw themselves off the cliff—in droves'," he read the headline.

Rev turned to look at him and said, "Seriously?"

He nodded. "It's happening...everywhere."

She turned her attention back to the road. Dylan was surprised, then worried, about her silence. As well as his own.

After a moment, she said, "Please don't tell me some of them are teenagers."

Dylan quickly read the rest of the story, closed his laptop, then simply said, "Okay."

Rev drove on for a bit, then abruptly pulled over and stopped the van. Dylan looked at her.

"I should've known," she said flatly. "Of all the people, I—"

"But you're not responsible for—"

She looked at him. "But if I hadn't've suggested, *dared*—"

"But if they hadn't've believed—"

"But—if it had've been me—the younger me—" She looked out the window, then turned back to face him. "I was going to become a nun. Right after my Confirmation. I was ready to give my life to God."

To say Dylan was surprised would be an understatement. He couldn't believe she'd give her life to anyone.

"But you were—"

"Thirteen. A very—earnest—thirteen."

Okay, that he could believe.

"But the roundtable consisted of adults, we were—"

"Yeah, but people were listening. In the audience and at home. People were listening," she repeated oddly.

"Switch," Dylan said after a moment. "I'll drive."

It took all of fifteen minutes for the first car to appear. Then the second. And the third. The driver of that one was wearing a lime green t-shirt. Half an hour later, they had a dozen cars following them. Some supporters, some not. Dylan's phone rang.

"Dylan's phone, Rev talking." She listened for a few moments, then said, "Okay." To Dylan, she said, "That was Phil. He's asked us to pull into the next truck stop or whatever and call him back."

"That sounds ominous."

She simply stared out the window again. "It's just—I'm not used to being taken seriously," she mumbled.

The next stop was ten minutes down the road. Dylan pulled over, and Tucker zipped in neatly behind him, having caught up. About twenty more vehicles followed. Rather less neatly.

"What's going on?" Tucker asked as he quickly went tc their side and looked out at the sudden, and mixed, convoy.

Dylan told him about the newspaper story he'd read.

His eyebrows raised. "But— Oh." He looked again at their sudden convoy, more carefully this time.

Dylan dialled Phil's number. Rev leaned in to listen. In a word, or six, the shit had hit the fan. The AAC had been inundated with requests for interviews, appearances, and lynchings. They were handling it. Mr. Lyon was handling it. If either Dylan or Rev got any direct calls, from anyone, they were to say 'No comment.'

"Rev?" Phil pointedly waited for a response.

"No comment."

They were excited, no doubt about it. This was the publicity they'd been waiting for. Sort of.

Tucker's phone rang, and he stepped away to take the call.

"Did you want us to do any of the—"

"No," Phil said. "I think you've said pretty much all that can be said. And I mean that in a good way. Mostly," he added. "Let's just see how this plays out."

A few minutes later, both calls finished, Tucker walked over to them.

"I've got orders to keep you in sight at all times," Tucker said. "Literally."

"But—"

"To provide protection as well as an alibi," Tucker said.

"Oh."

"The Chief is liaising with the local forces as we travel. We'll have assistance managing the convoy. And anything else."

"And apparently your guy is liaising with our guy to plan our route," Dylan said, "and we're to stick to it."

"Yeah, I got that too."

According to Mapquest, the drive through the desert from Los Angeles to Myrtle Beach took forty hours. It was a subdued drive, broken only by more subdued stays in Curadas along the way. Only partly because Tucker's round-the-clock presence made their stash inaccessible.

On the third day, the fall-out from their tv appearance disappeared almost as suddenly as it had appeared, so when, on the fourth day, they pulled into the driveway of the house that would be their home for two weeks, no one pulled in behind them except Tucker and Peanut.

They were pleased to find that the house was right on the beach. And easily large enough to accommodate the four of them. They went about settling in.

"You know what we need?" Dylan said as they unpacked.

"Yeah, but Tucker's here."

"My bubbles," he said.

"Yeah, but Peanut's here."

"Right."

Over the next few days, they made trips to the grocery store, the bank, the library, and a few beach shops—Dylan bought Peanut a Peanut-sized beach ball—but mostly they spent a lot of time just walking on the beach. Both Dylan and Rev were eager for the tour to be over. No doubt Tucker was too.

Although every day was warm enough for shorts, a fact that continually amazed them, their first weekend was particularly summery, and the beach was full of people. The water was actually warm enough for swimming. So they headed down with their towels to do just that. After all, back home, the ice was just starting to melt.

After a refreshing, but short swim, they sat on their towels to watch the world go by. Peanut batted his beach ball around for a while, amused that he couldn't actually grab it, then dug a hole in the sand beside Tucker and lay down.

"This is so weird," Rev commented. "Being at the beach. In April."

"It is, isn't it," Dylan agreed.

Suddenly Peanut got up, stared intently down the beach for a moment at absolutely nothing, then took off at full speed.

"Peanut!" Tuck called out, taking off after him. Dogs were allowed on the beach, but not unleashed. Let alone apparently unhinged.

Rev and Dylan followed, establishing the proverbial chase pack, but they were close enough to see Peanut bound into the water. A minute later, Tuck followed. When they got a little closer still, they saw Tuck help an exhausted girl struggling with two very small children. A cluster of people had gathered by the time Rev and Dylan got there.

A young couple took the children from Tuck, the man taking the little girl, and the woman, the little boy. Both kids were crying, a good sign.

"My boyfriend's still out there," the older girl gasped as she bent over to catch her breath. She couldn't've been more than fifteen or sixteen. "He's not a good swimmer. He needs help. There's one more kid," she sobbed, and looked as if she might try to go back in after him.

Tuck raced Peanut back to the water's edge, but he didn't understand that there were two more people out there.

"Go!" Tuck urged him, pointing out to sea. Where? Why?

"Rescue!" Tuck said, and ran into the water a little ways, calling to Peanut. But of course Peanut didn't know that word.

"What were you thinking, letting these kids go out so far?" someone asked angrily, as the two children continued to cry. "Do you have any idea—"

"They're not mine!" the girl replied with what little energy she had left. "Peter and I just saw them—they were really in trouble—"

A few murmurs rose from the crowd, as people looked around for whoever was to blame. Someone stepped forward then to the girl. "You did good," she said, "just breathe. That's it, Peter will be okay, you'll see."

"QUIET!!" Tuck suddenly yelled. In his Police Academy voice. "Peanut needs to hear them," he explained, a little apologetically.

In the silence that followed, Tuck looked out to sea. Peanut did likewise, if only because Tuck did. Ten seconds of silence. Fifteen seconds. Twenty. Twenty-five. Then suddenly, hearing what only he could hear, Peanut flew into the waves and started swimming out to sea.

Tuck took his cell phone out of his pocket. "Border Patrol Jon Tucker 13621 requesting Coast Guard to—" he pressed a button on his fancy watch and read off the satellite coordinates. "One young man, one child, needing rescue. One dog attempting."

"Tuck—" Dylan pointed out to sea. Peanut was coming back.

"No! Go!" Peanut didn't hear. Didn't understand. Tuck thought for just a moment, then raised his right arm and made a circle. Happy to be dancing in the water, Peanut swam in a circle, facing out to sea again for a few moments. Tuck repeated the gesture. Peanut swam another circle. On the third circle, he must've heard the cries again, because he started swimming out again.

Tuck turned and scanned the crowd that had gathered.

"You! Asafa Powell! And you! The guy that beat him!" Two young men, college athletes by the look of them, glanced over. They didn't know whether they were flattered or insulted.

"I need binoculars and a megaphone. There's a beach shop a hundred yards that way, and another one down that way." But they certainly knew what to do with orders from a white guy. No one spoke.

Then an older black man came forward to stand between Tuck and the two young men. "Ten seconds there, ten seconds back. Can you do it?" he asked. They nodded. "Step up, then." They had the grace to look a little ashamed before they took off like shots.

Peanut had in the meantime made two more course corrections, but was still swimming out.

Someone else stepped forward then. "I've called an ambulance." Tuck nodded.

"The siren," Dylan said, standing at his shoulder. "Peanut—"

Tuck looked inquiringly to the people tending the two children and the older girl. They gave him a thumbs up.

He made another call. "Border Patrol Jon Tucker 13621, ambulance en route to Ocean Drive and 11th Avenue is for stand-by only. Please instruct use of siren only if necessary. Dog attempting rescue needs to hear cries for help. Repeat, siren only if necessary." He ended the call and resumed looking anxiously out to sea.

Suddenly a loud, and obnoxious, voice cut through the tense quiet. "Hey! What are you doing with my little girl! Get your hands off her!" A man and a woman stumbled over the sand as they made their way from the nearby beach bar. "What the fuck do you think you're doing!"

The young man hastily put the little girl down. His wife set the little boy on the ground as well.

"I—" the young man started. The drunk took a swing at him, barely landing a blow.

A Linda-Hamilton-as-Sarah-Connor look-alike quickly stepped in and pinned the drunk's arms behind him.

"You let go of him," the wife said to her. "We got rights! You can't—where's Emily?" She suddenly broke off. "What did you do with our little Em?"

"QUIET!" Tuck screamed. Peanut had lost them again.

"I will not be quiet!" the woman screamed back.

Another couple, with 'Mom' and 'Dad' written all over them, or at least on the t-shirts they wore, stomped over to the drunk couple. Dad punched the drunk in the nose and Mom slapped the wife. Hard to say which action had the greater stun-factor.

Hamilton-Connor tightened her grip and hissed into the drunk's ear. "Your kids were drowning. That young woman and her boyfriend saved them. The boyfriend and your other child are still out there. That man's dog is trying to find them. And he can't hear them unless you shut the fuck up."

"You can't speak to us—" Mom slapped her again. Twice. She fell onto the sand. And stayed there.

"Hey! You can't do that to my wife—" Dad punched him again. He too went down.

By now 'Asafa' had returned with binoculars. Tuck took them and looked out. Silence. More silence. Then, "I see them. I see—two heads." A sigh of relief rose from the crowd. "Peanut can't find them," he added quietly.

Just then, 'Usain' sprinted up with binoculars and a megaphone. Tuck looked out again, took a moment to compose himself, then sang into the megaphone in the purest clearest voice, sounding exactly like Billy Joel, "'If you said good-bye to me tonight—'"

Many in the crowd looked confused, but ready to add the 'oo-oo-oooo-oo' bit, so Dylan quickly put his finger to his lips to shh them.

Tuck looked out, then raised the megaphone and sang again. "'If you said good-bye to me tonight—'" The line hung in the air. Tuck looked through the binoculars once again. Come on Peanut, you can do it, he said quietly to himself. He needed to swim on a diagonal, but the diagonal was hard for him, and it had taken a long time to get it. But he *had* gotten it. The opening of the new dance they'd been working on, to "The Longest Time", was a diagonal.

He sang the line once more, his voice trembling just a bit. "'If you said good-bye to me tonight—'" And raised the binoculars once more.

"He's there! He's found them!" A restrained cheer rose from the crowd, then quickly died as everyone waited for further reports from Tuck.

"Oh. I didn't know he could do that," he murmured. Peanut had made a little dive and come up under Emily so she was riding him like a pony. "He's got the child," Tuck said in the quiet. But there was no way a teenager could climb on too. Could he grab on without pulling Peanut under? "Okay, it looks like he's—pushing the boy. His head's above water. They're not moving very fast, but—"

Several people looked ready to swim out and help, but a woman seemed to be discouraging them.

Tucker looked out to sea again. "No," he moaned. "He's going the wrong way." He raised the megaphone to his lips and called out "This way, Peanut! This way!"

The woman ran up to him then and yanked the megaphone away from his mouth. "Leave him!" she said as she took his binoculars and looked out to sea. Tuck stood, confused. "It's probably a riptide," she explained, as she searched for him. "If he swims this way, he'll be swimming against the current. You're supposed to swim *parallel* to the shore until you get out of the current, *then* turn back in. There he is." She watched him for a few moments. "He's doing what you're supposed to do," she said with a smile in her voice. "He's doing it exactly right," she handed the binoculars back to Tuck. "But he looks tired."

"He needs—" Dylan was still at Tuck's shoulder. "At the bar that night—the chorus—the two lines where he just—that wasn't choreographed, right? It's just all energy and—" Dylan started madly singing through the song in his head to get to the lines in question, but Tuck, of course, picked the first note out of nowhere.

"'Come on, come on, come on and dance with me!'" he sang out to Peanut, pitch-perfect with spot-on tempo.

As he started to sing it a second time, Dylan turned to the gathered crowd and encouraged them to sing along, but not to go onto the next line.

"'Come on, come on, come on and dance with me!'" A few of the older ones recognized it and got it right away. The others caught on shortly after and soon the whole beach was cheering Peanut on.

"'Come on, come on, come on and dance with me!'" Everyone sang as loudly as they could. Tuck looked out. It was working! Peanut wasn't moving any faster, but he wasn't getting any slower.

But a few minutes later, he did get slower. Emily was still on his back, but Peter was no longer being pushed; he was behind, holding onto Peanut's tail. Tucker winced. Clearly that was all the boy could do, but he was dragging on Peanut terribly.

Tuck got out his phone again. "Coast Guard to—" he repeated the coordinates— "request ETA." He waited a moment, then shouted, "Well don't you have more than one boat?" His voice cracked.

Asafa nudged Usain. They conferred very briefly, then sprinted off down the beach. In fifteen seconds flat, they reached the beach store, and in another fifteen seconds they'd grabbed a couple flutterboards and picked up a paddle boat. Literally. They practically threw it into the water, then jumped in and started paddling. Their piston legs paddled the damn thing so hard, it rose out of the water and they were paddling air. Realizing the problem, they veered slightly toward a group of college-aged women frolicking in the waves. With a single steroid-pumped arm, Asafa scooped up the first one they came to and set her hundred pounds on the front of the boat to act as a counterweight. She had no idea what was going on. Because she gripped the paddleboat's prow with her knees, tore off her bikini top, and starting waving it like it was a lasso. "Woo hoo," she called out.

In the meantime, the proprietor of 'Bill's EVERYTHING Beach Store 843-888-4343 200 Ocean Drive Mon-Sun 8-8' had sent someone down to the beach in one of those three-wheeled sloop beach bicycles to distribute his entire stock of binoculars. Ya gotta love capitalism.

Rev gave hers to the girl, Susie, who had regained her strength and was standing anxiously at the water's edge.

No one gave theirs to the drunks. In fact, there was no shortage of lookers-on who simply shoved them back down whenever they regained consciousness and tried to get up.

Suddenly a cheer erupted from the crowd: the paddleboat had reached Peanut. Asafa scooped Emily off Peanut's back and carefully handed her to Usain. She teetered, but seemed okay as long as Usain held onto her. Everyone cheered.

Next, Asafa hauled Peter into the paddle boat. He seemed conscious, but barely. Everyone cheered.

Then Asafa tossed the bronco-riding young woman into the water. Everyone cheered.

He set Peter up front where she had been, tossed one of the flutterboards into the water after her, admittedly as an afterthought, and tied the other one to the back of the paddleboat before tossing it in as well. The young woman straddled her board, then lay down on it and started paddling like she was heading out to surf the pipe. Peanut studied her carefully, and as Asafa held his board steady, he actually managed to get it under him. Everyone cheered. He barked.

Tuck let out a sob of joy.

They slowly turned the paddleboat around then and started paddling back, the child and the boy safe, Peanut in tow. The young woman, in the meantime, had gotten to her feet, despite the lack of surf waves. Peanut had not missed that, and once the boat picked up some speed, it seemed possible…

"Oh," Tuck said, still watching Peanut through his binoculars. "I didn't know he could do that either."

"'Catch a wave and you're sittin' on top of the world,'" Dylan sang softly, as he looked out at Peanut, now visible even without binoculars.

Tuck grinned.

Since it took them several minutes to reach the shore, everyone was at their landing spot to greet them. As soon as Peanut saw that Asafa and Usain had Emily and Peter in hand, he flew into Tuck. Literally. Knocked him flat onto his back in the sand. Tuck wrapped his arms around him and gleefully submitted to the thorough face-licking that ensued.

All three children, as well as Susie and Peter, were quickly loaded into the waiting ambulance. Peter and Emily were probably okay, the paramedic assured the crowd, but may have suffered respiratory distress from swallowing too much saltwater. No such assurances were given to the couple still face-first in the sand some distance away.

Tuck managed, eventually, to crawl out from under Peanut. Who had decided he would just lay where he was for a while. Dylan and Rev sat down on the beach beside them. Several people were milling about, not yet wanting to leave the scene of excitement. Or Peanut. Who was getting lots of congratulations. And loving every minute of it.

"Hey look," Rev said, her pizza radar always in full force. A caravan of waiters from Mega Pizza were heading straight toward them. Fully loaded.

"We didn't know if your dog was a Meat-Lovers fan or a Cheese-Lovers fan," the first one said, "so we brought ten of each." She and the second waiter set the large boxes onto the sand. "We also brought a cooler of Pepsi," the third waiter stepped forward, "and a couple jugs of Evian. We figured he wouldn't like Pepsi."

"Hey, thanks!" Tuck was overwhelmed. And upset that he hadn't yet thought about water for Peanut.

A cheer went up from the crowd as the pizza boxes were opened, and soon everyone present had pizza and Pepsi. The Evian was poured into the empty cooler, and Peanut drank it all. Every last drop. He also consumed two large meat-lovers. But only after Tucker blew on them. Twice. And then he simply went to sleep.

Once the pizza, and the people, had gone, and Rev and Dylan had returned to the house, a man with a black bag approached Tuck and Peanut.

"Hi there. I'm Ron Severn. I'm here on holiday with my wife. I'm a vet. And I heard about—this is the famous Peanut?"

"Yeah," Tuck nodded, smiling.

"Mind if I give him a once over?"

"No, please do," Tucker started to get up, but since the vet had gotten onto his knees, he did the same.

"I heard he had quite a day. How's he been?"

"Well he ate a couple pizzas, drank a lot of water, and then went to sleep."

"Sounds about right," the vet laughed. "He kept the food and water down?"

"Yeah."

"And he's been sleeping since?"

"Pretty much."

The vet started to feel along Peanut's body. "How long was he in the water?"

"I don't know. It all happened so fast. And then so slow. Half an hour? An hour?"

"I see. Normally, that'd be a piece of cake for a dog this breed. But I understand he was carrying a child on his back?"

"And a teenager was holding onto his tail."

"Oh. I hadn't heard about the teenager. Well," he said, "I have heard stories of rescue Newfs tugging boats to safety, but not with their tails...." He ran his hands along Peanut's legs.

"Rescue Newfs?"

"Oh yes. They can be trained to be rescue dogs. They're extremely well-suited for it. What they do is go out with a special flutterboard or buoyancy ring that's rigged up to their harness. Though sometimes they use a tow handle, I think..." He lifted Peanut's leg and felt along his belly.

"Okay, let's check this tail...," he carefully felt every inch of his tail, "it seems okay. They can get what's called 'swimmer's tail'—even without a teenager dragging on it."

"He sprained it a few months ago. I was afraid—"

"He sprained his tail? How did he manage that?"

"He wags it too much."

The vet laughed. "I've never met a dog that sprained its tail by excessive wagging, but...." He opened his bag and took out a stethoscope. "Okay, let's give a listen." He listened to Peanut's heart. Then checked his breathing.

"Keep an eye on his breathing. If he swallowed a lot of saltwater, it's possible the lungs were damaged—he hasn't been coughing?"

"No."

"Well that's good."

"He'll be sore. Given what you said, his shoulders would've done most of the work. You might want to give him a massage."

"I will. Thank you. Anything else?"

"Well, don't overdo the food. The meat-lovers was good," he looked at the empty pizza box, with MEAT-LOVERS written on it, "because he'll need a lot of protein, but stick to small quantities for a while. Same for the water. Sucking on an ice cube would've been better than guzzling a couple gallons, but you said he kept it down, so I wouldn't worry."

He pulled a bit of skin at the side of Peanut's chest, twisted it, then watched it spring back. "He doesn't seem too dehydrated. His eyes look a bit red. That'll be irritation from the saltwater. Soak a cotton ball in fresh water and wipe them a bit, that'll help."

"Okay. Massage and eye wipe. Small quantities of food and water. Got it. Thank you so much."

"No problem. Here's my card. I'm staying at the Hilton. Room 204. Just in case. But everything looks good," he assured him. "You've got a fine dog here," he scratched Peanut's ears. "I do. Thanks again."

A while later, toward evening, Dylan walked down to the beach. Tuck and Peanut were still there, Tuck sitting in the sand leaned up against a post with Peanut's head in his lap. He was singing softly to him, a lullaby version of "Sweet Pea". Every now and then Peanut wagged his tail. Just the tip. A proxy wag. Dylan hoped that when Peanut died, years and years from now, it'd be like this. His head in Tuck's lap, Tuck singing to him, sweetly, tenderly.

"Hey, how's it going?" Dylan said quietly, having hung back until the song was over. He handed Tuck the sweatshirt he'd brought. It would be getting chilly. "He's still sleeping?"

"Yeah."

Dylan sat down beside him.

"Thanks," Tuck said, putting on his sweatshirt while trying not to disturb Peanut.

They sat for a bit, just listening to the waves.

"I thought I'd lost him," Tucker said then, and wiped away his sudden tears with a gesture of embarrassment.

"Hey, cry," Dylan said. "You almost did lose him. That's certainly worth crying about." Then he added, "The whole 'Be a man, chin up, feelings are for wusses' thing is just a conspiracy to get us to do awful things."

Tucker looked at him curiously.

"If we felt pain, about hurting others, about getting hurt ourselves," Dylan explained, "we wouldn't do half the shit we do. Emotion, emotional expression, it's good."

Tucker remained doubtful.

"And you *didn't* lose him. You sang to him. You saved him as much as he saved those kids. You two are a great team."

Tucker started crying again. "Yeah," he managed to say.

Just as the sun started to set, Rev joined them.

"Hey," she said, sitting down. "His tail's okay?"

"Yeah. Just a little sore, I think. Some guy, a vet, came by to check him out."

"Cool."

"He likes it here," Tuck said after a while, looking out at the ocean. "So do I."

"It is nice," Rev said, not taking her eyes off the late sun sparkling on the water, and the clouds just starting to pink and purple.

"You know how sometimes everything feels just—right?" Tuck asked. "How you finally find exactly where you're supposed to be? What you're supposed to do?"

Rev and Dylan exchanged a look. "Not exactly, no," Dylan said.

"Well, I'm thinking—it can get pretty hot here in the summer.

Too hot for a dog like Peanut. But I'm thinking somewhere a little further north, on the coast though—I think Peanut wants to be a Rescue Dog," he finished.

"I think you're right," Dylan said, looking at Peanut. "Either that or a Surfer Dog."

Tuck grinned.

"They're not mutually exclusive," Rev spoke up.

"He could be both," Dylan translated.

And Peanut wagged his tail.

A week later it was time to leave their housesit and continue the tour. Tucker convinced the Chief that Peanut needed a few more days of recuperation. At the beach. And so the four of them said their goodbyes there. Dylan assured Peanut, and Tuck, that they were always welcome to visit them in Sudbury. Always.

The drive from Myrtle to Massachusetts was a quiet one. Rev was still feeling sad, or at least guilty, about the whole Christians-throwing-themselves-off-the-cliff thing, and Dylan was feeling sad to have left his bestest-friend-ever.

"So," Dylan said as they pulled into the parking lot outside the Divinity School. "Our last gig."

Rev simply nodded.

"I don't suppose—I mean, especially since Los Angeles—this is probably a 'Know thine enemy' booking, yeah?"

"Probably," Rev said. "Unless it's a 'Kill thine enemy' booking."

They opened the van doors one last time to take out their boxes and set up.

"I've always wanted to go to Harvard," Dylan said, looking out at the campus.

Rev snorted.

"I know, I know, they don't have a good music program, and I never would've been able to continue my tambourine studies, but—

Harvard!"

It did indeed reverberate with reputation. They took in the architecture of Andover Hall, which was very old. And then they looked at the parking lot, which was very new. And, they belatedly noticed, very empty.

"Perhaps they already know their enemy."

They sighed, shoved their boxes back into the van, and closed the doors.

"Well, this is a rather unremarkable ending."

"It is, yes."

Several packed cars pulled into the lot then, and dozens of students tumbled out in a rush of excitement. A cloud of lime green jiggled toward them.

"Where is everyone?" the one in the front asked.

"What we said," Dylan replied.

They considered that for a moment, then almost unanimously burst into "PAR-TY! PAR-TY!" They changed direction, grabbing Dylan and Rev, and headed for the nearest student pub. Dylan and Rev grinned at each other.

"Pizza and beer on the AAC!" Dylan called out as they mobbed the place. It was the least they could do. It was, after all, their last gig. So, tables were claimed, chairs pulled up, pizzas ordered, pitchers and bottles of assorted beverages obtained, drained, and obtained again, and a jukebox put into service.

Shortly after the party was underway, one of the young women left, then returned, visibly upset.

"My parents just found out the insurance company won't pay," she said angrily to those near her who had inquired. "Acts of God are exempt." She carefully set her phone onto the table. Clearly she'd wanted to throw it against the wall.

Dylan and Rev looked to the students at their table for an

explanation.

"Her house was one of those hit by that tornado in Arkansas," the young man beside her said.

"Oh," Rev said. "We've been under a sort of self-imposed news blackout. Didn't actually know there'd been a tornado in Arkansas."

"We should sue!" someone suggested.

"What, for misrepresentation?"

"Could do."

"How about fraud?" someone from the next table had heard.

"No, that has to be deceit in order to manipulate someone to give something of value. Doesn't apply."

"Wait a minute," someone from another table had their ipad out. "Fraud includes concealing a fact from the other party which may have saved that party from being cheated. *That* applies."

"What, are you all pre-law?" Rev said a little sarcastically as she took a bite of her pizza.

"Duh. This is Harvard."

It took a moment. Then Dylan giggled. "Oh, this is perfect."

"But if the other party—"

"Actually," the young woman raised her voice, "what I meant was we should sue *God*. Not the insurance company. For the damages. If, as they say, it was his action that's responsible—"

There was just the tiniest second of silence before the tables erupted.

"Negligence?"

"What's he gonna say? 'I didn't know'? There goes omniscience."

"'I couldn't do anything'? There goes omnipotence."

The two young men clinked their glasses together in a toast to their cleverness.

"Can you imagine the compensation? He'd have to restore roads, buildings—"

"He'd have to bring people back to life."

"Could do." That got laughs all round.

"My guess is he just won't show." More laughs.

"But can you imagine the theatrical value of such a trial? I mean even if it doesn't—"

"Yeah, but isn't a representative required by law to show?" Most of the students were on their feet by this time, crowding the table that started it all.

"Oh, that's good. So priests and ministers across the country—either they show or, by their absence, confess they're not really his representatives!"

"So why don't we just sue *them*?"

"Yeah, a class action suit!"

"Everyone who's ever suffered property damage from a storm or flood or lightning—"

"By the time the churches finish providing compensation, they'll be bankrupt!"

The comments were coming from all directions, and Dylan and Rev struggled to keep up. Half the students had their droids or ipads out and were pecking away. Madly. It was a wondrous thing that was happening.

"Can we name them all in the same suit? There are differences between the various religions—"

"Better media value with one huge suit or a swarm of small ones?"

"Wait a minute, I didn't mean we sue just for the physical damage. I meant for all the psychological damage!"

There was another almost imperceptible moment of silence. And then the second bomb exploded.

"Of course! They're disseminating misinformation—or engaging in fraudulent advertising—"

"Oh don't stop there!" someone boomed. "Do you have *any* idea what it's like to be *raised* Catholic? For example?"

"It's like being in a fucking straightjacket!"

"What's the mental equivalent of foot binding?"

"Again, a class action suit? For child abuse?"

"Cult survivors have sued before, there must be lots of precedents." Yet another ipad was enthusiastically put into service. And a few more pitchers of beer summoned.

"And our *parents*!" The room practically roared. "They're the ones who took us to church in the first place."

"Where I was told I was *born* a sinner. Do you have any idea what a number that does on your self-esteem?" the young woman looked around her.

"It's a wonder any of us made it this far."

"I almost didn't." That punched a hole of silence in the bedlam for a second.

"To be discouraged from asking questions," a young man ventured.

"To be told these fantastic stories, without a shred of evidence or even credibility—"

"And threatened into accepting them—" The buzz resumed.

"Yeah, what that does to people like us! Thinking people, intellectually curious people!"

"I still have trouble with sex," yet another young woman said, not at all out of nowhere, "and this is the bloody 21st century."

"Tell me about it," the flamboyantly gay young man across from her said. They knocked their bottles together in a toast. To maladjusted sexuality.

"And not just that, but *any* pleasures in life. Religions aren't exactly joie-de-vivre philosophies."

"Everything's a test."

"Or something simply to be endured."

"Turn the other cheek. To injury, to injustice."

"God will provide—"

"I spent nights praying, *begging* for a sign, for some certainty—"

"The mental gymnastics I went through to—"

"—and then when I finally gave up, when I finally woke up, and said FUCK THIS SHIT!—"

A cheer rose from the tables and glasses were raised. Emptied. Refilled.

"There must be hundreds, thousands, of people like us. People who," the speaker searched for a clear definition, "who've been royally screwed by our religious upbringing."

Rev grinned. Sort of.

"What damages would we ask for though?" someone piped up. "You can't put a price on—"

"You must've missed Taval's lecture," a young man called out to her. "You *can* put a price—on anything. Emotional abuse—"

"Psychological abuse—"

"Cognitive abuse—"

"What about conspiring to—"

"We should make it illegal for parents to inculcate any religion—"

"To lie to their kids about such fundamental matters—"

"And the rituals. We've gotta include those. We're not exactly slaughtering goats anymore, but—"

"I can make a case for equivalence," someone put up his hand. "The holy water. Eat my body, drink my blood."

"And all those crucifixes in public places. They're symbols of Christianity and therefore of torture, murder, persecution—the Inquisition—"

"Are you suggesting hate crime?"

"Imagine every one of them replaced with a swastika, *that'd* be a no-brainer."

"Listen up!" A young woman climbed onto one of the tables. "Suing god, over there! Suing the churches, over there! Suing parents, here!"

The students grabbed their beverages and their pizza, their droids and their ipads, and scrambled to their chosen tables, talking a mile a minute.

"Lawsuits all round," Dylan said joyfully, impressed with the speed with which the idea took off and the students' can-do attitude.

"How American," Rev responded.

They just sat back then and watched, as various legal documents seemed to be in preparation before their very eyes.

"Now this was more the ending I was hoping for," Rev said. Smiling for perhaps the first time since Los Angeles.

"Actually," Dylan said, "it looks like more of a beginning."

Get your own lime green t-shirt

"There are no gods. Deal with it."

from www.cafepress.com!

(Just do a search for "Jass Richards There are no gods")